THE SILK

Volume 6 of 7

A NOVEL BY

JOHN M. BURTON QC

FOR MY MOTHER WHO HAS HAD A DIFFICULT YEAR BUT DESPITE ADVANCING YEARS HAS TAUGHT US ALL HOW TO DEAL WITH ADVERSITY.

Books by John M. Burton

The Silk Brief, Volume 1 of The Silk Tales

The Silk Head, Volume 2 of The Silk Tales

The Silk Returns, Volume 3 of the Silk Tales

The Silk Ribbon, Volume 4 of The Silk Tales

The Silk's Child, Volume 5 of The Silk Tales

The Silk's Cruise, Volume 6 of The Silk Tales

Parricide, Volume 1 of The Murder Trials of Cicero

Poison, Volume 2 of The Murder Trials of Cicero

The Myth of Sparta, Volume 1 of The Chronicles of Sparta

The Return of the Spartans, Volume 2 of The Chronicles of Sparta

The Trial of Admiral Byng, Pour Encourager Les Autres, Volume 1 of the Historical Trials Series

Treachery, The Princes in The Tower.

TABLE OF CONTENTS

CHAPTER 1

THE RUSSIAN INTERPRETER

He glanced at his watch which he had placed on the lectern in front of him. He read the date of 25th August 2017 and the time, 12:17pm. He had been speaking for close to two hours now and was finally coming to an end, which was good news as the eyes of some jurors were beginning to glaze over. They had been sitting on this trial since late April and they had now heard four defence speeches in addition to the prosecution's closing.

Soon Tatiana Volkov, the Russian interpreter he had first met on a boat in the middle of the Channel, would have her fate decided by the twelve faces all looking at him now. The case had originally been listed in January but had been adjourned until late April because the prosecution were not ready. They had failed to carry out their disclosure duties, a frequent problem with the Crown Prosecution Service these days. It was the duty of the prosecution to disclose to the defence everything that might undermine the prosecution case or assist the defence case. As this case had involved many thousands of documents, the prosecution had concentrated on picking out everything that assisted their case and had been somewhat neglectful in finding any material that did not. They had been given three months to sort their case out with the threat from the judge that if they did not, he would stay the case as an 'abuse of process'.

This had been fortunate for David and the other barristers as the case had then been 'contracted' with the legal aid authorities and had become a VHCC case, a 'Very High Cost Case.' Unlike ordinary 'graduated fee' criminal work where he was paid an amount per page and per witness regardless of the amount of work he had to conduct, he and his senior clerk, had been able to negotiate a healthy sum for the case with the legal aid authorities. He had even been paid two of the three instalments payable in the case and for almost the first time since his divorce, he was feeling flush, at least until the Inland Revenue came knocking!

The case had generally been boring with a few moments of humour. It had almost been derailed when a diminutive male juror had accused a large female juror of pushing past him with such violence that he had fallen over and fractured his wrist. It had taken considerable tact on the part of the trial judge, and physically moving the two to opposite ends of the jury box, before they were persuaded to continue to serve on the same jury.

A bigger drama occurred when a notebook was discovered in the dock by a security guard and passed to an usher who had taken it straight to the judge. One of the defendants was clearly an accomplished amateur artist and he or she had used their talent to draw a picture that was clearly of the judge and the prosecutor in a compromising sexual position. The judge had been furious when he found out and had insisted on an investigation as to who was the artist with a view to imprisoning the perpetrator for contempt of court. The prosecutor had merely made discrete enquiries as to whether he could have a copy of the drawing. The investigation had drawn to an abrupt halt when all defence counsel had asked to see the notebook, so that they could take instructions from their respective clients. The judge had clearly not wanted this particular work to be artistically scrutinised by the bar and had decided not to pursue the matter further and had refused the prosecutor's request to see the exhibit which he had then torn up in the presence of the lawyers and the defendants, threatening that any repeat of this conduct would be met with an immediate sentence of imprisonment.

David put these thoughts behind him and continued with his address to the jury, they were flagging so he said in a louder voice, "Please look at my client, Tatiana Volkov."

He paused whilst the jurors' faces turned to the weeping face of Tatiana who was in the dock surrounded by security guards and her hard-faced co-defendants, several of whom looked like they could have a career as extras in films involving the Russian mafia.

"She is no fraudster. She is an innocent dupe! Used by the one living man she thought she could trust in her life, not a husband, not a boyfriend or lover, but her own brother. A woman may not be able to trust a lover, a fiancé or even her husband, but she should be able to trust her own brother. A man she has known all her life; a man who was brought up with her in distant Moscow, a man who should have wanted to protect his sister, but a man, as the evidence has shown, who had no qualms about stealing large sums of money from his bank employers and their innocent customers. A man who cared nothing for anyone he used, whether it be a client, a customer or even his own poor innocent sister.

He asked her if he could use her computer and she agreed thinking nothing of it. Why should she? He asked her if he could use her name as a company director in what she thought was a legitimate enterprise and she agreed, because she trusted him implicitly.

He used her and then deserted her. Fleeing back to Russia and not having the decency to come back to protect his own loving sister who had trusted him implicitly. He would rather see her dragged through the humiliation of a trial and potentially punished for a crime that he committed, rather than come back and own up to his treacherous and dishonest behaviour.

He fooled many people in this case, his employers, customers, the authorities, the police who let him out on police bail, and even his closest family members.

Do not let him fool you.

Tatiana Volkov is guilty of one thing and one thing only, trusting her dishonest brother. She is not guilty of any of the charges brought against her by the prosecution and I ask you for the only proper verdict in this case.

'Not guilty', to the charges she faces."

He gave them each one last look before adding, "Thank you for your patience in listening to a speech that was much longer than I planned and no doubt far longer than you hoped for."

With that he sat down acknowledging the smile from the middle-aged woman on the front row who had cast him many a meaningful look throughout the long case, particularly just now when he made the comment about not being able to trust a husband. Maybe she fancied him or maybe it was just indigestion as Wendy had cruelly suggested when he mentioned to her earlier in the trial that the woman had smiled at him. Whatever it was, there was a chance it might assist his client and so he smiled directly at her as he knew Tatiana needed all the assistance she could get.

The evidence had in his opinion been nearly overwhelming and far more complex and concerning than his client had mentioned when she first asked him to represent her. Her involvement had not simply been limited to allowing her brother to use her computer and name on some company documents. She was involved in sending a wide range of money transfers to different people in many countries, some of which she must have carried out when her brother had returned to Russia. Coupled with her poor performance in the witness box, he was not expecting a result in this case.

It was a pity really! He had grown fond of Tatiana. She had an innate winning charm, although in his opinion, the same is usually exhibited by the best fraudsters. After all, if they were not charming and believable, fraud would hardly ever be successful. It was unfortunate that the charm had not extended to her appearance in the witness box when she had come across as arrogant, belligerent and downright rude to the prosecutor. Indeed, she had ignored every piece of advice that David had given her and almost seemed to court an adverse finding by the jury.

He had hoped to win the case, not least because it had made the newspapers and there had been a press following when Tatiana gave evidence. He suspected it was because she was extremely attractive and the newspaper editors had enjoyed publishing photographs of Tatiana as she made her way towards the court building, sporting a different designer outfit almost every day. On one occasion David had been pictured in the newspapers, smiling at Tatiana and holding her arm. A photograph that he had to explain to Wendy after she had seen it in three different newspapers in one day. It was not his fault that the press photographer had just managed to take a photograph the moment Tatiana stumbled and he had grabbed her arm to stop her falling. At least that was how he recalled the incident!

He turned around and smiled at Tatiana. There was no point in giving her his opinion of the result of this trial. After all, it was possible he was wrong, it had been known, and in any event, she would find out the jury's verdict in a few days from now. He had already told her that in his opinion she was facing about eight years imprisonment for her part in this fraud. He had told her that she would only serve half that time and hopefully, after the first few weeks, months at the outside, most of her time would be spent in an 'open prison' subject to her immigration status. It had not been comforting to her but at least he had done his job. Now all he had to do was await the verdict.

CHAPTER 2

DEATH IN THE STREETS

"Bastards"

Gerry Worthy was in his own words, 'thoroughly pissed off'. The day had started bad enough but then it turned into an awful evening. It was 25th August 2017, the end of the week with a day off on Monday for the bank holiday and he had been looking forward to a long enjoyable weekend, but that no longer seemed a possibility. He was aged twenty-seven and he worked in a storage company on the northern outskirts of Brighton in Sussex. He had worked for four years as a storage operator, a post one above a general dogsbody, but recently he had been given the job of trainee manager. He still found the work boring but at least it was a promotion and an increased status in the company.

His joy at the promotion had changed though. Recently a new trainee storage operator had joined the firm called Maureen O'Connor. She was older than most trainees and was in her early forties, having come back to work after her three children had grown up. She had been a nuisance from the moment she had started. At first, she had wasted his time by constantly asking questions about procedures that she should have known about, but in the last couple of weeks she had started to openly challenge the way he worked, even criticising him to other members of staff. He believed she wanted his job and would do anything to get it. He had not allowed her behaviour to continue for long before he confronted her and in a heated conversation on Monday of that week, he had called her a, 'rancid menopausal bitch'.

He had hoped that matters would end there and in future she would show him the respect he deserved. She had different ideas and had complained to his manager, Richard Brightman, the son of the owner of the firm. Sadly, in Gerry's opinion, he did not live up to his name and today he had summoned Gerry to a meeting and instituted disciplinary proceedings against him! Gerry claimed the comment he had made was merely banter between co-workers but his boss had ruled this was workplace harassment and sexual bullying and had issued him with a written warning saying that if it was repeated he would be dismissed immediately.

Richard claimed it was something to do with the fact that Gerry was 6 feet 4 inches and eighteen stone of well-built muscle, whereas Maureen was a mere ten stone and 5 feet 2 inches. Gerry thought the whole thing had been blown up out of all proportion and he was being discriminated against because of his size and sex. He was sure there would not have been a complaint if he had been arguing with a male colleague and used similar terms.

He hoped things would get better this evening but things had become even worse. He had driven his prize possession, a brilliant white, 1972 E-type jaguar motor car from his works to a pub in West Brighton. The pub was about two miles away from his work and was called the Prince of Orange. It was usually lively on a Friday night and he hoped to meet friends there.

He met Brian there, a coding clerk in his office who had introduced him to Shirley West, a friend of Brian's and together they had all consumed a great deal of beer and spirits before Shirley mentioned a party she was going to. Although drunk, Gerry drove them all to the area of the party near East Brighton park. Shirley told him to park near some garages that were at the rear of a row of houses. As soon as he stopped the car, Shirley quickly got out with Brian and promptly left Gerry who, in his drunken state, had difficulty parking the car without blocking one of the garages.

When he had finished parking and locking the car, neither Brian nor Shirley were around. They had clearly gone straight to the party and forgotten about him. The annoying thing was that Gerry had not been given the address and he could not tell which house it was at, as they all looked alike. It now looked like he would have to spend the rest of the evening trawling this estate looking for a house that had some sign that a party was in progress.

After fifteen minutes he was even more annoyed. The houses not only looked alike, they all had lights on in the rear of the houses and all looked like they had parties going on!

He had had enough, he was angry now and someone should pay. He could not help himself shout out as loudly as he could, "Where did you fucking bastards go to?"

He saw people in some of the kitchens moving the blinds and looking out at him. This only infuriated him more as he responded loudly with, "What the fuck are you lot looking at?"

Most of the blinds closed rapidly but the blinds in one house stayed open and he was sure he saw Brian hiding behind them

"Is that you? You fucking bastard, come out here now, I'm going to fucking kill you!"

The blinds closed and a few seconds later the rear door opened and Brian, Shirley and a group of youths came out towards him.

Brian reached him first with his hands extended in a seemingly placatory way. He came up close and blurted out, "I'm so sorry Gerry, I completely forgot about you."

Neither the gesture nor the words calmed Gerry down and he was about to shout some further obscenities at Brian when an obviously drunk Shirley appeared shouting, "What the fuck's your problem, screaming like a fucking kid, why don't you piss off, no one wants you here anyway!"

Without thinking Gerry swung his right fist in her direction connecting under her chin, lifting her off her feet and instantly knocking her out. She crumbled to the floor. He had a sudden pang of guilt but was unable to say anything because a young lad, probably 19 or 20 in age, was now confronting him and waving a knife in his face.

Strangely he was not scared, but was exhilarated by the sudden threat. He smiled, took a fighter's stance and shouted, "Come on then, give me your best shot."

Brian suddenly came between them, "Just stop, this, this is madness, let's just help Shirley, she's out cold."

At those words Gerry looked down at the prone body of Shirley who was laying on the pavement with her limbs splayed like a rag doll. He walked towards her but Brian stopped him. "Gerry, if I was you I'd just leave. We'll look after her, it's better you go before matters get worse."

Gerry looked at him with contempt and looked at the four lads around him, including the one with a knife, "I'm not scared of these prats, I can take the lot of them on anytime."

Brian nodded, "I'm sure that's right, but we don't want anyone else getting hurt, please just leave."

At that point a black youth came forward and announced in a clipped accent, "Brian is right, please just leave."

He put his arm on Gerry's shoulder and turned him away from the other youths. Gerry calmed down and allowed the black youth to usher him slowly away towards his car. They had only travelled a few yards when Gerry suddenly felt a sharp pain in the back of his right leg. He looked down and even in the poor light he could see his white trouser leg rapidly staining with blood. He looked at the black youth and exclaimed, "You fucking cheeky bastard."

He pushed the youth away and hobbled towards his car. He found it difficult to walk and was feeling faint and sick almost straight away. The pain was unimaginable at first but was beginning to ease now. He managed to stagger the twenty yards or so to his car and fumbled for his electronic key. He could not find it and after few seconds he gave up looking. Everything was going dark now but fortunately the pain was slowly diminishing. He did not notice himself collapse against the driver' door of his car. He felt immensely tired and he knew he needed to rest. He put his arms out to steady himself on the pavement, watching, with bemusement, the large amount of blood rapidly pooling around his leg. He grimaced a little, he had only bought these trousers recently with his expected pay rise and now they were ruined. He would have to get some more.

He was cold now and thoroughly exhausted. He looked towards Brian and the others who were looking at him strangely, he wondered what they were looking at as he slowly closed his eyes.

CHAPTER 3

THE SUSPECT

It was a Monday morning and Detective Inspector Bill Splinter, 'Splinter' to his friends and enemies alike, was seated in his office in Brighton police station looking out on the busy street below him. He opened the papers in front of him. It referred to yet another murder on the streets of Brighton that had taken place the previous Friday. The victim was a local man who had been out for the night drinking when he came across some yobs, one of whom had stabbed him in the right leg. The victim had lost an enormous amount of blood before emergency services had arrived and although the paramedics had done their best to stabilise him at the scene, he was pronounced dead at hospital at 2:12am.

Police interviewed people at the scene and it appeared that the incident, like so many murders he had investigated, had arisen out of nothing. The victim, Gerry Worthy had taken a couple of friends to a party, he had got lost and become angry as a result. People from the party, having heard him shouting and swearing outside, had come out to confront him. It appeared that at least two people in the group had armed themselves with knives. Mr Worthy had hit one of the girls who had confronted him, knocking her out. One lad had been seen 'dancing around' waving a knife at Mr Worthy and threatening to stab him. He had been identified as one Adrian Simons who had been arrested that night.

Another one of the party had then been seen to put his arm around the victim apparently to usher him away. However, although no one had a seen a knife in his hands, he clearly had one, because within seconds the victim was heard to say, 'You fucking cheeky bastard' and push the youth away, before hobbling away to his car where he lay down by the driver's door and slowly bled to death from a serious wound to the back of his right leg.

The people from the party had been unhelpful and it had not been until a couple of days later that the person seen ushering Mr Worthy away had been identified as Joseph Rogers, a university student at the local Sussex university. He had been arrested late last night at his university lodgings and was in the cells waiting for Bill to interview him. It seemed an open and shut case to him and unless his solicitor advised him to make 'no comment', he expected the lad to confess to the crime and be charged before lunch time.

Twenty minutes after reading the file and taking a quick swig of whisky from a bottle that he kept hidden in his desk, Bill was joined by Detective Constable Ben Sharpe and both went down to the cells to collect Joseph Rogers for an interview. As they arrived they saw he already had a solicitor present in the cells with him.

It was Graham Turner, a well-known, if not infamous solicitor, from the local firm of Gardeners. Bill inwardly groaned. There would be no confessions today and no doubt he would have to deal with some 'balls-aching' complaint. He disliked solicitors generally, they got in the way of good police work, but this one he loathed.

Within a few minutes the cell door was open and Bill was addressing the solicitor. "Mr Turner, always a pleasure to see you. We're going to take your client for an interview now, unless you need extra time with him?"

Graham Turner rose purposefully from the cell bench to his full 5 feet 4 inches and acted as if he was rising to address the Supreme Court, "You are not taking my client anywhere until you explain why he is being kept in such degrading conditions and why his human rights have been so badly infringed."

Bill nodded, it was going to be the usual set of complaints. Graham Turner had a reputation for making a lot of noise. Of course, none of it ever helped his clients, but it sounded good to them and they thought he was fighting their corner, when usually he was just delaying the inevitable and in some cases his client was kept longer in the police station than was necessary. That was not the case here though, Joseph Rogers was not going anywhere.

Bill put on his best smile and addressed a Graham, "You know the procedure Mr Turner. If you have any issues, raise a formal complaint with the custody sergeant. However, I need to interview your client. If you need further time with him, that's fine, if not, can we move to the interview room?"

Graham was not going to be placated, "I do not need further time with Mr Rogers. As far as I'm concerned, I've had wholly inadequate disclosure; it's obvious that this case has not been properly investigated, my client has been kept in degrading and unsettling conditions and cannot think straight, never mind answer detailed questions. I shall be advising him to make no comment to all questions asked and I shall convince a judge at court that no adverse inference should be drawn against his interests because of the several breaches of his human rights."

Bill sighed, "If you're saying your client is not fit to be interviewed, we can delay the process and get a doctor to see him and give an opinion."

Graham, stood back slightly and glanced at his watch, "That will not be necessary, we shall take our chances with the court."

Bill grinned, he had been through almost exactly the same conversation with this odious little man, on several occasions in the past. By the time the cases came to court, no barrister instructed by Graham Turner ever argued against a judge giving an adverse inference direction to the jury. They always accepted that there was no good reason for failing to answer questions.

Just over an hour later, all four of them were returning to the cells. Bill had asked numerous questions in the interview and Joseph, on the advice of his solicitor had refused to answer any of them. Graham Turner had made a brief statement at the beginning of the interview saying his client would not be answering any questions because of several breaches of the Human Rights Act. None of this bothered Bill. As far as he was concerned, he had enough evidence in any event to charge Joseph. The process was always the same, within the next hour he would leave the cells once more and hear that he was being charged with the offence of murder. Later that night he would be transferred to Lewis Prison and there he would stay until his trial.

CHAPTER 4

ALL AT SEA

"Cheers darling."

Wendy pushed her glass of champagne towards David's and their glasses clinked. It was Saturday 7th October 2017, and they were both standing on their balcony outside their port side cabin, watching as their ship, the Odin, made its way through the Solent on the way from Southampton towards Norway.

They had both decided that they needed a holiday and David had been able to finance one from the payments he had received to date for the Tatiana Volkov case. The case had ended as he expected. The jury had unanimously convicted her and the other defendants after just two days of deliberation. He suspected they had not taken long on her case and had spent most of their time deciding the guilt or innocence of two of the other defendants who had some points in their favour, however, weak.

On Friday 23rd September 2017, Tatiana received a sentence of six years imprisonment, which he considered was a good result. She could easily have received more. Fortunately, the judge had clearly not blamed her for the piece of unflattering artistry that he had come across earlier in the case.

Of course, the visit to the cells after the verdict had been traumatic. Tatiana had been distraught at the idea of being sent to prison and then probably deported and David's attempts to comfort her, had failed miserably. He finally left her stating that he would look through the papers and his notes of the trial to see whether there were any grounds of appeal. He knew it was unlikely that he would find any. The case had been overwhelming and none of the judge's important legal rulings had gone against Tatiana's interests. She had thanked him for his efforts and handed him a picture she had drawn. It was a perfect representation of him addressing the jury. She was clearly quite an accomplished artist!

He raised his glass in silent salute to Tatiana, after all, in a way she had paid for this cruise and the complimentary bottle of champagne that came with the cabin.

He looked back from the balcony into their home for the next week. It was a spacious deluxe balcony cabin. He could see Rose in her cot placed next to their king-sized bed. She was asleep, breathing deeply, still attached by nasal cannulas to her portable oxygen tank that had to be taken everywhere with her, along with a spare. The cabin had all that they required for a week complete with an ensuite bathroom which contained a jacuzzi style bath and a separate shower.

He turned back to Wendy who, unbeknownst to him, was watching a jet skier apparently racing their ship, crossing and recrossing the bow at a considerable speed.

"Idiot," she muttered loudly, before she turned around to face a startled David and asked, "How long is it before we arrive in Norway?"

He smiled realising that her first comment was not directed at him and answered, "We spend tonight and all of tomorrow at sea and should arrive in Bergen the following morning at around 9am."

She grinned, she was aware what time they arrived in Bergen, but it amused her to have David explain it. She knew he was overjoyed when he had been able to arrange this late holiday and find a decent cabin available on the ship. She also knew he had really looked forward to the trip and getting away from work and chambers for a week and that he had memorised the itinerary for every day of their voyage.

David began to refill their glasses as they watched the Isle of Wight pass slowly by. Their peace was momentarily disturbed when there was an annoying tannoy, announcing, "Could all passengers please collect their life belts and go to their muster stations for an emergency drill."

They both looked at each other, knowing how important it was to discover where they should muster in an emergency and that it was essential that all passengers complied with the drill. They also both looked at the sleeping Rose, grinned at each other like naughty schoolchildren and ignored the tannoy as David continued to pour the champagne.

One hour later they went to their designated dining hall, the Narvik Suite, for a welcome drink and canapés. They had finished the champagne long ago and felt it important to join their fellow travellers at this event. Rose had awakened from her afternoon nap and had been busy crawling around the cabin trying to pull her oxygen tank along with her, despite the fact they had attached an elongated cannula to it.

As they arrived in the dining room many heads turned to look towards Rose. She was in her pram with the oxygen tank hidden under her coat in the base. Nevertheless, a number stared at the cannulas and made hushed comments to each other. David and Wendy ignored them. They were very used to such reactions by now.

They seated themselves near a window where they were given glasses of Prosecco. Obviously, the ship's owners could not bring themselves to serve Champagne at such events, but the

Prosecco was of reasonable quality and was an acceptable alternative and David began to feel the pressures of the last few months slowly disappear.

He had one unusual case in the diary for November. It involved two old lag bank robbers and he anticipated the case would not take very long so he had no worries at the moment, save for the usual one of would there be any more cases coming his way for the remainder of 2017 and then 2018.

Putting aside such concerns, they talked to a few people during the get together but both soon became bored with the constant questions about Rose and her cannulas or the equally nauseating, 'how could they represent people they knew were guilty' when their fellow guests discovered they were barristers. After half an hour they returned to their cabin to relax before dinner.

At 7:30pm prompt they made their way down to have dinner in their allocated dining spot. They were allocated a pleasant table by a window on the port side of the ship with Wendy and Rose facing the direction of travel and David sitting exactly opposite them. It gave them an excellent view of the English countryside, just a few miles distant, bathed in the last vestiges of the evening sun.

No one was seated too near to them, which was merciful for other passengers, as Rose was a messy eater and felt the need to surround herself with scraps of food, up to a metre away from where she was seated.

David surveyed the other guests who were seated nearby, ensuring they were not within range of Rose's impeccable aim. For one so small she had an uncanny accuracy with a bread roll!

He did not recognise anybody but he did notice a black couple on a table nearby on his left hand side. They were mostly noticeable for their clothes. Both were very large and very well-dressed. The man wore a bright, white, remarkably clean, one piece-outfit like an Egyptian galibaya. He wore a small hat like a cut down fez and had very ornate shoes that looked like they were made from crocodile skin and ended in upturned silver points.

The woman wore a multi-coloured outfit which was stunning and seemed to have pearls sewn into the fabric which shone under the artificial lights of the dining room. She also wore a colourful scarf on her head which had diamond like stones set in it at regular distances. David noticed that the man was staring at him and as David caught his eyes, the man raised his glass.

It looked like the man recognised him but David was sure he had never seen him before. Nevertheless, he nodded at the man and then turned around to look towards Rose, who was busy propelling a piece of bread well over her usual one metre boundary, in the direction of another couple seated on a table near the couple he had just acknowledged.

After profuse apologies had been made, David and Wendy carried on with their meal with anything moveable carefully placed well outside the reach of little Rose, much to her annoyance which she remonstrated about by crying.

As the meal was ending, Wendy nudged David under the table and spoke to him in hushed tones, "Do you know that man at the table on your left? Don't look now but he keeps staring at you!"

David immediately looked in the direction of the man as Wendy scowled at him. The man again raised his glass and David once again nodded at him before turning to Wendy and answering, "No, I haven't got a clue who he is. I don't recognise him and there's no reason for him to recognise me. I suspect he's simply being polite and won't bother us. We have the best anti-people deterrent around in this little one."

He looked at Rose who had stopped crying and now smiled at him, and then, as if in silent agreement with his comment, hurled a small piece of bread, she had been hiding, towards him with her usual impeccable accuracy.

CHAPTER 5

THE TREATMENT

All he had wanted was a haircut but Wendy had different ideas.

"It's been a hard year for both of us, you deserve a bit of pampering, as do I!"

David had left Wendy to book them both, 'a bit of pampering,'

It was day two of the cruise and they were now in the North Sea, making their way slowly towards Norway. The weather was good and the sea unnaturally calm for this time of year so they were enjoying the cruise.

They spent the day mainly in their cabin or in one of the dining rooms, adding numerous unnecessary calories to their diet.

Eventually at just before 4pm David went to his allotted appointment. He made his way from their cabin on deck 4 at the rear of ship, to deck 12 at the front of the ship, where the beauty salon was located. He had noticed that the ship advertised its staff by proudly showing their photographs around the ship. Maria was the chief hair stylist. Her photograph showed a picture of a beautiful, well-endowed woman in her mid to late thirties, sporting a beautiful smile. Perhaps, this would be an enjoyable experience after all, he thought.

He made his way into the reception of the ship's 'Elysian Spa.' An attractive receptionist showed him to a comfortable seat and told him his stylist would be there any moment.

After a fifteen minute wait a high-pitched voice called out to him, "Mr Brant, I'll only be a few more minutes, I hope that is ok?"

David looked up from his phone which he had been idly playing with to see Julio, his hair stylist and chief pamperer. His face dropped. Julio looked hurt, "You were expecting someone else?"

David quickly responded with a smile, "No, not at all."

"Good, I will be with you in a minute, darling."

David looked towards the pretty receptionist with a distinct look of regret. A few minutes later Julio reappeared, "Please come with me."

David followed him, silently cursing Wendy.

Julio sat him in a chair facing a mirror and a basin. "This will be a wonderful experience for you!"

David gave an unconvincing nod.

"Let me begin by cutting your hair and then we will move on to the shave and the face mask."

"Face mask?" David responded rhetorically.

"Oh yes, your partner, Wendy, isn't it? She came to see me and insisted you have the best treatment possible and it is my job to ensure that is what you receive."

David gave another nod.

After fifteen minutes of touching David's hair and removing minute amounts, Julio looked at the finished product, "You look like a movie star now, you have such lovely hair."

David gave an uncomfortable, 'Thanks' as Julio moved on to the topic of shaving. "How do you shave David?"

David looked surprised at the question, "Like everyone I suppose."

Julio looked serious, "With the grain or against it?"

David thought for a moment before answering, presuming he had the right answer he said, "Against the grain."

Julio looked horrified, "No, no, no. You must always shave with the grain."

Julio then drew him a diagram showing David how he had been shaving improperly for the best part of 45 years.

After two hot towels, two cold towels, pre-shave, shaving gel, a thorough shave and the application of an aftershave balm, Julio looked at David's face as if he had produced a work of art.

"Wonderful. You look like a Greek God."

David squirmed in his seat.

"Now we must apply the facial scrub and then the face mask."

David noticed the balding man in the chair next to him grinning as he was having a simple haircut from the chief hair stylist, Maria, that for obvious reasons was concentrating on his sides. How David envied him at this moment.

Julio scrubbed away vigorously at David's face before applying a white cream which hardened quickly into a mask.

"Beautiful." enthused Julio.

Twenty minutes later Julio unpeeled the mask and scrubbed away at any parts that failed to be removed by a simple peel.

"Wonderful. Just feel your skin David. Doesn't that feel smooth. You must keep it that way if your skin is not to age prematurely."

He paused before adding, "I have a selection of products for you here."

David, shook his head, "No, I don't think so. I'll see how things go for 24 hours before I think of purchasing anything."

Julio adopted a hurt look. "No David, you look wonderful but if you don't buy these products you will soon revert to the state you were in when I first saw you today."

He shook his head, "Shocking that such a handsome man could let himself go in that way."

He picked up a bag of products, "I cannot allow that to happen. I will apply a 10% discount to the products just because I know you need them. Your partner, Wendy, would never forgive me if I allowed you to leave without them."

Ten minutes later David entered his cabin where Wendy was lying on the bed watching a movie and little Rose was sleeping in her cot. Wendy looked at him, beaming and then whispered, "Wow, you look ten years younger!"

He just grunted a reply as she noticed the bag he was carrying, "What have you got there?"

David looked at the bag in his hand which had just cost the best part of £80 and which he had felt under duress to buy.

"Oh, just a few essentials to keep me looking ten years younger." He quickly placed the bag in the side compartment of his suitcase, knowing it would probably never leave that location again.

CHAPTER 6

ARRIVING IN BERGEN

David rose at 6am to watch the ship travel up the Hjeltefjorden. He had never been to Norway before and had woken up when the Sun shone through a small gap in the cabin's curtains. He immediately, but quietly, made his way past Rose's cot and went onto the balcony to watch as the ship slowly made its way down the deep fjord. With the sunlight breaking over the mountains and the gentle lapping of the waves against the hull of the ship, he felt mesmerised and sat down to enjoy the thrill of his first trip in a fjord. It reminded him of all the films he had seen of Viking ships travelling home from one of the many raids on England, although fortunately his journey was considerably more peaceful.

At just before 8am, Rose awoke and made herself known to the world. That caused Wendy to wake, who, upon seeing the sunshine streaming in through the gap in the curtain, gave Rose a cuddle and a bottle of milk to consume, before she joined David on the balcony and put her arm through his, whispering, "It's so beautiful and surprisingly warm for Norway at this time of year."

He nodded and put his arm around her as they watched the ship pass the few houses that could be seen on the shoreline.

At almost exactly 9am the ship docked in Bergen, Norway. David, Wendy and Rose were all seated in the deck fourteen restaurant, enjoying a large breakfast. They had booked a walking tour of Bergen which started at 11am and they had wanted to ensure that they all had a satisfying meal inside them on what might prove to be a long journey. Wendy had heard that the dock at Bergen was not pram friendly as there were too many cobbled streets and so she had opted to carry Rose in a chest harness that both would take turns in wearing. They had a small oxygen cylinder to take with them that was carried in an article resembling a small rucksack.

At 11am they received their embarkation cards and left the ship to join their guide Elizabet, who would take them round and explain the history of Bergen and point out the interesting sites.

The tour commenced at the fortress, the Bergenhus Festning. The guide told them that it had only ever been involved in combat once in 1665 when an English fleet had chased a Dutch treasure fleet into Bergen harbour and tried to seize it. Elizabet seemed to take delight in explaining that the English fleet had suffered heavy casualties, before adding, "We give our

English visitors a much more welcoming greeting these days!"

David was quite interested in the history of the place but noted Wendy stifling a yawn and looking around at the trees and grassland which she was far more interested in than the historical fortress.

As he followed her gaze, David noticed that the well-dressed couple, that he had seen the night before last, were on the tour. The man was wearing another long flowing galibaya, this time coloured bright blue. He wore the same fez that he had worn at dinner. At least David thought it was the same fez. The man's wife was in another multi-coloured dress, though she was wearing a coat, presumably in case the weather changed.

David had seen the couple on the ship since the night the man had acknowledged him but they had always been some distance away. This time, as their group made their way round the castle, the man seemed to edge his way closer to David. Eventually, just as Elizabet was informing the group that a Dutch munitions vessel had blown up in the harbour during the Second World War, damaging most of the buildings in the castle, the man acknowledged David again. This time he came within a couple of feet of David and said, "Mr Brant QC, I hope you do not mind my introducing myself to you and your lovely wife?"

David had no intention of giving the man a potted history of his relationship with Wendy and why they had not married, so he just acknowledged the man and asked, "How do you know my name?"

The man beamed at him, "Of course I know the famous Queen's Counsel, David Brant. I followed your recent case, the case of the Russian lady who was charged with fraud. I saw your photograph in the newspaper."

David noticed the slight frown that appeared on Wendy's face but ignored it and addressed the man. "Clearly, you have the advantage over me. This is my better half, Wendy and tied to her is our daughter Rose. I'm sorry but I don't know your name."

The man took his fez off and bowed, "My name is Dr Frances Ignatious Sanda and this is my wife, Grace Wilhelmina Sanda."

David acknowledged them both as did Wendy. Rose simply cried as she struggled violently with the baby harness, without achieving any notable success. The couples passed a few words before Elizabet indicated they should move on as she now wanted to take them to the German Hanseatic houses built by the German Hanseatic league, traders, who, she told them, had first set foot in Bergen in the 13th Century AD and then colonised the area.

After a further one hour of walking around the streets of Bergen; visiting the Holy Mary Church, the wooden Hanseatic houses, the Hanseatic museum and the lake, which Elizabet proudly told them was made from a glacier, Elizabet announced that she would now take them up the funicular railway so that they could receive a panoramic view of Bergen.

It was at that stage that Wendy announced that she was returning to the ship with Rose because her shoulders and back were hurting from using the harness and carrying the oxygen. David offered to wear it but Wendy said she thought that taking the harness off her and then putting it on David would cause too much stress to Rose and it would be better for her to simply return to the ship. In any event she told him in a lowered voice, she had seen enough of Bergen and she could not bear any more history about Bergen.

David mildly protested but in fact welcomed some time to himself. A few minutes after saying goodbye to Wendy and Rose, he caught the funicular railway to the top of Bergen and did enjoy spectacular views of the city. Elizabet announced that they would have some free time in this location, so he took the opportunity to go around the area taking several photographs to show Wendy what she had missed. As he set off away from the tour group, Dr Sanda approached him again.

"I see you are alone Mr Brant QC. If you wish, you would be welcome to join my wife and myself on this tour."

David hesitated before replying. He would rather be on his own but did not want to appear rude. He started by saying, "Please, call me David. Thank you for your kind offer, but I wouldn't want to impose. Anyway, I promised to take photographs up here for Wendy who has had to return to the ship with our little one. I will have to move at quite a pace to ensure that she can see everything."

Dr Sanda smiled and bowed to him. "I perfectly understand. My wife and I have five children. All are grown now but we remember when they were young and how difficult we found things with them."

He paused before continuing with a sad expression, "Unfortunately, even when they grow up they can cause severe problems for their parents."

David tried to be light hearted, "I know, I have two grown up children who still cause me problems."

Dr Sanda gave him a faint smile and moved away with his wife. David noticed that she took very little part in their conversations and never seemed to smile, as though she was seriously troubled by something. He soon dismissed the thought. He was on holiday and enjoying himself and did not have time for other people's problems. That was his occupation, he did not want to have to deal with people's problems on his vacation as well.

He took a few photographs and a video of almost the whole of Bergen that could be seen from this vantage point. As he was filming, he saw a goat climbing up a steep incline towards him and marvelled at its dexterity. He put all concerns about the Sanda's potential problems out of his mind and aimed his camera at the goat. Even if Wendy might not be interested in the photograph, Rose probably would be!

CHAPTER 7

A TRIP TO THE GLACIER

Two days later the ship docked in the pretty port of Olden so that the passengers could visit the impressive Briksdal Glacier. David had not seen the Sandas again except from a distance and he had not made any real effort to communicate with them. He had seen that Mrs Sanda continued to look morose and quite frankly he wanted to enjoy his holiday and thought her company might be slightly depressing. It was therefore with some degree of concern that he saw the Sandas enter his coach for the journey to the glacier.

They had a new guide, Lars, who told them he was a former school teacher and had lived in the region all his life. He clearly had considerable knowledge about the area because it seemed to David that the man never stopped talking. David was relieved when the coach stopped by a lake so that the coach party could get some photographs of the area and David could get away from the constant commentary.

David made his way across the road towards the glacial lake that had formed at the base of the nearby mountains. Wendy appeared to enjoy the guide's commentary because she followed him with Rose attached to her by the chest harness. Lars pointed out some stone structures which visitors seemed to have created by piling small stones onto one another. 'No doubt there's an interesting reason why they've done that,' thought David, showing no interest whatsoever.

After ten minutes they were all ushered back onto the coach as it took them closer to the Briksdal glacier. Now the guide was regaling them with stories about how many hundreds of people had died over the last century during avalanches in this area, "But don't worry, there's no danger of that happening today," he added cheerfully as everyone looked nervously around them at the mountains.

Eventually the coach stopped in a beautiful location where they were surrounded by mountains and waterfalls with a fast moving glacial stream nearby. Here they were told the walk to the glacier and back would take no more than forty five minutes and then they would be treated to cakes and coffee in one of the local cafes.

The walk to and from the glacier took them just over an hour. It was an upward climb on the way there and they took it in turns with the chest harness, Rose seemingly enjoying the attention when they disturbed her to change over, rather than complaining vociferously as Wendy had feared.

David was on harness duty as they crossed a bridge that was under a roaring river. The spray from the river was like a cloud and he had to make considerable efforts to keep Rose dry, getting saturated himself, but he thought the journey well worthwhile and to him, the trip to the glacier was the highlight of the cruise.

Eventually they came as close as they could to the Briksdal glacier. It had receded greatly from the time that photographs in their travel brochure had been taken, but it was still impressive. In front of them there was a high cliff with a small part of the glacier visible at the top and then a great deal of ice and rock cascading down from the top, stopping about thirty feet above the glacial lake. They were told that the glacier was constantly feeding the lake and river with something like 10,000 litres of water a second. The ice was so dense that it did not let light through and so the glacier looked like it was a dreamy light blue in colour.

It was too good an opportunity to miss and David tried to manoeuvre his camera to take a selfie of the three of them with the glacier, mountain and lake behind them.

"Here, let me help you, I can take the photograph for you."

David looked round to see that it was Dr Sanda addressing him.

He responded with thanks as Dr Sanda took the camera and took a few photographs of them from different angles so that they had a number to choose from when they returned home.

Dr Sanda returned the camera and asked, "I wonder if you can do me a favour, Mr Brant?"

Thinking he wanted a photograph, David quickly replied, "Of course."

Dr Sanda beamed at him, "My wife and I are dining in the Valhalla restaurant tonight next to the Spa, we find it boring on our own and would greatly appreciate it if you could both join us, with your beautiful daughter ... as our guests of course."

David's face fell, he was willing to take a photograph but spending a whole evening with the Sandas had not been in his thoughts at all."

Wendy quickly spoke for him, "That is so very kind of you, of course we would love to attend as your guests, but are you sure you will be able to get a reservation, we've tried and been told there are not tables available this cruise?"

David gave her a look that she recognised, but as usual ignored. The Odin was like most cruise ships, the food was inclusive and there was a choice of standard restaurants. However, it also possessed three exclusive restaurants where you paid extra for the dining experience. The Valhalla was the most exclusive of the lot and charged an extra £50 a head to dine It was apparently small and although he had tried to get a table, he was told that they were fully booked for the whole cruise.

Dr Sanda did not appear to notice David's look as he continued, "It is an intimate dining room and is sold out quickly. I managed to speak to the Head Waiter though and he reserved for us a large table for every night of the cruise except for our first, when we dined in one of the ordinary restaurants."

David had no doubt how the talk with the Head Waiter went. It no doubt cost Dr Sanda a great deal more than £50 each but from the look of his and his wife's clothes, he could afford it.

David knew he had no choice in the matter, "Of course we would be delighted to be your guests, providing we can reciprocate in some way during the voyage."

Dr Sanda grinned at him, "Excellent, shall we say 7:30pm for cocktails in the Valhalla bar, followed by dinner at 8pm."

Wendy again answered for them both, "That will be lovely."

Dr Sanda took off his fez and bowed slightly to her before he and his wife left them. It might have been David's imagination, but he was sure that Mrs Sanda was smiling for the first time he could remember on this trip."

CHAPTER 8

A POTENTIAL BRIEF

David, Wendy and Rose attended the Valhalla bar promptly at 7:30pm. They were immediately shown to a table where Dr Sanda and his wife were seated. They were both sipping large Pina coladas. Dr Sanda immediately got up when he saw them coming and grabbed David's hand, in both of his, "Thank you, thank you so much for accepting our invitation."

David was slightly taken aback by the enthusiastic welcome but managed to say, almost convincingly, that they had been happy to accept.

They seated themselves and ordered two Pina coladas for themselves with an orange juice for Rose. Wendy had insisted they all get dressed up for a meal in the Valhalla restaurant and she was wearing a long flowing blue dinner dress whilst David wore his black dinner jacket and trousers and sported a blue bow tie. Rose was dressed in what looked to David like an expensive dress. He had never seen it before and doubted Rose would ever wear it again. He tried to put aside the thought of how much it had cost to be worn just once on this cruise!

Dr Sanda was wearing a dinner jacket and trousers as well and was also sporting a black bow tie. Mrs Sanda was wearing yet another brightly coloured dress with matching headdress.

They all sipped at their cocktails and swopped pleasantries. They discussed the cruise so far. The quality of the food and the excursions they had been on and which ones they enjoyed best. Dr Sanda did most of the talking for him and his wife and Wendy did most of the talking for them. Rose was quite quiet and sipped on her orange juice until she found more pleasure in knocking her glass over and joyously watching the juice travel from the table to the floor in a small waterfall.

David was about to apology when Dr Sanda just smiled and with the slightest hand gesture ordered a waiter over to clear up the mess and provide another orange juice so the entire process could be repeated.

At 8pm they made their way to their table. It had five settings and David found it hard to believe that Dr Sanda had managed to book a table this size for almost the entire duration of the cruise for just himself and his wife. 'It must have cost him a fortune,' he thought.

As if on cue, the head waiter appeared and enthused over Dr Sanda. 'Yes, it cost an absolute fortune', David observed to himself.

The head waiter served them all night and was particularly attentive to Rose and Wendy. David had not doubt that this was on instruction from Dr Sanda. He wondered if Dr Sanda wanted something from him at the Briksdal glacier or was just a generous man. Now he was convinced Dr Sanda wanted something from him, but he could not think what it was. It was not as if he had large sums of money to invest in some dubious scheme, though he supposed Dr Sanda might not think that. He might have the public's impression that all criminal silks were loaded.

As if Dr Sanda knew what he was thinking, he suddenly turned to David and asked, "Are you all right David, you look like you are apprehensive about something?"

David's expression quickly changed, "I'm sorry I was somewhere else, thinking about one of my cases," he lied easily.

"Oh yes, your cases. You must conduct some very interesting cases as a criminal Queen's Counsel?"

David smiled, "Some are very interesting, some are very boring. I suppose it's like many jobs really."

Dr Sanda shook his head, "I cannot believe that your job is boring at any time. You must have interesting cases, interesting clients. Do you ever conduct murder cases?"

David nodded, "Yes, most of my cases are murder cases, although as you saw from the newspapers, I also conduct fraud trials as well."

Dr Sanda looked deep in thought, "How many murder trials have you conducted?"

David paused before replying trying to think back to almost forty years of practice at the bar, "I don't know, I've never really kept count. I suppose over my career it's been close to a hundred."

"They must be very difficult cases to conduct. I suspect the police and the prosecution make an extra effort to win in murder cases?"

"They do, it is after all the most serious crime out there."

Dr Sanda nodded and then added, "Have you ever won a murder case?"

David smiled at him, "The police and the prosecution do make an extra effort in murder cases and you're right, they are difficult to conduct and often very interesting. They often involve expert witnesses who are used to giving evidence in court and are quite a challenge, but yes, I have won a few."

Wendy intervened, "David is being modest, he has won a considerable number of murder cases. Probably more than most criminal silks. Of course, I am biased, but I was a solicitor before I became a barrister and I have seen many criminal silks in murder cases and I can say, David is one of the best."

Dr Sanda looked at his wife and simply answered, "I thought that would be the case."

They all moved onto other subjects whilst they enjoyed the food and wine. Dr Sanda chose the wine and David noted that none of the bottles he chose were under £250 in price. He really enjoyed the experience and acknowledged to himself that he was glad he had not had to take Wendy here at these prices.

Rose was good for most of the meal enjoying the attention of the waitresses who all exclaimed how cute she was. She finally dropped off to sleep in the high chair as they enjoyed their main courses. Fortunately, the high chair was an expensive one not found in other parts of the ship and they were able to recline it so Rose could get some proper sleep before they took her back to their cabin.

After the dessert, Dr Sanda asked Wendy if she would mind if he took David out onto the restaurant's private balcony, so they could enjoy a fifty year old brandy together. Wendy managed to persuade Mrs Sanda to open up about herself and talk to her now, so she readily agreed. It was David who was more reluctant as he had anticipated that this moment was coming. Still the lure of a fifty year-old brandy had its effect and he followed Dr Sanda outside onto the balcony.

It was cold outside but fortunately the restaurant had provided heaters and David enjoyed the sea breeze and the night's sky. Although there was some light pollution from the ship, it was limited and the sky was full of stars and David could make out several constellations, even if the only one he could name was Orion.

After a few seconds Dr Sanda turned towards him looking serious. 'Here it comes', thought David.

"David, I have marvelled at how good your daughter has been tonight. Children are such a blessing to us."

He paused before continuing.

"You told me you had two grown up children who you rarely see these days. I have a son, Joseph, who is aged 21. He has caused me many problems in the past. He rebelled as a teenager. He refused the opportunities given to him.

We sent him to a public boarding school in Kent but he was expelled. We managed to send him to another public school in London where he did well. I wanted him to go to Oxford or Cambridge universities but he refused. He wanted to go to a university in Sussex where some girl was attending who he was enamoured with. I argued with him of course but to no avail. He even changed his last name by deed poll, as if embarrassed to be associated with the family.

He then went to the university to study engineering rather than law which I hoped for and refused further contact with my wife or myself. We had not heard from him for over a year … until recently."

David nodded sympathetically, not knowing what he could say or do.

Dr Sanda continued, "Now he has finally contacted us. He has got himself into trouble and is to appear in Lewes Crown Court for a trial. He already has lawyers but they are telling him he should plead guilty. I want someone who will fight his case and give him every chance of an acquittal. I wondered if you might be able to help him?"

David's fears of being asked to invest in some dubious scheme were clearly unfounded. Indeed, it sounded like he was going to be briefed on a private case, probably some minor affray or criminal damage charge, but if it paid privately, what did he care.

"Of course, if I can help, I will. What's he charged with?"

Dr Sanda looked him straight in the eyes as he silently mouthed the word, "Murder."

CHAPTER 9

HOMEWARD BOUND

"Their son is charged with murder! I can't believe it. They seem such a nice couple, what a terrible thing to happen to them."

Wendy had been like this since David had told her about Dr Sanda's request to represent his son, two days ago now. It surprised David a little for a criminal barrister to react in this way, having seen what Wendy had seen in her practice and how perfectly decent, honest people can easily get caught up in crime due to a close relative or friend. He put it down to the fact that she had been away from chambers and criminal practice for over a year now. She really needed to get back, but that was hardly likely to happen with Rose still needing very close care and Wendy not trusting nannies or wanting to be away from Rose for any length of time.

The day following their dinner with the Sandas they had visited the port of Stavanger in Norway. He had found it a little bit of a let down after visiting the glacier. He opted for, 'the Viking tour'; which had turned out to be a coach journey to some radio tower for a view of Stavanger, a trip to a fjord to see three large swords sticking out of the ground commemorating some Viking battle from an unknown date, followed by a trip to a small, distinctly uninspiring museum. He wished he had not bothered by the end of the day and had spent the day with Wendy, who said she had an enjoyable time visiting the Stavanger flower island.

He had only seen Dr Sanda and his wife in the distance and not spoken to them again. The case might not find its way to him. He had received hundreds of promises of cases in his career and knew only a fraction of the promises turned into actual briefs.

In this case there was the added difficulty that Dr Sanda was not the client. His son was the person charged with murder and he might like his lawyers and have faith in them. Further, the solicitors would no doubt try to keep the brief with the silk they had instructed who they no doubt trusted and had a good relationship with. In any event the silk would undoubtedly work hard with his clerk to keep the brief. David might as well forget about this offer.

The ship left Stavanger four hours after its allotted slot due to the 'reserve engine' malfunctioning. The Captain of the ship sent a cheery message to them all that they would not thank him if he set off for the North Sea with a broken engine and they would have to wait for the engineer to fix the problem. As a result, some of the passengers had assumed a waxen ashen pale visage as they walked around the ship, worried that they might be set adrift in one of the world's notoriously bad seas. It did not encourage them that the next port was Southampton and they would spend the next day and a half at sea.

The prospect of breaking down had not unduly worried David or Wendy who assumed that the reserve engine was not needed unless one of the others broke down. David did take the precaution of checking that the lifebelts were in place in the cabin and he also checked where their muster station was, temporarily regretting sipping champagne when they should have been fully involved in the drill on the first day of their voyage.

Fortunately, there were no mishaps on the return to Southampton and the North Sea had been friendly to the ship. On the last day they had only seen the odd ship and a solitary oil rig and no land, so they were quite happy as they returned to Southampton, although sorry the holiday was over.

At 9am they went down for their last breakfast on the ship and then had to wait two hours before they could disembark. As they did so David bumped into Dr Sanda and his wife. Dr

Sanda was his usual cheery self, though his wife had returned to her former depressed state.

Dr Sanda grabbed David's hand and told him, "I will arrange for Joseph's solicitors to send his papers to you as soon as I return home. Please look out for papers in the name 'Joseph Rogers.' Thank you so much for agreeing to help him."

David beamed at Dr Sanda and clasped his hand, "Not at all, I am looking forward to meeting him and helping in any way that I can."

With a final wave he said goodbye to the Sandas, fully expecting not to have anything to do with them or their son again.

CHAPTER 10

THE CIVIL PARTNERSHIP

Even though it had only ended three weeks ago, the cruise seemed a distant memory as David entered court room 4 at Inner London Crown Court on 6th November 2017. Now he had been instructed privately to represent William Hargreaves and Benn Fright, known affectionately as the 'Bill and Ben crew' to their criminal associates. Both were aged in their late sixties and had a long history of bank robbery recorded against their names. It was something that ran in the family as both had fathers who had been bank robbers and all of them had spent close to half their lives in prison.

Bank robbery was not a popular crime amongst the criminal fraternity these days dues to the heavy sentences handed out to convicted bank robbers and the security measures employed by banks that had discouraged such activity. However, Bill and Ben had never learnt any other professional or even criminal trade and had been planning another bank robbery when they had been arrested. They had entered into a simple agreement. They would both 'employ' a get-away driver and then rob a small bank in Clapham in South London. It was an independent bank and they had both assumed that it would have limited security. They had both only recently been released from fifteen year prison sentences which they had received for their last bank robbery. Both qualified for legal aid but their extended families had insisted that they be represented by a 'silk' and hence David had been instructed.

Although the trial was listed for two whole weeks, David's fee was not a large one. The evidence was overwhelming as they had not known who to approach as a get-away driver as many of their previous contacts were dead or in prison and they had been led by an underworld informant to an undercover police officer who had taped their conversations. They had then promptly been arrested. They pleaded not guilty because they had one highly novel legal argument that they hoped would stop the trial. If it failed, they had told David that they would both plead guilty.

David entered the robing room on the second floor and changed his jacket for a silk waistcoat and gown and placed his wig carefully on his head. Looking in the mirror he could not help noting how torn his silk gown was and how the cuffs of his silk jacket were becoming worn. His wig was looking the worse for wear as well. He decided the next time he had about £3,000 to spare, he would replace them!

As he was contemplating his attire an in-house Crown Prosecution Service barrister walked into the room.

"Hello David, ready for your unique legal argument, or are your boys ready to see sense and plead. There's still some credit for plea available?"

David turned to face Geoffrey Carter. He was just about six feet tall, slightly overweight and sported a beard. Quite jovial and friendly and on the two previous occasions David had met him, had never engaged in trying 'robing room tactics', the attempts at one-upmanship that lesser advocates usually engage in.

David grinned back at him and took this for what it was, a little bit of banter, "I'm definitely ready Geoff and I can say now if you were to drop the case, my two would not seek any costs against the Crown Prosecution Service."

After a friendly chat about the case they went their separate ways. Geoffrey to find the police officer in charge of his case and David to visit his clients in the cells.

Twenty minutes later David was seated in a cell when the two defendants were brought in. Both were grinning which surprised David. If the legal argument was not successful they were facing another lengthy sentence of imprisonment and as both had only served half of their last sentence they had half of that sentence left to be added to it.

"You two seem cheerful! You do realise that today is the first day of your trial?"

Bill was the one to reply, "Oh that Mr Brant, we've both treated trials as a form of 'occupational hazard', a kind of unpleasant tax system which applies to people in our line of work.

We were both laughing with the guards. You see, we've both been sharing a cell in Wandsworth prison. As the guards pointed out, it's the first time they have ever heard of a married couple sharing a cell in an English prison!"

David smiled, it was certainly the first time he had heard of such an arrangement as well.

Half an hour later he was in court 4 with his clients behind him in the dock. He was in front of HHJ Joseph Tainworth, one of the most stoic and least friendly judges in London.

"Are we ready to swear a jury Mr Brant?"

David rose from his seat to answer, "No, your honour, there is a legal argument that we would both like to raise with your honour before a jury is sworn. If successful there will not be a need for a trial and selecting and swearing a jury would be an unnecessary waste of time."

Tainworth was clearly not impressed, "If there is a legal argument that might end the case, why have you waited to raise it at the last minute on the very first day of the trial. I trust it is not for a reason that affects your fees?"

David's expression clearly conveyed his anger at the suggestion. If he was legally aided and the case was listed for trial then his fee would be higher than if a successful legal point had been taken earlier in the proceedings. However, as he was privately instructed, with the client's family paying the fee, it made no difference when the legal argument was raised. In any event it would have been unprofessional to wait until this stage to raise a legal argument with clients both languishing in prison and he did not like the implication.

"Certainly not! I have been instructed on a private basis and my fee is not affected in any way by the timing of this application. Indeed, we tried to have this application heard much earlier, not least because my clients have been remanded in custody, but we were told that there was no court time available and the earliest such an application could be heard would be in front of the trial judge when the case was listed for trial."

"So why can't I swear a jury?"

"Because as I've pointed out it may be a complete waste of their time. They would be sworn and the defendants put in their charge. They would then have to wait until the legal argument was over and then, if successful, your honour would have to have them assembled again for you to direct them to acquit. That would be a complete waste of everyone's time, particularly if the jurors could be utilised in other courtrooms."

Tainworth ignored the latter argument and ceased on one issue, "Did you say that your clients instructed you on a private basis? How could they afford your fees, they've were both in prison for over seven years, then released and then committed this offence, they've had no time to earn enough to pay for representation by Queen's Counsel?"

David looked at him coldly, "I did not say they were paying, I said that I was privately instructed. They have an extended family who have no doubt struggled to put together sufficient funds to pay for the legal services for family members who are of course innocent until proven guilty."

Tainworth was clearly not impressed. "I suppose the real reason you do not want a jury sworn is that it will count as the trial starting and if they then plead guilty the discount will have reduced even further!

Your clients are obviously aware that the discount for a plea at the first opportunity is a one third reduction in sentence, thereafter it goes down to a one quarter reduction until the day of the trial when it is reduced to one tenth and after the trial has started but before the jury concludes, even less than that at my discretion!"

David was becoming even more annoyed at the judge, particularly as he was right about the latter point!

"We have not reached a point where we can discuss pleas. My clients have the utmost faith in the legal argument that applies to their unique circumstances. Has your honour read the skeleton arguments?"

Tainworth answered gruffly, "No, when I logged onto the computer system this morning I had difficulty finding the skeleton arguments. You had better take me through them!"

David nodded, the whole point about the digital case management system operating in all the Crown Courts now, was that the parties could upload documents before the hearing for the judge to read. He had uploaded his own skeleton argument personally and could see it now, clearly on the system. He had no doubt what the real reason was why the judge had not read the arguments, however, he simply nodded and added, "I'm delighted to."

He took a printed copy of his skeleton argument and handed a copy to the usher for her to give to the judge. He then slowly took the judge through it.

"The defendants are both charged with one offence of conspiracy to commit a robbery. It being alleged that they agreed together to rob the Clapham Independent Bank on a date sometime between 1st June 2017 and 29th July 2017.

The main evidence in this case derives from a statement made by an undercover police officer who has been given the name 'Michael' for this case. The defendants were put in contact with him by a criminal associate. He claimed that he was an accomplished getaway driver and they were allegedly looking for a getaway driver so that they could rob the bank.

The defendants met with Michael on one occasion on Friday 28th July 2017 in a back room of a public house called the Dog and Dart, in the Mile End Road, London. Michael was wearing what is colloquially called 'a wire' or more properly, a digital recording device and their entire conversation has been recorded and transcribed. The relevant parts of the transcript can be found at pages 31 and 32 of the exhibits bundle."

Tainworth negotiated his way to page 31 of the exhibits on the computer screen in front of him as David continued, "The defendant, William Hargreaves is alleged to have said, 'You see

Michael we have been doing a bit of a 'reccy' since early June and we reckon they have a cash delivery after 3pm, every Friday. We want to strike at 3:05pm; go in with the shooters, make a bit of a noise, shoot a couple of rounds into the roof, grab the cash, get out of the bank and get straight into a car driven by you. You'll then take us to Brixton at speed where we ditch the car and get into another one which we've stolen that day and parked up before and then ride slowly away. It's really quite straightforward. We will count the usable cash, you always lose some to dye or spillage, then we split it twenty per cent to you and forty per cent to each of us as we're taking the major risk.'

As you will note, Benjamin Fright is then alleged to have said, "Is that alright with you Michael?'

Michael came back with the response, 'There's still a great deal of risk for me and the sentence will be the same for all of us, what about giving me 30% and you two taking 35% each?"

Benn Fright responded, "No, it's our plan, we've done the reccy, we do the hard work, the most we are offering is 20%. There are other drivers out there you know."

Before Michael could answer, five uniformed police men burst into the room and 'arrested' all three.

Both defendants were interviewed and on the advice of their solicitors they made no comment to all the questions they were asked. Since then they have both served defence statements in which they do not deny the accuracy of the transcripts and admit the attribution of the conversation to themselves. However, both raise the same defence. They cannot be guilty of conspiracy to rob because they are in a 'civil partnership'. Both were released from prison on Friday 5th May 2017. They then entered into a civil partnership on 20th May 2017."

Tainworth looked aghast, "Are you claiming that your clients are both gay?"

"No, in fact they are not. They simply entered into a civil partnership because they had made joint wills leaving their property to the other in the event of their death, thus avoiding inheritance tax. It also has the unexpected benefit of protecting them from a conspiracy charge."

Tainworth was almost apoplectic with rage, "What absolute nonsense, two heterosexual men cannot claim the benefit of a law that protects married or gay couples! In any event, how can they legitimately possess enough property to worry about inheritance tax. I forget the exact amount but the limit is several hundred thousand pounds."

As usual David put his head around the clerks' room door and gave a cheery, 'Hello'. Strangely none of the clerks looked busy, something that made him deeply suspicious. The clerks' room always looked busy even if they had nothing to do. He suspected it was something to do with the fact that none of them had received a rise in the last two years because chambers' income was falling and there simply were not the funds available to pay for a rise. He had heard that the clerks were complaining to junior members of chambers about the difficulties of making ends meet, ignoring the fact that the juniors' incomes were decreasing at the same time as their costs of being in chambers were increasing. He assumed the clerks were showing their dissatisfaction at the situation by having a 'go slow'.

John Winston returned David's greeting and just as David was leaving the room he shouted out, "Mr Brant, good news, a murder brief has come in for you. It's from a new firm to Chambers, Gardeners, in Brighton. Do you know anyone in the firm, sir?"

David replied candidly, "No, I think I've heard of the firm, they are a busy criminal practice, aren't they? But I don't think I know any of the partners."

John Winston beamed, "It's a firm I've been targeting for some time now, but they've been wedded to Michael Bell, so I'm happy they've instructed you on a murder."

David knew of Michael Bell's reputation. He was a senior clerk in Ravensbourne Chambers. A set of chambers just outside the Temple and north of Fleet Street. The chambers were very busy mainly due to Michael Bell, who was reputed to have a large 'slush fund' given to him by his chambers so that he could 'wine and dine' solicitors in order to secure briefs for his barristers. There was a suspicion amongst other sets that he used the funds to pay back handers to solicitors to secure the work. Of course, David did not know whether the allegations were true, the stories could be apocryphal, spread by jealous clerks or members of the bar, but then again, a considerable number of solicitors did brief those chambers instead of others and the general opinion at the bar was that the barristers in that set were below average, so there may be an element of truth in the allegations.

David tried to put thoughts of Michael Bell out of his mind. He had once been approached by him and asked before he was awarded silk and asked to join the set. David had declined as he was happy in chambers at the time as a busy junior barrister and he had also heard of Bell's reputation and did not want to be associated with him. There were many times since, when he had months without work, when he wondered if he had made the right decision, after all, Bell might have just been a good clerk!

David inwardly laughed at the concept of a 'good clerk', he had yet to meet one! He turned to John with a grin still on his face and asked, "What's the name of the case?"

John looked suspiciously at David wondering what he was grinning at. Not being able to fathom the reason, he ignored the grin and picked up the brief that was in front of him.

"The client's called Joseph Rogers. The case is listed in January 2018 with a two-week time estimate."

He smiled as he added, "You might have to give up skiing next year sir!"

David nodded, skiing had already become a distant memory since the birth of Rose. His expression changed as he recognised the name of the client. He decided to put an end to John's attempts to take credit for obtaining another brief.

"Oh yes, I met the client's father when I went on that cruise in October. I've been expecting this brief for some time now, especially as there is, as usual, very little work in my diary."

John made a feeble attempt at a smile. "Well I suspect I helped you secure it from the solicitors, through my pestering them for work for months now."

David just nodded, picked up the brief and turned to make his way out of the Clerks' room. Before he went through the doorway he turned back to face John.

"I know you are all busy but I have a lot of reading to get through, could you get someone to bring me a coffee?"

The look of horror on John's face that one of his barristers, even a silk, had the audacity to ask a clerk to make him coffee, was almost worth David jeopardising his chances of receiving the next silk brief from him.

Ten minutes later David was seated comfortably behind his desk sipping at a coffee that had been brought to him by chambers' most junior clerk, Ryan. He had untied the pink tape that was tied around the brief and noted the endorsements from Michael Woodsill QC, who had previously been instructed.

He knew Michael quite well and almost felt bad at stealing a brief from him. Michael was a good advocate, far better than most in his set and would have done an excellent job, but the client had been persuaded by his father to brief David, and David was not about to complain. The fee would be quite useful just after Christmas.

He spread the papers out in front of him and turned on his laptop before taking another sip of coffee. There were about fifty pages of papers in front of him but another thousand or so pages online on the Digital Case Management System. He knew he had a lot of reading ahead of him.

CHAPTER 12

THE CLERKS ROOM

David had read all he needed to by 5pm the following day. The case was not as straightforward as Dr Sanda had suggested. Indeed, the evidence against his son, Joseph Rogers, was quite strong and he understood why previous counsel and solicitors had advised the client that he ought to consider offering a plea of guilty to the offence of manslaughter, though, David doubted the prosecution would accept such a plea and thought they would probably hold out for a murder conviction.

He packed his belongings and made his way to the front entrance via the Clerk's room. As he said a cheery goodbye to them, John Winston looked up.

"Before you go, sir, I've just had the Head of Chambers on the phone. He wants to arrange an emergency chambers meeting for tomorrow night to discuss finances. I hope you'll be able to attend, sir?"

David inwardly groaned. He loathed attending chambers meetings where a few vociferous souls would rant and rave for hours and little would be achieved. He also did not like the reference to 'finances'. That usually meant that someone was suggesting an increase in the amount the tenants pay into chambers' account. After his recent payments in the Tatiana Volkov case amounting to twelve and a half per cent of his fee, he thought he was paying more than enough to chamber's and resented the idea of paying any more. Also, the fact that John seemed interested in him attending the meeting suggested the clerks were seeking more money.

He nodded and replied, "I'll be happy to attend. Is there anything I need to know in advance!"

John got up and pushed his chair back, "Perhaps, I can have a quick word before you go, sir."

There had been too many 'sir's in the last few minutes, it was definitely about a proposed increase in the clerks' pay.

David agreed and a few minutes later he was seated in his room with John seated in a chair in front of David's desk.

"You see sir, it's like this. We all know there has not been an increase in legal aid fees for years now. Indeed, we've suffered constant reductions and chambers' income has suffered."

David quickly intervened, "What about privately funded work, haven't you been trying to increase that into chambers."

John paused for a few seconds, "We have sir, and we've had quite a few successes. I managed to get Mr Wontner QC a nice private brief the other day."

'Typical', thought David, 'as usual the only decent silk work in chambers is pushed in the direction of 'Want more QC'.'

John carried on, not noticing that David was deep in thought.

"The problem is everyone is out there looking for more private work, and as you know there are some hard hitting silks out there who are likely to attract it to their chambers before we do."

David looked at him coldly whilst thinking, 'So it's my fault you cannot attract more silk work, forget any idea about a raise!'

John noticed the look and changed tact, "Of course sir, you attract a great deal of work in your own right but that cannot be said about everyone in these chambers."

David nodded, thinking, 'Keep talking, you're still not getting a rise.'

John carried on oblivious to his unreceptive audience, "I know some of the junior members of chambers are struggling, but they have the potential to earn a great deal in the future. The clerks room is different. Our contracts give us a base salary, that hasn't been increased in years and a percentage based on chambers' gross turnover, which has been falling. It means all our salaries are falling in real terms before you consider the effect of inflation. I'm worried that some of our clerks will be looking elsewhere for a job if their salaries are not increased."

David looked at him closely, "Are you suggesting you might leave us if we don't raise your salary?"

John looked aghast at the suggestion, "No, sir, not at all. I'm a chambers' man. I'm here for the duration, but I'm worried about my first junior clerk, Nick and young Asif."

David feigned surprise, "Surely junior clerks are always moving chambers. Usually a first junior obtains a job as a senior clerk in another chambers when there's a vacancy?"

John paused for a few seconds before replying.

"That's true sir, but I'm concerned that Nick and Asif might go to another chambers and retain their current positions, because we're not paying them enough. That could hurt our reputation around the Temple. It might suggest we are not doing very well and we don't have a future."

David wanted to say that it might indicate that chambers had useless lazy clerks, but he just nodded and added, "So you want us to have a chambers' meeting to discuss the possibility of increasing their salaries."

John hesitated before replying, "Well I have suggested to the Head of Chambers that we discuss all the staff salaries as there hasn't been such a discussion for a long time."

"So, you do want us to discuss your salary as well?"

"Well it makes sense to discuss all the salaries at the same time rather than just one or two individuals' salaries. Otherwise some of the other staff may be concerned that they are being unfairly treated and may look elsewhere.

David had had enough time winding up his senior clerk although he could not resist saying, "No, I can see that, that's clearly quite sensible. Rest assured that I will attend tomorrow and I will be more than happy to discuss your salary!"

CHAPTER 13

THE CHAMBERS' MEETING

On Wednesday evening at precisely 6pm, David walked into chambers' large conference room. Many tenants were already seated there, though as usual, there were some seats available at the very front. He smiled to himself as he thought about the irony that people who make a living drawing attention to themselves, always avoided the front row in a chambers' meeting if they could. It was probably a throwback to their studies when, if you sat in the front row at college, you were often the first to be picked on to answer awkward questions.

He seated himself at the front opposite James Wontner QC who sat at the head of the room facing most of the members of chambers, although he was flanked by members of the management committee. Tim Adams QC was there beaming at David. He had recently been appointed as chamber's Treasurer and so now added control of chamber's finances to his growing résumé. David's friend Graham was also a member of the management committee, in charge of Human Resources, probably the worst position to put him in!

David received several greetings with many asking after Wendy and Rose. He acknowledged them all before James Wontner QC, who had been most profuse in his own greeting, suggested they start the meeting. He waited for silence before addressing the ensemble of barristers,

"Ladies and gentlemen ..."

There were a few audible groans from some juniors who thought he should address them all on a neutral gender basis. He ignored the noises and carried on, political correctness was not a strong point with him despite all the diversity training he had been encouraged to conduct in the recent past.

"These are challenging times for us all..."

There were a few more stifled groans from juniors who knew that James was rich, busy and fed large private fee paying work from the senior clerk.

"The Criminal Bar is struggling and these chambers are struggling. The Management Committee has done its utmost to keep chambers' costs down and the rent each individual pays into chambers has not risen in three years. This is even though, as we all know, legal aid payments to barristers have not increased since 2012 ..."

"Except in VHCC cases," butted in Graham, winking at David.

James Wontner QC ignored the interruption even though a few members of chambers laughed at the comment.

"We are all hit by the reductions. Legal aid fees..."

He now turned to Graham, "...save in a very few VHCC cases, which are sadly very few..."

He turned back to address the meeting, "... are now at pre 1997 levels, so clearly with rising inflation, we are all being paid less than was thought to be, 'fair and proper remuneration,' back then.

In this climate, we obviously do not want to increase rents for any reason, but sometimes a cost arises, or a concern arises that needs to be faced head on. As a management committee we were going to have our usual budget meeting in April, where it was likely that we were going to seek an increase in rent payments. However, I have called this chambers' meeting because one such concern now faces us that we cannot ignore.

Because we have tried to keep costs at a minimum, we have not raised chambers' rent for the best part of three years now. Equally in that time, we have not given our clerks any increases."

David knew the relevant period was just over two years but he was not going to interrupt, yet!

James carried on, "Few can doubt that the bedrock of a chambers is its clerks room. It is the first port of call to visitors, the first voice someone hears on the phone is a clerk's voice and they are the ones out there doing their best to fill our diaries. It is often said that a barrister is no better than his clerk's room."

There were a few more groans from around the room, including one from Graham, David winked at him. James ignored the noises and carried on.

"If our clerks are unhappy, it is noticed by solicitors who phone or visit chambers. They are less likely to send work to a set which has unhappy clerks, in which case the work reduces, the money the clerks receive from their percentage payments are reduced, they become unhappier, which leads to less work and so on.

John Winston spoke to me the other day. He is a chambers' man and he has made it plain to me that he will stay with chambers whatever happens ..."

A barely audible voice from the back of the room whispered, "That's because no one else will have him!"

There were a few laughs but again James ignored the hecklers, intent on finishing his speech, ".... and John has promised that he will continue to boost the morale of the clerks' room if he can, but he did tell me he is worried. The junior clerks, Nick and Asif have told him they cannot continue to live on their salaries and they will have to move elsewhere if they don't receive an increase this year.

I told him I would raise this with chambers which is why I am addressing you now, in what I believe to be the long term interests of chambers. I have spoken to our Treasurer, Tim here, ..."

He acknowledged Tim who looked suitably solemn.

"... he has told me there is no room to increase their incomes from members' current contributions to chambers, even in the short term. If we are to increase their income it must come from an increase in members' contributions."

He paused, expecting an audible groan from around the room which he received with a couple of members expressing, "Told you so"

James waited until there was calm.

"Chamber's' income last year was just over £3 million. Members contributions vary, the most junior paying a relatively small base fee whilst the more senior pay a much larger base fee. All then pay twelve and one half per cent of their gross income into chambers. Many chambers have a much more draconian rent system so we are lucky that we have kept it so low."

There were more groans around the room

"We were already considering raising the percentage payment in April to thirteen per cent. My suggestion is that we raise rents now. We do not believe we should alter the base fee that members are paying, but that we should increase the percentage by a mere one per cent which will be paid by those who are receiving fees and inevitably means that the higher earners will bare most of the cost..."

Graham could not help himself blurt out that, "I suppose it won't make much difference to me, thirteen and a half per cent of nothing is still nothing."

James frowned at him. How he wished he had ignored David's suggestion to put Graham on the management committee when David resigned. He replaced the smile with a grin and continued, "The extra one per cent on current projections, will generate about £30,000 a year. £15,000 of that will be needed to cover basic increases in chamber's expenses, stationery, photocopiers, printers, telephones etc. The remaining £15,000 we can then distribute to the clerks in any way we see fit. We could increase their base salaries or their percentages or have a combination of the two.

Of course, if we are to consider the clerk's salaries, we should consider all of them at the same time, otherwise we may find that there are problems between the clerks. I suggest that to keep them happy we increase all their salaries. Say £1,000 to Ryan, £2,000 to Asif, £3,000 to Nick and £6,000 to John. The remaining £3,000 will then cover employers' national insurance contributions on these sums as well as the increased pension contributions we will have to make."

He quickly added, "These are just suggestions and of course I welcome your views. Some of you may think that John should receive a larger increase because of his central role in the clerks' room."

With that he sat down as the meeting erupted with everyone wanting their say. There were few voices supporting the proposal, many moaning about their own straightened circumstances. A relative newcomer to Chambers, Andrew Warren, even stated, "I have a massive debt from my studies at university and the bar course. I have other large personal debts from paying for such luxuries as transport and food! My practice is mainly in the Magistrates court so I'm lucky if I make the minimum wage some days. I can't afford any increase. If there is going to be an increase, surely it should be borne by those who can afford it..."

David knew what was coming next.

"... the silks. After all they're the highest earners. Any increase to them is also tax deductible because they all pay forty to forty-five per cent tax. But any increased payment by me is not tax deductible because my meagre earnings don't even reach the minimum tax threshold!"

David looked thoughtful at this obvious iniquity whilst at the same time wondering why they had taken this individual on. He had been in chambers over a year now, so, if he was any good, even with the difficulties facing the junior bar, he should be earning above the minimum wage. In any event David noticed he was very vociferous for one so young, and his comments were usually against the silks' interests.

Eventually after most people had their say, James looked towards David. He had noted that David had been writing down figures throughout the meeting. "Our Deputy Head is very quiet, what do you think David?"

David knew that any thoughts he had would be unpopular with some faction in the room, if not all of them, but he did not like the suggestion that he should be one of the four silks in chamber's bearing the cost of paying increased salaries to the clerks.

He paused until everyone was quiet. "These are hard times as has been graphically represented by Andrew when he addressed us. Ideally, we need to increase chambers' income, in which case the three clerks on a part percentage would benefit. We can increase income by recruiting good busy barristers, particularly silks, but we are unlikely to attract any, if they see that we have a separate percentage for silks which is greater than that for juniors. After all, by the nature of practice these days, many leading juniors make more than silks. By all means silks should pay more into chambers than very junior members of chambers, but they already do by paying larger base rates than very junior members and paying more from their percentages because on the whole they have larger incomes.

However, in the short term we are not recruiting any silks or busy juniors from other chambers, so the question is, do we need to increase the clerks' salaries at this stage?

There are many arguments both ways. Chambers is struggling, the barristers, particularly the juniors are struggling. Should the clerks be in any better position than the people they are employed by? My opinion is they should not. We should hold out the carrot that if chamber's income increases in the next year, their percentages will produce an extra income and there will be extra money available to give to Ryan, who does not receive a percentage of chambers' income.

However, if people are on the whole favourable to giving the clerks a salary increase, it does not have to be in the amounts suggested by James. I would suggest lesser sums. A half percentage increase for members, which takes effect from January rather than in April is surely enough. We should look to reducing our expenditure in other areas. For example, in a digital age, we should have considerably less photocopying, printing and stationery costs. Raising our rents by a half percent in December, will raise about £5,000 more for the year, than if we raised it in April. Out of that sum, Ryan could receive £500, his salary is only £15,000 a year so I see no reason to suddenly increase it by a thousand pounds. The remaining money can be distributed between the other three clerks in any way that chamber's sees fit. For example, £2,000 to John, £1,500 to Nick and £1,000 to Asif. Of course, we would have to pay extra towards our national insurance contributions for them and their pensions, but we should seek to make savings in other areas and review the situation in April. Personally, I would inform the clerks that we are increasing their money but not make it start until the new year.

David grinned as he added, "Of course we could always take John up on his offer. It seems to me he is not threatening to leave or operate a go slow policy, quite the opposite. Perhaps we should not increase his income at all but tell him we will monitor what happens in the clerks' room over the next year and if there is a significant improvement in morale and attitude he can expect a hefty Christmas bonus, indeed we could suggest to all the clerks that if we see significant improvements in attitude, they all will receive 'hefty' bonuses in a year!"

CHAPTER 14

A CONFERENCE WITH THE CLIENT

The lights of the indicator board at London Victoria station grabbed David's attention. The 7:47am train to Lewes, was leaving from platform 17, so he made his way along to the platform, stopping on the way, to buy a hot coffee from one of the many kiosks in the station. The coffee never tasted any good but at least it was steaming hot and he needed the heat in this weather. It was now Thursday 23rd November and he was fully prepared to meet the client, Joseph Rogers and the junior, Gavin Peacock and the solicitor, Graham Turner. Both Gavin and Graham were from the solicitors' firm, Gardeners in Brighton.

The chambers' meeting had gone much as expected, no one, save for James Wontner, supported a one per cent rise. Some liked David's idea of a hefty bonus at Christmas if the staff improved, but the compromise of a half per cent increase in chamber's rent was the one finally decided upon. David would have rather given the clerks a 'hefty' bonus in the form of a £50 'hefty' Christmas hamper, but he voted for the half per cent increase as he suspected that would be the result and he did not doubt that everything said in the meeting would be related back to the clerks. There was no reason to needlessly antagonise them. He might need them to give him a brief in the future. He did not doubt that James Wontner QC did not want a one per cent increase in fees but had voted for that rise so that he could tell the clerks he had supported their claims in full in a chamber's meeting. 'Oh well, chambers' usual miserable politics,' is all he could think.

The train was slightly delayed due to 'signalling failures' at Clapham junction. David had been delayed on this route many times over the years, for various reasons ranging from 'track fires' to 'the wrong type of snow', so it did not concern him in the slightest.

At shortly after 9:30pm David's taxi, which he had caught from outside Lewes station, drew up outside Lewes prison. David made his way to the visitors' centre and after giving his details to security and being searched and scanned, he met the solicitor, Graham Turner and his junior, Gavin Peacock.

He had seen Graham in court over the years but never passed anything other than a few pleasantries. Now they both made more of an effort.

Graham held out his hand whilst announcing, "Mr Brant, nice to finally meet and work together."

David nodded in reply. He knew Graham Turner had originally instructed Michael Woodsill QC from Michael Bell's chambers, where he might have received an unlawful, but undoubtedly welcome, 'financial reward' for the brief. The most he would receive from David was a cup of coffee, or if he was really lucky, a pint of the local Sussex brew in a nearby pub!

Graham carried on and introduced Gavin, "This is Gavin Peacock, one of our in-house barristers. I don't know if you know each other?"

David looked at the skinny, sharp face of Gavin. He recognised him from the courts but they had never conducted a case together. They shook hands both acknowledging that the custom of barristers not shaking hands because of a pretence that they all knew each other, was rapidly disappearing.

David thought he should clear the air as soon as possible. "Look I know neither of you had me in mind for this case. I know you had already instructed Michael Woodsill QC who already conducted a consultation with the client. As you know the client's father asked me to conduct the case and as he is a persuasive man, I agreed."

Graham laughed in response. He knew how persuasive Dr Sanda was. Dr Sanda had phoned him to tell him that he insisted that David be briefed in place of Michael Woodsill QC or new solicitors would be instructed. He had protested that he had never heard of David and that Michael Woodsill QC was an excellent silk and in any event, if they wanted another silk, he knew some brilliant silks who he was used to working with. He emphasised that clients usually took his recommendation.

Dr Sanda had put the phone down on him before he had finished his sentence and within 24 hours the client had contacted him from prison and was demanding that he either instruct David Brant QC or Joseph would be instructing a new solicitor. Although Michael Bell had promised him a cash payback representing about 5% of the value of the Silk's brief, he had no choice but to instruct David or lose the case and his own solicitor's fee.

"Not at all Mr Brant. I've had you on my radar for some time now and your clerk frequently contacts me pestering me to brief your chambers. It was only a matter of time before we instructed you."

With the initial lies out of the way, the three made their way across a courtyard in the prison and then up some stairs to the interview cells where they could conduct a conference.

Within five minutes of being seated in a particularly small cubicle, Joseph Rogers was brought in to see them, wearing a yellow vest over his prison attire, just in case he might sneak out of the prison pretending to be a solicitor or barrister!

After a few pleasantries had passed, David asked his first question, "Why did you change your name to Rogers?"

Of course, it had nothing to do with the case and he was not really interested in the answer, but he thought it might break the ice. Joseph looked surprised at the question but answered quickly, "I had a falling out with my parents as I did not want to follow the life they were planning for me. I was so annoyed with my father that I changed my name as well. We had a massive argument before I changed my name. My father called me a 'drunken fornicator.' I was so annoyed with him that I chose the surname of one of the few teachers I ever respected, 'William Rogers'.

As a result, my father never contacted me again until this happened. Now he is a great support which is why I took his recommendation and instructed you as my leading counsel."

David did not bother taking a note of any of this family history. He was happy that father and son were reconciled, not least because he had received this brief. He did acknowledge to himself that it was unfortunate that it took a murder to unite the family!

David took him slowly through the case papers, pointing out the difficult evidence, and the lack of any evidence supporting his version of events.

"Joseph, I appreciate that in the past the strength of the prosecution case has been pointed out to you and indeed you have been advised about the credit available for a plea of guilty."

Joseph frowned at David, who immediately added, "I am not going to cover those matters with you again as you have made it quite plain that you are adamant that you are not guilty of murder or manslaughter. What I must deal with though, is how the injury was caused to Mr Worthy.

No one alleges that they saw you with knife at any stage, but the evidence suggests that you had one and caused the fatal injury. You have the witness who attended the party with Mr Worthy, who states that he saw a person who must be you, ushering Mr Worthy away when he shouted out "You fucking cheeky bastard."

Perhaps more importantly, you have two of your own friends giving evidence, that they also witnessed Mr Worthy saying the same words, just before he reached down to touch his right leg and limped away towards his car. What I want to know is the answer to two matters; firstly, did you ever have a knife in your hands? Secondly, did you stab Mr Worthy, albeit in what you saw as some type of self-defence of yourself or another?"

Joseph's expression changed to one of anger as he rose from his seat, "No, no, no. I'm sick of answering this question. I never had a knife and I never stabbed him."

David quickly tried to calm him down.

"Very well Joseph, but I have to ask to make sure that we have covered every eventuality. If you did not stab him, someone else did. All along you have avoided saying that you saw someone else stab him. If you did see someone else commit this murder, now is the time to say."

"No Mr Brant, I'd like to say I saw someone else stab him but I never did. Obviously, I saw Adrian Simons dancing around threatening him with a knife, but I never saw him stab him. All I remember is I was ushering him away so there wouldn't be any more trouble. There were a number of people around us. I don't know where Adrian Simons was at the time but I heard Gerry Worthy, say 'You fucking cheeky bastard.' He was obviously talking to me and thought I had done something to him but at the time I had no idea what he was talking about. I let go of him and noticed he touched his leg, then he staggered away toward his car. I didn't see how he got injured or who did it."

purchasing a brand new coffee flask for him which was now in his bag, containing his favourite Italian brand filter coffee. The flask was guaranteed to keep the coffee hot for four hours so it should certainly last until close to lunchtime.

Eventually after queuing for fifteen minutes David was ushered forward by a burly, ginger-headed security guard manning the court door. David had never seen him before. He looked early twenties but carried himself as if he was in charge of security at the MI6 building in London. David saw his name badge gave the name Gary, so he gave him a smile and said, "Hello, Gary," in the hope that a little friendliness might mean that the search of his bags and person would not take long and he could go about his business.

The security guard took one look at David, frowned, stopped chewing his piece of gum for a moment and in a strong East Sussex accent asked, "You a lawyer?"

David replied politely that he was, now convinced that the search would be a cursory one.

However, Gary had different ideas and demanded that David unzip every zip on his bag and then insisted that he take out every item whilst he examined them closely. Finally, his eyes fell on David's new flask. "What's that?" he asked in seeming innocence as if he had never seen such an object before.

David was annoyed that his search was taking longer than everyone else's but in an effort to ensure that it ended sooner rather than later, he politely replied. "It's a flask. It contains coffee as I understand there are no longer any facilities in this building."

Gary assumed a blank expression.

"You can't take that in here. I'll have to confiscate it. I'll give you a ticket though and you can collect it at the end of the day."

David was startled, not least because he doubted that this particular individual had known the word 'confiscate' until he used it.

In a somewhat less polite voice than usual, David demanded to know, "Why on earth would you confiscate my coffee flask?"

"It's a dangerous object."

"What are you talking about, it's a coffee flask!"

Gary hesitated whilst he engaged his thought processes. It was clearly difficult for him. Finally, he came up with, "You could use it to throw hot coffee over a judge."

Any pretence at politeness was now lost as David replied, "That's absurd, I am a barrister, a

Queen's Counsel, I would hardly have survived in this job for close to forty years if I was prone to throwing coffee at judges! In any event, in the past this building used to serve hot coffee in plastic cups, there was nothing to stop me throwing those at judges if I was that way inclined!"

Gary pulled himself up to his full 6 feet 2 inches and threw out his chest like he was training in a gym and in a voice, that he thought was as menacing as possible, but actually came out as a high pitched squeal, he responded, convinced in his own mind that he was correct, "You are not taking that into the court building and I am taking it off you now."

David knew that the battle was lost. He could have asked for this idiot's supervisor but that would take time and it did not seem worth it especially as he was conducting a murder trial today and had far more important matters on his mind than a simple coffee flask. He resigned himself to losing the flask for the day.

"Very well, please give me a ticket so I can collect the flask later."

"I don't think I've got any tickets here."

David started to turn red, but managed to say, "Well please get some."

After receiving the ticket and piling all his belongings back into his bag, he resolved never to have to deal with this idiotic jobsworth again. There were two security guards on duty that day. How he wished he had chosen the other one!

A few minutes later David was in the robing room looking longingly at a flask of coffee that a young female barrister was drinking from. He had to ask her, "How on earth did you get that through security."

She looked at him for a few seconds in surprise before replying, "I've never had a problem, I just smile at Gary, the nice, tall, ginger-haired security guard and he always lets me through with just a cursory search of my bag."

David was about to say he smiled at Gary and had been detained for almost a full intimate body search, but he chose not to. It was obvious that Gary was far more likely to respond to a smile from this particular barrister rather than from him.

She looked at him closely, "You're David Brant QC, aren't you?"

He looked at her quizzically, "Yes, I am."

"Hello, I'm Emilia Johnson, I'm the junior for the prosecution."

David was surprised. "I thought the prosecution junior was a man, I saw a name on the draft opening saying that Walter Young was junior for the prosecution."

She grinned, "He was but Walter is a very busy member of chambers and he had a major clash so I was instructed in the case a week ago,"

David nodded, it was unusual for anyone to return a murder case these days, clearly Walter Young was very busy. "Has your leader changed as well, or is it just you?"

He knew that the leader was Richard Thornbrite QC. He had come across him a few times in his career. In David's opinion, Richard was too serious, pedantic and a bore and he hoped there was a change of leader.

"Oh no, Richard is still leading for the prosecution. He's just gone off to see the officer in the case He obviously would like a word once you've changed."

David nodded, "No problem, I would have joined him for a coffee, although I understand there are no facilities available in this court anymore."

"No that's wrong, the WRVS are still serving coffee, but I always bring my own flask of coffee."

She grabbed her cup and put it to her lips as she said, "Cheers."

CHAPTER 17

THE PROSECUTION OPENING

Mr Justice Christopher Holdern QC was a civil judge who had been sent to Lewes Crown Court for a few weeks to try serious cases. It was not the first time he had sat in Lewes. This was going to be the eighth murder case he had tried it Lewes in as many years. He liked conducting judicial business in what he considered to be a sleepy Sussex town. The pace was not the same as the High Court in London being far more relaxing, even though he was dealing with disputes concerning human life rather than multi-million pound contracts. Murder cases were much simpler to conduct. The law, with a few exceptions, was relatively straight forward and if he made a few mistakes in his conduct of the case, the Court of Appeal was likely to support him and state that despite a slight, 'unimportant' error by the judge the conviction was still safe. It was so unlike the civil Court of Appeal that seemed to take delight in picking at his judgments, regardless of how long he spent crafting them.

The case was listed at 10:00am. He had come down the night before and was staying in a reasonable hotel in Brighton just a few miles away. Every day an official car would pick him up and drop him of at court and at 4:45pm every day the car would return to take him back to the hotel where he would consume a passable meal and a half bottle of good French red selected from a small but surprisingly adequate wine list.

He was married and had been so for thirty-five years. His children had grown up and as his wife, Lady Holdern and he had barely exchanged a word since the children had left home, he was quite happy with the nomadic life style of being a judge travelling to Crown Courts around the country.

This morning, sleepy Sussex had lived up to its name and the start of the trial had been delayed. Mercifully, there were no legal points to be decided in the case before the trial commenced. He had read all the papers and it seemed a straight forward case to him. The only issue was whether the defendant had stabbed the victim and whether he intended to kill him when he did so, or cause him really serious harm. There were no issues of 'self-defence' or 'loss of control', a subject he still had difficulty with, as had been demonstrated in one, almost caustic judgment of the Court of Appeal where his directions to the jury had been seriously challenged in that court. Fortunately, although their lordships had criticised some of his comments, they had nevertheless upheld the conviction. It would not have helped his career if a conviction for murder had been quashed because he had made a simple mistake.

Although there were no points of law to consider, the prosecution had served some further evidence quite recently and he had acceded to defence counsel's request for extra time to consider the statement with his client. Apparently, it involved an alleged confession. If he was lucky the defendant might plead and he could get away quite early. It was too cold for a round of golf but he was sure there were plenty of things he could do in Brighton. He could contact an old friend of his who lived here and if he was not available, he could always finalise his judgment in a multi-million pound copywrite action, Smirnov v Ivonov, that he had tried recently in London involving Russian oligarchs. He shuddered at the thought. Whatever care he took in writing the judgment he knew one side or the other would appeal him.

It had been a difficult case and for some weeks he had really had difficulty determining who, if anyone, was telling the truth. Thank God for a criminal trial where such matters were easily determined. It was invariably the defendant who was not telling the truth!

An hour later, Richard Thornbrite QC rose from his seat in the front row of Counsel's bench, to address the jury. David had used the hour to go through the troublesome statement of Jamie Anderson with his client. Joseph had shown that he was worried about the statement but was still adamant that Jamie was lying for reasons best known to her and was still adamant he was not guilty.

Richard adopted a stern expression as he addressed the jury demonstrating, he hoped, the seriousness of this matter, "Ladies and gentlemen, I, together with my learned friend, Emilia Johnson, who sits behind me, represent the prosecution in this case. The defendant, Joseph Rogers, who sits in the dock at the back of the court, is represented by my learned friends, David Brant QC who sits closest to you and his junior, Gavin Peacock who sits behind him.

Ladies and gentlemen, this is a case of murder!"

He paused for the word to have its effect.

"It is the prosecution's case that Mr Rogers murdered Mr Worthy on Friday 25th August 2017 by plunging a knife into his thigh with such force that it cut through the femoral artery and severely damaged the femoral vein, leading rapidly to him bleeding to death."

He paused again as he scanned the jurors' faces.

"Shortly, we will call the evidence before you, but this is our opportunity to address you and tell you what you are about to hear, so that you can put it into context when you hear the evidence. Before I do that, there are a few documents that I have asked the usher to hand out to you. They are held together in a bundle that Ms Johnson helpfully created. They include; the indictment, just a legal word for the charge sheet, a plan of the area where the murder took place, a diagram of the area showing where certain items were found, some photographs of the area and a body map showing where Mr Worthy was injured. You will be happy, no doubt, that we will not be showing you any actual photographs of the deceased, as we consider such matters are too distressing for jurors and would serve no useful purpose in a case where the issues are relatively straight forward."

He waited until all the jury had been given the documents and acknowledged the smile of a silver haired lady in her late sixties who was sitting in the front rank of the jury. He then resumed his opening.

"The circumstances which have given rise to this tragic death and the charge of murder against this defendant, are as follows: The 25th August 2017 was a bank holiday weekend. Gerry Worthy was looking forward to having the next three days off work. Unfortunately, his Friday at work did not go as planned. He worked for a storage company called Brightman and Co, based in the north of Brighton. Earlier in the week he had an altercation with a female co-worker called Maureen O'Connor, which resulted in his being disciplined on the Friday. There is no doubt this had an effect upon him because he was annoyed that evening as will be testified to by a close work colleague of his, Brian Williams, a coding clerk working with Mr Worthy for the same employers.

That evening, Mr Worthy drove his prize possession, a 1972 jaguar motor car, to a public house in West Brighton, on the way to Hove, called 'The Prince of Orange'. There he met Mr Williams and a friend of his, Shirley West. It is clear that they all consumed a significant amount of alcohol. Ms West then suggested that they attend a party that she knew was on that night in East Brighton. Mr Worthy was clearly over the legal limit for driving by this stage, but he agreed to drive the three of them to the party.

After a short time, they arrived at the rear of some houses in Sangster Street in Brighton at around 10pm. I will ask you now to look at the jury bundle and turn to tab 5 where you will find a diagram of the area. You will see that a car has been drawn on the map at the rear of some houses in Sangster Street. That was Mr Worthy's vehicle and that is where he parked it.

Mr Williams and Ms West got out of the car and left Mr Worthy to park it. Unfortunately, they did not tell Mr Worthy where the party was, nor did they wait to show him. He was undoubtedly the worse for having consumed so much alcohol and it appears he had some difficulty parking the car and took some to me to do it. After he had finally parked the car, he found himself quite alone in an area of Brighton he did not know.

Mr Worthy had been annoyed at the start of the evening, now he was clearly angry that he had been abandoned and he started to walk around the area trying to find out where the party was being held. You will hear from people who lived in the area that around 10:20pm they heard Mr Worthy making a great deal of noise. You will hear from some occupants from the area Lynn Turnbull and Carl Williams, that they heard an angry man shouting out names. That was Mr Worthy who was shouting out Mr Williams and Ms West's names in generally unflattering terms.

The party took place at number 84 Sangster Street. Loud music was being played and the occupants did not at first hear Mr Worthy's shouting. However, there came a time when they did, sometime around 10:25pm.

Present at that party that night was the son of the owner, Steven Denley and a number of guests. Those guests included Joseph Rogers, and earlier in the evening, his girlfriend Caroline Jennings, although she apparently left before Mr Worthy arrived. It appears that she and Mr

Rogers had an argument that undoubtedly effected the mood he was in that night.

By the time Mr Worthy arrived, Brian Williams was also present at the party as was Shirley West, Carl Turnbull, a young man called Adrian Simons and his girlfriend Jamie Anderson.

They heard Mr Worthy shouting out for his friends in an aggressive tone. It was then that Brian Williams realised he had forgotten about him and he went outside to speak to Mr Worthy. He was followed by Shirley West.

Other guests were concerned that Mr Worthy was trying to crash the party or was intent on hurting these two guests and they went outside intending to confront him. Adrian Simons armed himself with a knife, which was clearly seen by others. It is the prosecution case that this defendant, Joseph Rogers, also armed himself with a knife, but slyly, he kept it hidden from the other party goers and presumably, also from the unfortunate Mr Worthy.

Outside the property Brian Williams tried to placate Mr Worthy but it was to no avail. Shirley West, who was clearly drunk by this stage, confronted him and challenged him, asking why he was shouting and making it clear he was not wanted there. Mr Worthy was in a rage and he responded by hitting out. We will never know what his intention was or whether he intended to hit anybody, but he caught Ms West under her chin, lifting her off her feet and knocking her out.

If you look at tab 3 you will see an area at the rear of the houses with a drawing of a prone female. That is where Ms West ended up after being hit by Mr Worthy.

Of course, this act incensed the crowd of youths who had left the party and were all probably now fuelled with copious amounts of alcohol.

Adrian Simons started dancing around in the street, waving the knife and making threats to stab Mr Worthy. Mr Worthy apparently accepted the challenge. Fortunately, Mr Simons, whose behaviour was otherwise reprehensible, did not use the knife and caused no injuries whatsoever to anyone that night. His girlfriend, Jamie Anderson had been able to intercede and walked him back to the house before he caused any injury to anyone, or, was injured himself.

You will hear that he later pleaded guilty to the offences of affray and possessing an offensive weapon at an earlier hearing, because of his conduct that night, namely, waving the knife around and making threats to use it.

Even though Mr Worthy had assaulted and knocked out Ms West, Brian Williams still tried to placate him. It also appeared that this defendant, Mr Rogers, was trying to placate Mr Worthy as well. He was seen to stand on Mr

Worthy's left side, place his right arm around Mr Worthy's shoulders and apparently usher him away from the scene.

However, that was clearly not his intent. Although no one saw him or, should I say, admits to seeing him with a knife, it is clear that he had one. He was the only one close to Mr Worthy when Mr Worthy suddenly shouted out, "You fucking cheeky bastard," and immediately pushed the defendant away and lent down to touch his right leg.

He had been stabbed in the back of the right thigh, severing the femoral artery and cutting into the femoral vein. Mr Worthy staggered away and managed to make it to his car. There he collapsed, through loss of blood.

You will see on the diagram at tab 5 of the jury bundle, a drawing of a prone man. That is where Mr Worthy collapsed to the ground next to his vehicle. You will also see a trail of blood marked on the diagram leading towards where Mr Worthy collapsed. We say that the start of this trail is where Mr Worthy received the fatal wound at the hands of this defendant.

Paramedics arrived a short time later and Mr Worthy was taken to hospital. There at 2:10am he was declared dead. He had bled to death from this serious wound and the doctors, despite extensive efforts, had been unable to repair the damage.

The prosecution say there can be no doubt that Joseph Rogers is responsible for inflicting that wound and is guilty of murder.

After causing the fatal injury, Mr Rogers and the others returned to 84 Sangster Street.

You will hear from Jamie Anderson in this case. She is Mr Simon's girlfriend, the man who was waving a knife around and threatening Mr Worthy. She will tell you that she saw that her boyfriend was acting, as she puts it, "like an idiot", and she persuaded him to come back into the property. There he threw his knife into the kitchen sink, which is where a long kitchen knife was later found by police. No traces of blood or tissue were found on that knife.

Ms Anderson will also give other important evidence in this case. She will tell you that Joseph Rogers returned to the property with a smirk on his face. When she asked him why he was smirking, he told her he had "shanked" the man in the leg.

You may not be aware of the term, I believe it was originally a prison term for using a "shank" on someone, namely a homemade knife. It has developed overtime to mean, stabbing someone. Mr Rogers admitted to her that he had stabbed Mr Worthy in the leg. It appears that he also told others at the party that he had stabbed the man.

He went further and even indicated to Jamie Anderson where the injury was located. He told her it was in revenge for what Mr Worthy had done to Shirley West. Mr Rogers also told Jamie Anderson that he had thrown the murder weapon into the bushes, outside the house. That of course is where the murder weapon was later recovered from.

You will hear that the police were called to the address and attended whilst Mr Rogers was there and the other witnesses were still there. None of them assisted the police at that stage, including Ms Anderson.

However, the police did have information that a man had been seen outside the house waving a knife about and threatening Mr Worthy. Mr Simons answered the description of this man and he was arrested. The details of everyone else were taken but they were allowed to leave after a cursory check.

Because of their refusal to assist the police Mr Rogers was allowed to go free at that stage. He walked Ms Anderson home to her address and repeated to her that he had stabbed the man.

Mr Rogers arrived home at his university lodgings and presumably disposed of or washed any clothing that he was wearing that night, that might have had evidence that could have incriminated him. Indeed, when he was later arrested at his lodgings two days later, on the

Sunday night, the clothes he was wearing that night had been washed and stacked neatly in his room.

Dr Mark Lumley, a very experienced pathologist, conducted a post mortem examination of the body of Gerry Worthy on 1st September 2017. He observed a deeply penetrating stab wound to the right leg. The wound divided the femoral artery completely and partly transacted the femoral vein too. The knife had been moved whilst in the leg so as to produce two separate tracks. This might suggest that the knife was plunged in, partially withdrawn and plunged in again. The wound almost penetrated the full thickness of the leg. The doctor concluded that the perpetrator of the injury had held the knife firmly on the way in and on the way out. It appeared that Mr Worthy had tried to grab the knife as he had what the doctor describes as a classic defence wound to the forefinger of his right hand.

The knives were recovered from the scene and sent for forensic analysis. As I have said, the knife from the kitchen sink revealed nothing at all. There were no traces of DNA or blood or tissue and no fingerprints. Fingerprints may have been washed off the handle when the knife was placed in the sink which was partially full of water.

The knife from the bushes revealed a lot more. Blood and fatty deposits were found on one side of the blade stretching all along the blade and close to the hilt. DNA strands were taken from this area and found to match Mr Worthy's DNA, with a match probability of one in a billion.

Police became interested in Mr Rogers after they had talked to some of the other witnesses from the party and he was arrested two days later at his university lodgings he was staying at in Brighton. There he was asked what clothes he was wearing on the night of the incident and he pointed to the freshly washed clothes that I have already mentioned.

He was taken to the police station where he was interviewed. He had the advantage of having a legal representative present. The police cautioned him, telling him that he need not answer any questions but that it may harm his defence if he failed to mention to them anything that he later relied upon at court. His legal representative read out a short statement on behalf of his client at the start of the interview, raising matters that now appear to be irrelevant."

He turned to David and smiled. David had told him already that he did not think that Joseph's human rights had been infringed and he was not taking any issue on the interview.

Richard continued, "In response to all questions about his movements, actions and the situation in general, Mr Rogers elected to make no comment.

What then are the issues for you to decide?

Firstly, Mr Rogers denies that he murdered Mr Worthy. He denies having a knife and using a knife to inflict that fatal wound. He presumably also denies that he confessed to Jamie Anderson that he stabbed the victim and to throwing the knife into some bushes, where it was later found.

The prosecution case is that this is exactly what happened and he is now trying his best to distance himself from his involvement.

What is the law for you to consider? You will take the law from his lordship as he is the judge of law and anything I say, or anything my learned friend says about the law is subject to correction by his lordship. However, as I am the first to address you about the case, it is perhaps helpful if I give you a little guidance on what I anticipate his lordship will direct you is the law.

In this case I anticipate that the law will be relatively simple. In relation to the offence of murder, the prosecution has brought this offence against Mr Rogers, it is therefore for the prosecution to prove it. The prosecution will have to prove to you that Mr Rogers stabbed Mr

Worthy and when he did so he intended either to kill him or intended to cause him really serious harm. We say that if you plunge a knife into the back of someone's leg with force, severing both the femoral artery and cutting the femoral vein, you must at the very least intend to cause really serious harm. If as appears to be the case here, the knife was partly withdrawn and then plunged into the leg again, it is clear the intent was to kill.

What is the standard of proof in this case? You will already have been informed about the standard of proof in the video you watched before you were selected for this jury. Nevertheless, it is of fundamental importance and I should mention it here. As I have said, the prosecution bring this case, it is therefore for the prosecution to prove it and to a very high standard, you cannot convict Joseph Rogers of any offence unless you are satisfied so that you are sure of his guilt. Please bear this in mind when you consider the evidence I am about to call in front of you.

CHAPTER 18

THE FIRST WITNESS

Brian Williams walked slowly into the courtroom. It was obvious to everyone present that he was not happy to be here. In truth he had agonised over the death of Gerry Worthy, blaming himself. Since Gerry's death he had asked himself countless times whether he could have avoided it. If he had not gone to the pub that night; if he had not introduced Gerry to Shirley, if he had not suggested driving them all to the party, if he had not left Gerry to park the car alone and if he had not forgotten about him. The list went on and was never ending. He had thought he was getting better and managing to bring some normality back to his life, but walking into this court brought it all back and he was almost in a daze when he strolled into the witness box and took the oath.

He was staring blankly when the prosecutor asked him his name. He gave it automatically without thinking.

Richard could see that the witness was struggling. Having conducted many personal injury cases as a junior and seeing witnesses dealing with death and serious injuries, he believed the witness was showing the signs of post-traumatic stress disorder and would need careful handling. He had recently conducted 'Vulnerable Witness' training at his Inn of Court, so he knew all the new rules about handling such witnesses.

The course was going to be compulsory for all barristers handling vulnerable witness cases in the future and he had decided to conduct the course before others, to get a head start. As the new rules basically restricted anything but the most anodyne questioning, he was going to ignore those rules in this case, but he would be careful with the witness.

"Mr Williams, I understand that in August last year you were working at Brightman and Co, in Brighton as a coding clerk?"

Brian stared at him as if the question were irrelevant, but then answered with a quiet, "Yes."

"Please speak up Mr Williams, the microphone in front of you records your evidence, it does not amplify your voice. Do you still work there?"

Brian stared at the microphone for a few seconds before saying "No," in a slightly louder voice.

"When did you leave?"

"After Gerry was killed."

"Why?"

Brian stared at him as if the answer was obvious, "I couldn't stay there after Gerry was killed. It brought back too many memories."

Richard nodded sympathetically, "I am sure we are all sorry to hear that. I am sorry that you have to relive that terrible night and I will try and keep my questioning to a minimum."

Brian just nodded.

"When you worked at Brightman and Co, did you work with Gerry Worthy, the deceased?"

Brian looked down at his shoes, realising he had forgotten to clean them. He shuffled uncomfortably in the witness box before answering, "Yes, I did. He was a Storage Manager, I was a Coding Clerk and I worked in the storage area with him."

"Were you friends."

Again, Brian looked down at his shoes before answering, "Yes, I liked him. He was a few years older than me but we got on well. We often had a drink together after work."

"I want to ask you about the Friday before the August bank holiday last year. The day of the incident that led to Mr Worthy's death."

Richard could not see the tears welling up in Brian's eyes as he asked the question.

"I understand that there was an incident that week at work involving Mr Worthy and a female colleague, Maureen O'Connor. Did you witness that incident!"

"No, but Gerry told me all about it."

Richard nodded, "I won't ask you what he said as we have certain rules of evidence, but did you become aware that Gerry was disciplined that Friday?"

"Yes, it was common knowledge around the office."

"Again, I won't ask you about what others said, but you met Gerry that night for a drink. What mood was he in."

"He was angry, he thought Maureen was after his job and was trying to get rid of him."

Richard smiled, "Did you meet anyone else in the pub that night?"

"Yes, I met Shirley."

"Is that Shirley West."

"Yes."

"Did there come a time when Shirley suggested that you all go to a party together?"

"Yes."

"What was Gerry's demeanour like then?"

Brian looked confused, "Sorry?"

Richard tried again, "Was he still angry?"

Brian thought for a moment before replying, "No, he seemed quite happy at that stage. We'd all had a lot to drink by then though."

"Did you know where this party was?"

"No, they were friends of Shirley's. She directed Gerry to a car park behind some houses, near East Brighton park."

"What happened when you all arrived at the car Park?"

"Shirley got out of the car and went to the party and I followed."

"What about Mr Worthy, what was he doing?"

"When he first stopped the car, he was parked at an awkward angle, blocking another vehicle. After we got out I heard him revving the engine and I presumed he was parking the car."

"Why didn't you wait for him?"

Brian again examined his shoes, "I really don't know. I guess I was so drunk that I wasn't thinking straight. I never even thought whether Gerry knew where the party was. I just followed Shirley."

He choked back a few tears, "I wish I had waited, he wouldn't be dead now!"

Richard gave him a sympathetic look before asking, "Did you follow Shirley into 84 Sangster Street?"

Brian was still looking down as he mumbled a reply, "I did."

"Mr Williams, I appreciate that this is difficult for you, but please look up, face the jury and speak up so everyone in court can hear you."

Brian looked at the jury and almost shouted, "I did."

Richard smiled, "That's much better. Can you tell us what time you arrived at the party?"

Brian hesitated as he tried to recall, "I think it was just before10pm."

"When did you realise that Mr Worthy was not with you?"

"I don't know how much later it was. Someone offered me a bottle of lager, I sat on a sofa drinking it and then started to doze off. The next thing I remember was hearing a lot of noise outside. I realised it was Gerry and then realised we had left him parking the car."

"What did you do?"

"People in the party were rushing to the windows and into the kitchen asking what was going on. I got up and left with a few others. I rushed out to try to get to Gerry first to avoid any problems."

"Why did you think there would be any problems?"

"Gerry sounded aggressive and some of the youths sounded like they might want to cause trouble."

"Did you know any of the youths at the party?"

"I knew Shirley and I thought I recognised a few faces from local pubs, but I didn't know anyone there."

"Can you describe the youths who sounded like they might want to cause trouble?"

"Not really, it was all noise. I did see one of them with a knife outside."

"Can you describe him?"

Brian hesitated to answer, trying his best to describe the man he had seen, "He was about one metre eighty tall, with dark hair, wearing a black jacket and blue jeans."

Richard turned to David, "I don't think there will be any dispute in this case that Mr Williams is referring to Adrian Simons."

David stood, "That is agreed my lord." He was obviously keen to establish that the only aggressive youth carrying a knife who could be named was Adrian Simons.

Richard continued, "Did anyone else have a knife that you saw?"

"No, I never saw anyone else with a knife."

"Did you see anyone else acting aggressively?"

"Shirley was a bit drunk and she went out and started shouting at Gerry."

"Tell the jury about the people at the party. Can you describe anyone else?"

"There was another girl there, quite pretty. I think she was the girlfriend of the lad who had the knife."

"Mr Simons."

"I didn't know his name."

"No, but he is the man you described earlier?"

"Yes."

"Anyone else?"

"To be honest I didn't look much at any of the others. I do remember there was a black lad there but that was it."

"Again, I believe there will be no dispute, but the only black man there was Mr Rogers."

David again rose to his feet and smiled at the jury, "That is agreed as well."

"Did you see whether Mr Rogers left the house?"

"I didn't see him leave, but I saw him in the car park so he must have left after me."

"What was his demeanour like in the car park?"

"I wasn't really watching him, but he seemed quite calm from what I saw."

"What happened when you went out into the street?"

"I went up to Gerry to apologise for leaving him and to try and calm him down."

"Did you succeed?"

"Not at first, it didn't help that Shirley was shouting at him and the youth with the knife was dancing around threatening to stab him."

"What was Shirley shouting?"

"She was asking him what his problem was and telling him to go away, no one wanted him there."

"Were those the words she used?

"No, she swore at him."

"Tell us the words she actually used, don't worry we have heard worse in these courts."

"She said something like, "What's your fucking problem, what are you fucking screaming about. Piss off, nobody wants an old fart like you around here."

"What was Mr Worthy's reaction?"

"He got angrier and he lashed out, knocking Shirley out. I don't think he meant to hit her. It was an accident."

"What did the other youths do?"

"They got angry, the one with the knife started threatening him with it and jabbing the knife at him and the others started shouting at him."

"Did you see what the black man, Mr Rogers was doing?"

"Not at that stage, but a little later I saw him put his arm around Gerry and lead him away."

"What did you do?"

"I was worried about Shirley so I went to see if she was ok."

"What is the next thing that you recall?"

"I remember hearing Gerry shouting something like, 'You cheeky fucking bastard.'

I looked around and I saw the black boy backing away and Gerry hobbling towards his car. He was touching the back of his leg with his right hand."

"Could you tell if he was injured?"

"The lighting wasn't good but he was wearing light trousers and I could see the right leg turning dark. I ran up to him and he said something like, 'The fucker's stabbed me.'"

"Did you know who he was talking about?"

"I assumed he meant the black youth."

"Why?"

"Because he was the last one with him."

"What happened then?"

"He managed to get to his car but then he collapsed and passed out..."

He took a handkerchief from his pocket and blew into it to try and mask the fact that he had tears in his eyes, "...the police and ambulance came a short time later and I never saw him again.

CHAPTER 19

A GENTLE APPROACH

David had not conducted Vulnerable Witness Training yet. He was putting it off until it was absolutely essential that he attend a course. After close to forty years at the bar cross examining witnesses of all ages and descriptions, he resented having to 'learn' how to cross-examine, especially as he had been told by those who had attended that the new rules effectively tore up the rule book and prevented any effective cross examination. However, he could see that Brian Williams was a nervous witness and that he would need to deal with him sympathetically so not to alienate the jury.

"Mr Williams, I am going to ask you some questions on behalf of Joseph Rogers. The gentleman who you have already described as the black man at the party. I don't have many questions so please bear with me."

Brian looked relieved, "Thank you."

"I understand that you were a close friend of Mr Worthy?"

Brian stared at him wondering where he was going with this, but he simply answered, "Yes."

"We have heard that on the day that he died, Mr Worthy was disciplined at work for …"

David looked down at a sheet of paper that was in his hands, "… 'intimidation, harassment and abusive behaviour towards a co-worker.' Were you aware of that?"

"Everyone knew it was because he had challenged Maureen and been rude to her."

"It was a little more than that wasn't it. He had been grossly abusive to a female co-worker, calling her a 'rancid menopausal bitch'?"

"I wasn't there, so I don't know what he said."

"I understand that but obviously he told you what he said and it was common knowledge in the firm."

Brian paused but then answered, "Yes."

"Did Mr Worthy tell you that he had called Ms O'Connor, a 'rancid menopausal bitch'?"

Brian hesitated before answering, "I believe he said it was something like that."

"Mr Worthy was a large man, wasn't he?"

"Yes."

"I believe we have a height and weight for him somewhere…"

David paused again whilst he appeared to look for a document that was in fact just in front of him, he picked up the pathology report and read out, "Mr Worthy weighed 115 kilos, about 18 stone and was 6 feet 4 inches tall, 1.93 metres."

"I don't know."

"I don't expect you to know his exact weight and height but do those figures sound about right?"

"I suppose so."

"Well I am sure they will be agreed by the prosecution as they come from a prosecution document."

David turned to Richard Thornbrite QC who nodded in agreement. He then turned back to address the witness.

"Ms O'Connor is a much smaller person?"

"Yes."

"About 5 feet 2 inches tall, approximately 1.6 metres and a mere ten stone or approximately, 60 kilos?"

"Something like that."

"You met Mr Worthy in a pub that night?"

"Yes."

"He was obviously upset with what had happened that day?"

"Yes."

"And no doubt he moaned to you and Shirley about his treatment at work."

"Yes."

"He was clearly upset, was he angry when he was in the pub?"

"Yes."

"Was he angry when he drove you to Sangster Street?"

Brian was boring himself with his monosyllabic answers, "I think he was a bit happier at that stage, he was calming down."

"Undoubtedly, but when he had driven to Sangster Street and you and Ms West left him to go to the party, he obviously got upset and angry again?"

Brian was about to answer when Mr Justice Holdern QC intervened, "Mr Brant, this is all very interesting but does it matter whether Mr Worthy was angry or not? I have read your client's defence statement, he is not suggesting that he stabbed Mr Worthy in self-defence or that Mr Worthy was aggressive or threatening towards him. He states that it is his defence that he did not have a knife and that he did not stab Mr Worthy."

David turned to face the judge, "My Lord, it is no part of Mr Rogers case that he was acting in self defence. As your lordship rightly points out, Mr Rogers is adamant he did not have a knife and did not stab Mr Worthy. However, the charge is one of murder, it is important to establish whether this is murder or whether the perpetrator might have believed he was acting in self-defence of himself or another. In any event, the prosecution led this evidence and I submit I am entitled to investigate Mr Worthy's state of mind at the time of and just before the incident."

David did not want to say in front of the jury that the jury might not believe his client and may conclude he was the stabber and in those circumstances, he wanted them to consider the possibility that he was acting in self-defence.

The judge turned to the prosecutor, "What do you say Mr Thornbrite?"

Richard rose slowly from his seat, "I have not objected to this line of questioning, nor do I. Obviously there must be limits, particularly as your lordship has pointed out that the defence is not one of self-defence."

Mr Justice Holdern QC nodded, "Very well Mr Brant, as the prosecution does not object, I will not stop this line of questioning. However, as Mr

Thornbrite stresses, there must be limits. Please consider that as you continue your questioning."

David bowed slightly, "Of course my lord."

He then turned back to the witness who seemed bewildered by what he had just seen and had no idea what was going on.

"Mr Williams, I was asking you about the state Mr Worthy was in when you and Ms West left him in Sangster Street. It is right that he was clearly very angry and upset when you returned to him?"

"I don't know."

David looked surprised, "Mr Williams, we know he was screaming and shouting in the street. We know that when Ms West approached him, he knocked her out. It must have been obvious to you that he was upset and angry?"

Brian was not looking well as his face turned pale, "I suppose so."

"You tried to calm him down."

"Yes."

"Unfortunately, he was not interested in calming down at that stage and he lashed out and knocked Ms West out?"

"It may have been an accident."

David paused before asking the next question, "Obviously Mr Worthy was a friend of yours. He has also sadly died and it is understandable that you want to protect his memory, however, do you really think that his knocking out Shirley West was an accident?"

Brian looked down at his shoes again, "No."

"It was then that Mr Simons started dancing around in front of Mr Worthy, threatening him with a knife?"

"Yes."

"He was the only person you saw that night with a knife?"

"Yes."

"You never saw the black youth, as you describe him, my client, with a knife at any stage?"

"No."

"You saw Mr Simons though. He was waving the knife around and threatening to use it against Mr Worthy?"

"Yes."

"Mr Worthy did not seem afraid of this, he seemed to almost welcome it?"

"I don't know about that."

"You knew him, you were there that night, you saw him. He stood his ground and looked like he was going to fight with Mr Simons?"

"I suppose so."

"It was then that my client intervened. He tried to usher Mr Worthy away?"

"I saw him put his arm around Gerry but I looked away as I was concerned about Shirley. I don't know what he was doing."

"Mr Williams, earlier you told us, 'I saw him put his arm around Gerry and lead him away.' He was clearly ushering Mr Worthy away?"

Again, Brian paused before resignedly answering, "It looked like that at the time, but I don't know what he was doing now."

"Mr Williams, you never saw my client with a knife at any stage?"

"No, I didn't."

"You never saw him stab Mr Worthy?"

"No, I didn't."

"There were other people around and near to him, when Mr Worthy shouted out, 'You cheeky fucking bastard'?"

"Yes."

"Did you see where Mr Simons was?"

"I don't remember now."

"I suggest he was very near to Mr Worthy, probably backing away at this stage?"

"I don't know. I can't remember where he was."

"But you remember my client. According to you he was backing away. He wasn't running away?"

"No."

"You didn't see anything in his hands at that stage?"

"No."

"Did he seem to be in shock?"

"I don't remember now."

"I suggest he had the expression on his face of someone who had just been shocked by what had happened?"

"I can't remember now."

David thanked him and sat down. He had done what he could with the witness but he had no idea what the jury were making of the case. He could only hope they were keeping an open mind at this stage. There were far more difficult witnesses going to be called soon.

CHAPTER 20

THE FIRST VICTIM

Shirley West entered the courtroom and stopped to look around at the judge, the barristers and the public gallery. She had clearly made an effort for court with a new hair style and a new outfit especially purchased for the day. She worked in a bakery shop in Brighton and was bored with the day to day drudgery of selling fresh bread and cakes to disinterested and frequently rude people. Her boyfriend had run off with her best friend just a few weeks before Gerry Worthy had died and she felt life in general was letting her down. She remembered how it had really annoyed her to see him at the party that night, kissing and cuddling his new girlfriend in front of her. She saw this as her one opportunity to star in the limelight and she was going to make the most of it.

She walked over to the witness box where the usher directed her and took the oath and gave her name in a loud confident voice. One of the men from her workplace had told her he was going to take the day off work to give her moral support and she searched through the public gallery from this new position to see if he was there. He was not.

In reality she knew he was just trying to get her into bed behind his wife's back and had just been pretending to be interested in her life. She wished she had not accepted that drink with him last Friday and the inevitable sexual fumbling that had occurred in his car afterwards.

'Bastard,' she muttered under her breath.

Mr Justice Holdern QC looked up from his computer and turned to his left to address Shirley, "I'm sorry, what did you say."

Shirley turned bright red and coughed, "I didn't say anything, sir."

The judge looked at her, knowing full well what he had heard. His hearing might be failing a little but he could still make out what was said from the witness box a few feet away from him. However, his judicial training kicked in, better to ignore it and let the trial continue rather than blow up an unimportant incident and potentially derail the whole process. He turned towards the prosecutor, "Carry on Mr Thornbrite."

Richard who was probably the nearest to the witness box in this archaic court room, had also heard the witness' exclamation. He had no idea who she was talking about and had no intention of finding out. He too ignored it as he saw no point in alienating this witness. He had not wanted to call her in any event as her evidence supported the proposition that Gerry was angry that night. He had no choice though, as her witness statement had been served as used material on the defence weeks before he became involved in the case and he could hardly refuse to call her now as she had been with Gerry almost all the night and could give some relevant evidence.

"Ms West, I am going to ask you some questions on behalf of the prosecution. There will undoubtedly be some further questions from my learned friend to my left, Mr Brant of Queen's Counsel, who represents the defendant."

She nodded.

Richard raised his voice, "I'm sorry, the recording devices do not pick up nods and gestures, so you will have to speak."

"Alright," she replied.

David thought that Richard was being a bit harsh on the witness, after all, he had not even asked her a question.

Richard carried on without realising this, "Ms West, I am going to ask you questions about August last year, the Friday before the bank holiday when I understand that you met the deceased, Gerry Worthy."

"Alright."

"I believe you met him in the Prince of Orange public house that night?"

"Yeah."

"Had you ever met him before?"

"No."

"Did you know his friend who was also there, Brian Williams."

"Yeah."

Richard was becoming a little tired of the monosyllabic replies so he tried another question, "How did you meet Mr Williams."

She looked coldly at him and he realised it was probably a mistake and against all his training to ask a question that he had no idea what the answer would be.

"He was just someone I use to see in a pub where I used to go to with my ex-boyfriend, the b..."

She stopped suddenly and looked at the judge before continuing, "After I split with my boyfriend I still visited the pub and Brian became a friend of mine and supported me."

She did not add that Brian had wanted something more than a platonic relationship and she had to reject his unwelcome advances on more than one occasion.

"Thank you, now could you tell us about that evening. What was Mr Worthy's temperament like that night?"

She looked confused, "His what?"

"Sorry, his demeanour, his attitude. Was he happy or sad or what?"

"He was angry. He said he'd been given a written warning because of something that happened at work with a woman."

"Did he discuss the incident with you?"

"Yeah, he seemed to have a downer on women. He kept on calling this one a bitch ..."

She stopped and looked at the judge, "Can I say that?"

The judge looked over his glasses and stared at her, "If you are reporting someone's speech, yes ..." He paused before adding, "... but not otherwise."

Richard continued with the questioning without acknowledging the judge's answer, "Did he discuss the incident with you."

"Did he! It was all he would talk about."

"You've told us he was angry when you first met him. Did this change."

"He seemed to get worse. I knew I had a party to go to at Steven Denley's house and I decided to leave him as I didn't like him."

Richard was not happy with where this was going.

"However, you did go to the party with him?"

"Yeah, I couldn't afford a taxi and the buses are rubbish around there at that time of night. He offered to take me and Brian."

"Had Brian been invited to the party as well as you?"

"No, but he was a mate so I was happy for him to come along."

"What about Mr Worthy!"

"Well he offered to drive us, so I told him he could come as well."

"Mr Worthy drove you both to the party, what happened when you got there?"

"I left the car with Brian and we walked to the party."

"What happened to Mr Worthy?"

"I don't know. I'd had a lot to drink by then, five or six double vodka and cokes and I wasn't really thinking. I walked to the party with Brian and thought Gerry would follow us."

"But he didn't?"

"No."

"Can you recall what time you got to the party?"

"Not exactly, I think it might have been around 10pm."

"When did you realise Mr Worthy hadn't joined you?"

"I don't know how long it was, but it was some time, probably twenty or thirty minutes or so."

"What happened for you to remember that Mr Worthy was not with you?"

"I could hear a lot of loud noises from outside. The music was loud at the party but we could still hear screaming and shouting outside. That was Gerry and that was when I realised that he hadn't joined us at the party."

"What did the people at the party do?"

"Everyone wanted to know what was going on out there, so we all left to go outside."

"Did you see anyone take anything with them when they left the party?"

"What do you mean!"

Richard smiled, he was trying not to lead the witness, "Was anyone carrying anything!"

"Oh yeah, I saw Adrian Simons pick up a knife in the kitchen from a knife rack. We had to go through the kitchen to get to the car park."

"Did you see anyone else with a knife?"

She paused for a moment and even looked towards Joseph Rogers in the dock, before she answered, "No."

"Are you sure?"

"Yes."

"What happened when you went outside!"

"I thought Gerry was acting like an idiot. Brian tried to calm him down, but he wouldn't calm down. He was ranting and raving. I went up to him to tell him to just leave and he decked me!"

Richard paused and looked around the faces of the jury.

"Some members of the courtroom may not know what you mean by the word 'decked'. Can you explain?"

"Yeah, I went up to him and told him to go away. The next I knew was I saw his fist coming at me! I was lifted off my feet and knocked out. The hospital said I was lucky that my jaw wasn't broken."

Richard interrupted, "We have rules of evidence, so please don't tell us what someone else said to you."

David stood as if to assist, "I don't object, on this occasion."

Mr Justice Holdern QC looked at him coldly and then addressed the witness, "Nevertheless we do have rules of evidence which bind both the prosecution and the defence."

He turned to Shirley, "Please do not tell us what someone else said to you."

Shirley shrugged her shoulders, "Alright, sir."

Richard faced her again, "Do you remember anything else that night?"

"Yeah, I remember waking up in the ambulance."

She looked quickly towards the judge before adding, "My jaw was really hurting, I thought it was broken."

Richard gave her a slight frown before he continued, "Can you tell now whether the blow to you was deliberate or may have been an accident?"

He knew what her answer was likely to be but he thought he would raise the issue of an accidental blow with her because of Brian William's evidence.

"It looked bloody deliberate to me!"

"Just before you were knocked out, you have told us a number of youths had left the party to see what the disturbance was outside."

"Yeah."

"Did you know the defendant in this case, Joseph Rogers?"

"Yeah, I'd seen him around a few times."

"Did you see him that night?"

"Yeah."

"Did he leave the party?"

"Yeah."

"Did you see what he was doing outside?"

"No, I think he was behind me when I got hit. I didn't see him do nothing."

CHAPTER 21

HELPFUL EVIDENCE

David wondered if there was any need to ask any questions of this witness. She had already given him everything he needed and there was always a danger that if he questioned her she might retract something or give an unhelpful answer simply because she did not like authority figures and associated wigs and gowns with authority.

He looked at her carefully as she looked in his direction. There seemed minimal risk, she was here and he might be able to gain some benefit for his client by asking a few further questions.

"Ms West, I am asking you some questions on behalf of Joseph Rogers."

She looked behind him towards the dock and gave a hint of a smile. That was promising, so he continued.

"Did you know Mr Rogers before that night?"

"I'd met him at other parties a few times."

"Were you close friends?"

"No, we'd spoken on a few occasions but that was it."

"You have given evidence that on the night of 25th August, the night of the incident we are dealing with, you never saw Mr Rogers with a knife?"

"That's right."

"You never saw him stab anyone?"

"That's right."

"You never saw him act in an aggressive way towards anyone?"

"That's right."

"He did not seem angry at any stage?"

"No, he never."

"You have told us you did see one person with a knife that night. You told us Adrian Simons picked up a knife as he went through the kitchen?"

"Yeah."

"You told us he picked it up from a knife rack?"

She paused whilst she thought, "I think it was from a knife rack."

"Did you see him threaten Mr Worthy with the knife?"

"He was waving it around and making, 'tough boy' noises."

David looked at her closely, "What do you mean by 'tough boy noises'?"

"From what you witnessed, you cannot tell us what the defendant's reaction was to seeing you deliberately floored by the angry and aggressive Mr Worthy?"

"No, of course I couldn't, I was out stone cold."

CHAPTER 22

THE FRIEND

The final witness for the day was Steven Denley, a friend of Joseph Rogers. David had hoped that this witness might be helpful to his client but Steven had made a couple of witness statements to the police. The first had been neutral, saying he had not seen anything, but the second was distinctly unhelpful and it was not clear which version he would adopt now and in any event, David was sure the prosecution would take Steven to his second statement whatever he said now.

Richard had the same thoughts and had decided that he would not give this witness a chance of detouring from his first statement. He waited until Steven was sworn and had given his full name before asking, "Mr Denley, you have given two witness statements to the police in this case. Firstly, one on 27th August 2017, two days after the incident and then one just over a week later on 5th September. In the first statement you claimed you did not see anything outside the house. In your second statement you say that you did. Which is correct?"

Steven looked nervous as he answered looking towards Detective Inspector Splinter, the police officer who was in charge of the case and was sitting behind prosecution counsel. He took one look at the stern face and blurted out, "The second."

"Before I ask you to go into detail about the incident can you tell the court why your two statements differ?"

Steven hesitated before answering looking around to see if anyone might come to his aid. No one did so he answered, "Yeah, I didn't want to get my friend into trouble so in the first one, I told the police I hadn't seen anything. Then a week later the police came to my home to ask me about my first statement and I decided I'd better tell the truth."

"Who was the friend you did not want to get 'involved'?"

He looked towards the dock and answered quietly, "Joseph Rogers."

Richard raised his voice as he asked, "Sorry could you say that again, I'm not sure everyone could hear you?"

Steven shouted out the answer this time, "Joseph Rogers."

Richard nodded and paused for a few seconds so the jury would take his answer in, then he began again.

"Mr Denley, I want you to tell the court what you witnessed that night. Firstly, I understand that 84 Sangster Street is your parent's address. Where were they that night?"

"They'd gone on holiday for a couple of weeks to stay in their caravan in the Lake District."

"So, you had been left in charge of the house?"

"Yes."

He looked sheepish as he answered. Clearly his parents had a great deal to say to him about how he had looked after their house.

"When did you first decide to hold a party at their house?"

"Before they left."

"Were they aware that you were going to have a party?"

He looked slightly embarrassed as he answered, "They told me I could have a couple of friends around whilst they were away, provided I kept the place tidy."

"Did they know that you were going to invite a large number of friends around?"

"No."

"What time did the party start?"

"I told people to come around after 7pm."

"Did anyone arrive at that time?"

"No, my mate, Scott Robson arrived at about 7:30pm, the others arrived later."

"Can you recall who arrived and at what time?"

"Not everyone, no."

"Tell us what you recall?"

"I remember Adrian Simons and his girlfriend arriving next, at about 8pm."

"Who was his girlfriend?"

"Jamie Anderson."

"Who arrived next?"

"I think it was Joseph Rogers and his girlfriend, Caroline Jennings."

"What time did they arrive?"

"I'm not sure, it wasn't so long after Adrian Simons."

"What was Mr Rogers like when he arrived?"

Steven looked puzzled, "What do you mean?"

"Was he happy, angry, upset or what?"

Again, Steven hesitated, "I think he was alright."

"Did he remain like that?"

"I think so."

"Think back now, did his girlfriend Caroline stay with him at the party?"

"No."

"What happened?"

"About an hour after they'd arrived, Caroline left. I didn't know why but when I spoke to Joseph, he said he'd had an argument with her. He said she claimed he kept looking at Jamie Anderson. He said she was stupid, he didn't fancy Jamie, but Caroline wasn't having it and she left."

"Did his attitude change because of this argument?"

"No, he seemed alright about it."

Richard paused looking at Steven's statement in front of him. "Did your second witness statement record your recollection of the matter at that time?"

Again, Steven looked puzzled before he answered "Yeah."

"Is your recollection of the matter likely to have been significantly better at that time than it is today?"

"Yeah."

Having used the statutory formula to ensure his previous statement was admissible, Richard asked, "Please refresh your memory from your statement, page 2 at the bottom."

A copy of his statement was passed up to Steven. He read it then Richard asked, "What does it say there about Mr Rogers' attitude after his girlfriend left?"

"Yeah, alright, he seemed upset and angry because he had an argument with his girlfriend."

"Did he remain angry and upset?"

"He wasn't happy, he did complain a bit about her being a bitch to him."

"Do you know Brian Williams?"

"No."

"Do you know Shirley West?"

"Yes."

"How do you know her?"

"She's just one of the group that regularly meets. She used to go out with another one of our group."

Richard looked quizzical, "Who's that?"

"Adrian Simons."

David looked up from his computer screen where he had been taking notes. The fact that Shirley West was an ex-girlfriend of Adrian Simons had not been mentioned in the papers nor had his client told him. It would obviously colour her evidence against Adrian Simons and he wished he had this information when he had cross-examined her.

Evidently Richard was also unaware of this fact as he asked with a puzzled expression, "When were they boyfriend and girlfriend?"

Steven hesitated before answering, "I don't know. They went out together for about a year I suppose and they broke up a few weeks before the party, but I can't give you exact dates."

"Do you know what effect the breakup had on them?"

"Well Adrian dumped her and he didn't seem to care about her. He used to make a point of snogging Jamie in front of her."

He paused again before continuing, seeming to be reluctant to go into any detail but eventually he added, "I think it affected Shirley a lot. At first, she was always crying when she saw Adrian with Jamie. Then she started drinking a lot more and getting drunk every night."

"Did she ever tell you how she felt towards Mr Simons?"

Again, Steven seemed reluctant to answer, "Just a few days before the party she told me she hated him and would do anything to get back at him and Jamie."

Richard nodded, he had got what he wanted so he moved on.

"We have heard that Shirley West and Brian Williams arrived much later at the party, around 10pm, do you recall them arriving?"

"Yeah, I don't remember the exact time but that sounds about right."

"Did you notice anything about them when they arrived."

Steven looked puzzled, "What do you mean?"

"How did they appear to you?"

"I didn't really notice. But by that time, we'd all had a lot to drink."

"What is the next thing you recall?"

"I remember someone, I can't remember who, telling us to be quiet because there was a lot of noise coming from outside at the rear of the house. I turned the music down and I could hear shouting and swearing."

"Did you hear what was said?"

"I didn't hear all of it. I did hear a voice say something like, 'Fucking bastards, where the fuck did you go?' Most of it just seemed to be rambling though."

"What did you do?"

"A number of us decided to see what was happening so we went outside."

"Now the jury have plans of your property. They are in the folder in front of you at tab 5."

He waited for everyone to pull out the plans.

"If we look at them, we see that to get to the rear of the house you had to go through the kitchen, is that right?"

"Yes."

"When you were outside, did you see anyone with a knife?"

Steven shuffled his feet in the witness box before mumbling, "Yes."

"Sorry, can you speak up, when you were outside, did you see anyone with a knife?"

Steven almost shouted, "Yes."

"That's better, who did you see with a knife."

"I saw Adrian Simons."

"Do you know where he got the knife from?"

"No, but it looked like one of the knives my mum has in her kitchen."

"What was he doing with the knife?"

"I didn't see it at first. It was only when the big guy knocked Shirley out that I saw Steven waving the knife at him and threatening to stab him."

"It's probably obvious, but just for the record, who is the 'big guy' you are referring to?"

Steven looked puzzled, he thought everyone would know who he was referring to, "The guy who was making all the noise outside. The guy who died."

Richard ignored the implied rebuke.

"Did you see Mr Simons use the knife on the man?"

No, he was dancing around and threatening him, but he never got close. The big guy looked like he could handle himself and Adrian was really backing away from him."

"Did you see what happened to that knife?"

"No, I think the police took it away because a couple of weeks later they came around to my address to show me photographs of two knives. They asked me if I recognised them. I said they were both similar knives and looked like ones from my mum's kitchen."

"You have told us that Mr Simons was backing away from the big man. What happened next?"

"That's when I saw Joseph Rogers go up to the man to try and calm things down."

Richard almost shouted his next comment, "Don't tell us what you thought his intention was, just what you witnessed."

Steven shrugged, "I saw Joseph Rogers put his arm around the big guy's shoulders and lead him away to the car park behind the houses."

"Did you see anything in Mr Rogers' hands."

"No, but I could only see his right arm which was around the man's shoulders."

"Was anyone else near to them at that stage?"

"Adrian Simons was a few feet away from them."

Richard paused, "Please look at your witness statement which was made much nearer the time of the incident. Please look at the bottom of page four."

Steven did as he was told.

Richard stared at him with cold eyes, "What does it say there?"

Steven read the section, "There was no one else close to them."

"You have just told us that Mr Simons was a few feet away from them, which version is correct?"

Steven looked at the ground as he mumbled a reply.

Richard quickly asked, "I'm sorry, I doubt anyone in the court heard that answer."

Steven spoke up, "My second statement's correct."

"So, no one else was near to them?"

"No."

"What happened next?"

"I thought everything was over so I looked towards Shirley, as I did I heard the big guy shout out something like, 'You fucking cheeky bastard'. I looked around quickly and saw Joseph Rogers backing away and the man holding his leg and hobbling away."

"What did you do?"

"I didn't think anything had happened, so I went to see if I could help Shirley."

"Did you eventually return to your home?"

"Yes, I did."

"Who was there when you returned?"

"A few people had gone back earlier than me because I stayed with Shirley until the paramedics arrived. When I got back, most of them were seated in my living room. Adrian Simons and Jamie were there, as was Joseph Rogers."

"What did they look like?

"Everyone seemed to be in shock."

"Did anyone say anything?"

"Everyone was talking at the same time, so I can't really remember any conversation."

Richard looked at him sternly and almost shouted, "You can refresh your memory from your witness statement, page four, paragraph three!"

Steven looked at his witness statement and then tried to adopt an expression suggesting that he had just remembered something. "Oh yeah, I did hear Joseph Rogers say something like, '... stabbed him,' but I couldn't hear any more. I asked him what he said but just then the police arrived."

"We have heard that the police arrested Adrian Simons for attempted murder. Did you speak out and say he was nowhere near?"

"No, I did not."

"Why not?"

"I was still in a state of shock. Anyway, I thought dancing around with a knife threatening to stab someone was an attempted murder!"

Steven adopted a proud expression thinking his answer was a good one.

"Why didn't you tell the police you had seen Mr Rogers near to the big man just before he was stabbed?"

"I didn't think Jo had done anything wrong. Anyway ..."

He did not finish his sentence.

"Please continue?"

"Well he's a mate, you don't grass a mate up to the police!"

CHAPTER 23

SOME ASSISTANCE

David looked at his watch, it was 15:50, too early to ask to adjourn until tomorrow and yet quite late in the day for the jury who had heard a prosecution opening and the evidence from three witnesses and been told they would be going home sometime after 4pm. He could be some time with this witness but the jury would not appreciate being kept late so he was going to be relatively short. As he observed the witness for a few seconds he noticed, even in the poor light of the courtroom that Steven was sweating, even though it was quite cold in the courtroom.

"Mr Denley, please help me with a few basic details. Firstly, you never saw Mr Rogers with a knife that night?"

"No, I didn't."

"You never saw him stab Mr Worthy?"

"No, I didn't."

"You never saw him act aggressively towards anyone?"

"No, I didn't."

"You have told us you made two statements in this case. In the first you claimed ..."

David picked up the statement and read from it, "'I went outside and saw the large man hit Shirley and knock her out cold. I was concerned for her and went over to her. I didn't see what happened after that.'

Is that the first version you gave in this case?"

"Yes."

"You have told this jury you gave that version because you did not want to get Mr Rogers into trouble, is that correct?"

"Yes."

"Is Mr Rogers a close friend?"

"I know him, we're not particularly close anymore."

"You are better friends with Mr Simons, aren't you?"

"I suppose so."

"You've known him longer, haven't you?"

"Yeah."

"You spend more time with Mr Simons, don't you?"

"Yes."

"You both went to the same schools?"

"Yeah."

"You've known him since you were both very young?"

"Yes."

"In your first witness statement, you mention that Mr Simons was at the party, but you don't mention him again. For example, you don't mention him dancing around and threatening to stab Mr Worthy with the long knife he had armed himself with?"

Steven looked in the direction of the officer in the case. David deliberately followed his gaze.

"Why are you looking at the officer in the case, Detective Inspector Splinter, he can't help you can he?"

Steven quickly looked away.

David pressed the point, "The police came to your home a week after you had made your first statement, what did they say to you?"

Again, Steven looked towards Detective Inspector Splinter, who this time looked away. David noted that the jury had seen the gesture this time and he again commented.

"Please do not look at the police officer, just tell the truth. What did the police officers say to you?"

"Splinter ..."

"Splinter, do you mean Detective Inspector Splinter, the officer in charge of this case?"

"Yeah, he told me to call him Splinter, he said everyone calls him that. He told me that the police had taken a large number of statements from people and they didn't think I was telling the truth. They said they thought I was trying to protect Jo."

"What else did they say?"

"They told me it was an offence to lie to the police and that I should tell them the truth or I could get into trouble."

"So, it was the police who first told you they thought you were trying to protect Mr Rogers by not giving the whole story!"

"Yes."

"Was that the truth?"

"What do you mean?"

"In reality your first version protected Mr. Simons, he was the one armed with a knife and he was the one threatening to stab Mr Worthy, after all, as far as you were concerned Mr Rogers had not done anything wrong?"

Steven paused and physically stopped himself looking at the police inspector before he replied.

"Yeah I was protecting Adrian ..." He paused before adding, "... as well."

"As well, or, was he the only one you were protecting when you gave your first statement!"

"I was protecting them both!"

"Very well, let me ask you a few other questions. You have told us that Mr Rogers came to the party with his girlfriend but that she left and he became angry and annoyed."

"Yeah."

"This would have been around 9pm according to your timescale, about an hour after they arrived?"

"Yeah."

"We know people left the party to go outside to see what was happening at around 10:20pm. What was Mr Rogers' attitude like then?"

"He seemed alright to me."

"He had calmed down?"

"Yeah."

"Let me ask you about what happened outside. When you were first asked by my learned friend, you stated that Adrian Simons was very close to Mr Worthy and Mr Rogers, a few feet away as Mr Rogers was escorting Mr Worthy away. You were then reminded of your statement and said he was not near. Why did you change your account?"

"I was scared. I was told if I'd said anything in my second statement that wasn't true, I could be done for perjury. I thought I could be done for not including it in my statement."

"Thinking back now, is the truth that Mr Simons was just a few feet away from Mr Worthy and Mr Rogers as Mr Rogers escorted him away?"

"Yeah, he was really close."

"Touching distance?"

"Yes ..." He quickly added, "... but I never saw him do anything."

David shrugged his shoulders, "He was still carrying the knife, the one he had threatened to stab Mr Worthy with?"

"Yes, but he didn't use it."

"How can you be sure, you've told us you turned away to look at Shirley when the stabbing occurred?"

Steven could not think of any reply.

"Is that correct, you turned away and then heard the man say something like 'You fucking cheeky bastard', you then turned back and saw that Mr Rogers was backing away and the man was holding his right leg?"

"Yeah."

"Where was Mr Simons?"

"He was still there."

"Within touching distance?"

"Yes."

"Still holding the knife."

"Yes."

"Did you notice if Mr Simons was wearing a pair of black gloves when he was holding the knife?"

Steven thought for a moment before stating, "I can't remember."

"Are you sure you can't remember or are you still trying to protect him."

Steven looked puzzled, "I told you I can't remember!"

"I'd like to move on now to when you went back to the house and everyone, understandably, was talking at the same time. You have told us that you heard Mr Rogers say, '... stabbed him'?"

"Yeah."

"You heard him use the word, 'stabbed'?"

"Yes."

"Did you ever hear him say anything else about the stabbing?"

"No."

"Did you ever hear him use the word 'shanked'?"

"What?"

"Have you heard the word, 'shanked' before?"

"No."

"So, it follows you never heard Mr Rogers use that word?"

"No, I never."

"You heard, "... stabbed him?""

"Yeah."

"May he have said, 'Someone stabbed him'?""

Steven again looked at Detective Inspector Splinter who was deliberately looking away.

"Don't look at the officer, just tell us the truth."

"I suppose he may have said that, I just heard, '...stabbed him.""

"Can you recall now if Mr Rogers was looking at anyone, for example Adrian Simons, when he said this?"

"I can't remember where he was looking."

Richard gave David a scowl which he completely ignored.

"Let me move on to a different topic. You have told us that you were shown two knives by the police and you identified them as ones from your mother's kitchen."

"Yeah, that's right. My mum was annoyed that two knives were missing after the party."

David nodded, "I think we can all understand that. I want you to look at some photographs that the police took of your property after Mr Simons had been arrested and everyone but you had left."

"OK."

"If you turn in the jury bundle to tab 7 you will see some photographs of your home."

Steven did as he was instructed as David continued.

"You will see at photograph four, a picture of one of the knives in the kitchen sink. You will see that it is partly submerged under water. Can you see that?"

"Yeah."

"And you have no doubt that is one of your mother's knives?"

Steven looked as if he thought the question was stupid, "Yeah."

"Now if you look at photograph 4 you will see a view of the kitchen sink area."

Steven looked and nodded.

"You can see that in the draining area is a chopping board with what looks like the remains of a lemon."

"Yeah."

"Do you know who cut the lemon up?"

"No." He thought for a moment before adding, "I remember one of the girls, I can't remember which one, saying she would like a lemon in her drink and I told her where the lemons were. She may have chopped it up."

"Using the knife we see in the sink?"

"Could be."

"And whoever chopped the lemon up could have then placed the knife in the sink and given it a brief wash?"

"I suppose so."

"Was this before the incident that occurred outside the house with Mr Worthy?"

"Yes, I don't think anyone had a drink after the stabbing."

"Now let me ask you to look at photographs of the other knife that was found. These you will find at tab eight of the jury bundle."

Steven turned to the appropriate section and looked at two photographs of the knife.

David turned to the jury, "You will see there is red staining on the knife. We will hear evidence in due course that Mr Worthy's DNA was found on the blade of this knife and without doubt, it must have been the one used to stab him."

He turned back to the witness, "We can see that this knife is similar in shape and size to the one found in the sink."

"Yeah."

"I want you to think back now to that night. You saw Mr Simons waving a knife around and threatening to stab Mr Worthy?"

"Yeah I did."

"Could this be the knife he was holding?"

Steven hesitated before answering. Eventually he said quietly, "Could be."

"You are dropping your voice, could you repeat your answer?"

"Could be."

"You have told us that Mr Simons was within touching distance of Mr Worthy when you turned around to see how Shirley was. In other words, he was within touching distance just before Mr Worthy was stabbed?"

"Yeah."

"It follows he was within stabbing distance, doesn't it?"

Again, Steven hesitated and looked towards Detective Inspector Splinter before answering "Yes."

"And that he could have been the one who stabbed Mr Worthy?"

David sat down before the witness answered. The answer was irrelevant, he had made the point he wanted to.

CHAPTER 24

ANNOYING TIMING

Steven left the witness box a few minutes later and Mr Justice Holdern QC sent the jury home for the day. Just as he was about to rise, Richard stopped him, "My Lord there is a short point of law that I seek your Lordship's assistance upon."

David frowned and looked at his watch, He had hoped to catch the next train to London, now he knew he would miss it and possibly the next one. He stared at Richard as he thought, 'Why couldn't he raise this at 10:00am tomorrow!'

Mr Justice Holdern QC clearly had a similar thought. Looking at David he stated impatiently, "How long will this take Mr Brant? I do have other important business to attend to."

David stood up, "I'm afraid I have no idea. I don't know what point of law my learned friend wants to raise at this late hour. If it is likely to take any time, we could always deal with it tomorrow?"

Mr Justice Holdern QC turned towards Richard, peering at him with a frown, "How long will this take, Mr Thornbrite?"

Richard responded slowly, demonstrating, he hoped, that he was not intimidated by the judge's cold stare.

CHAPTER 25

ANOTHER FRIEND?

The following day Richard was still reeling from the judge's refusal to sanction David for what was clearly, to him, going much further than his instructions. He had seen the effect the cross examination had on the jury and was already worried about his case. This was the first time he had prosecuted in Lewes Crown Court and he was hoping to obtain more prosecution work from the local Crown Prosecution Service. That was unlikely to happen if he lost this case, particularly as the Crown Prosecution Solicitor had told his clerks that the case was 'open and shut.' Hopefully today's witnesses would prove to be better than yesterdays.

At 10:00am, he called Scott Robson, another friend of Joseph Rogers to give evidence. After Scott was sworn and had given his name to the court, Richard pursued a familiar line.

"Mr Robson, you made two witness statements to the police in this matter. Firstly, one on 26th August 2017, one day after the incident and then one just over a week later on 4th September. Is that right?"

Scott Robson was another man in his late teens. He was about six feet tall and very skinny demonstrating that food was not something he regularly indulged in. His demeanour and general condition suggested that he more than made up for this with other indulgences. He looked at Richard with a bored air as he answered, "Yeah," roughly translated as, 'so what'.

"In your first statement you stated that you were drinking heavily that night and smoking cannabis and did not see anything, is that correct?"

"Yeah, though I didn't say 'cannabis', I told them it was 'weed'."

Richard shrugged at the irrelevancy of the answer, "In your second statement you stated that you had been drinking and smoking ..." He paused before continuing, "... weed ... but that you had gone outside and seen the altercation with Mr Worthy. Which statement is correct?"

Scott hesitated for a few seconds before replying with a smirk, "Both. I was drinking and smoking and I didn't see much, but I did go outside and saw what happened."

"Why in your first statement did you say you had not seen anything?"

"Cause, I didn't want to get involved. It's not healthy talking to the police where I come from."

Richard ignored the answer and continued, "I want you to tell the jury what happened on the night of 25th August 2017, leaving out nothing."

It was Scott's turn to shrug his shoulders, "Alright."

"Firstly, we have heard that there was a party at 84 Sangster Street, Brighton, that night. The party was organised by Steven Denley whose parents were away for a couple of weeks. I understand he is a friend of yours, is that right?"

"Yeah."

"How long have you known him?"

"Since school."

"Can you recall what time you arrived at the party?"

"No."

Richard looked at him sternly, "Would it assist you to look at your witness statement that was made nearer to the time?"

"Maybe."

"Did your second witness statement record your recollection of the matter at that time?"

"Yeah."

"Is your recollection of the matter likely to have been significantly better at that time than it is today?"

"Yeah."

"Please look at your second statement then."

A copy of his statement was passed to Scott as Richard continued, "Please look at page two of your statement, paragraph two."

Scott opened the statement and peered at it.

"What time does it state that you arrived at the party?"

He read a few lines before answering, "I got there about 7:30pm."

"Thank you. Were you the first guest to arrive?"

"Yeah."

"We have heard that others arrived after you, including this defendant Joseph Rogers and his girlfriend Caroline Jennings. Do you recall them arriving?"

"Yeah."

"Refreshing your memory from your statement, if you need to, can you recall what Mr Rogers' attitude was when his girlfriend left the party?"

Scott again looked at his statement, "Yeah he was a bit annoyed."

"Does your statement say he looked angry?"

Scott paused before saying, "Yeah."

"Did he say what he was angry about?"

"I can't remember much about it. He said something about having an argument with his girlfriend. She'd been a bitch to him!"

"We have heard that eventually Brian Williams and Shirley West arrived, did you know them?"

"I knew Shirley, I didn't know the bloke she was with."

"How were they when they arrived?"

"They seemed happy, probably a little drunk ..." He paused before grinning and adding, "... like the rest of us."

"Do you recall hearing a noise from outside the house?"

"Not really, no. I remember Steven turning the music down and saying something was happening outside. I then heard some shouting from outside."

"Did you hear what was said?"

"No."

"What did you do?"

"Everyone went outside to see what was happening."

"What did you see happen outside?"

"When I got out I saw the bloke who had been with Shirley was facing this big guy."

"Did you hear what was being said?"

"The big bloke was complaining about being left alone. Shirley then went up to him and told him to piss off and the bloke flattened her."

"Did you see what others were doing?"

"Yeah, everyone thought the bloke was right out of order. Adrian Simons faced up to him and told him to fuck off."

Richard picked up Scott's statement, "Please refresh your memory from page four of your second statement if you need to."

Scott looked at his statement, "Yeah, Adrian Simons was waving a knife at the guy at threatening to stab him, but I think he was just trying to scare the man. The bloke was much bigger than Adrian."

David cast a glance at Richard who nodded and said, "Please do not tell us what you think but what you saw."

"Alright, Adrian was threatening to stab the man."

"What happened next?"

"Joseph Rogers put his arm round the man and led him away."

"Did you see what happened to the man next?"

"No, we were all looking at Shirley."

"Did you hear the large man say anything else?"

"I heard him call Joseph a 'fucking cheeky bastard', and push him away, then he seemed to hobble away holding his leg."

"Did you see anything in Joseph Roger's hands?"

"No."

"Where was Adrian Simons at this time?"

"I saw him with his girlfriend. She led him into the house."

"Did you see where he was when the big man shouted, 'cheeky bastard' to Mr Rogers?"

"He was with his girlfriend, Jamie. She was trying to get him to go into the house."

"Was he anywhere near the large man or Mr Rogers when the large man called out 'cheeky bastard'?"

"No."

"What did you do next?"

"I stayed with Shirley until the ambulance arrived to take her away."

"Did you return to the house?"

"Yeah, just as the police arrived."

"Did you hear Mr Rogers say anything in the house just before the police arrived?"

"No, I went into the house just behind the police."

"The police started questioning everyone at the party. They were asking about the man who had been stabbed. Did you tell them what you had seen?"

"No."

"Why not?"

"I didn't want to get involved."

CHAPTER 26

A HELPFUL WITNESS?

David again had to make a speedy but important decision. This witness was supposedly a friend of his client and may be willing to assist him. However, he had given unhelpful evidence and if David probed too deeply, he might make the case worse.

"Mr Robson, I am going to ask you some questions on behalf of Mr Rogers."

David reflected to himself, 'It can't hurt to tell him that I'm on the side of his supposed friend.'

Scott just shrugged his shoulders as if to say, 'so what'.

"As we heard, you made two witness statements to the police in this matter. In the first you claimed you saw nothing. In the second you gave a version similar to the one you have given today."

"Yeah."

"Why did you make a second statement?"

Scott looked vacant and then answered, "The police came around and told me they thought I'd lied in my first statement and if I didn't make another I'd be charged with perjury."

David paused for the jury to take in the answer.

"Which officers came to see you and said that?"

Scott looked around the courtroom till he saw Detective Inspector Splinter and then pointed at him and said, "Him and another copper. I can't remember his name."

David looked at the witness' second statement and saw that two officers had witnessed it, "Your second statement was witnessed by Detective Inspector Splinter and Detective Constable John Rice. Are those the officers you are talking about?"

"Yeah, I think so."

"Did they tell you what they wanted you to put in the statement?"

"Yeah, they told me they thought I'd lied and that Joseph Rogers had stabbed the man and they wanted me to tell them what I saw."

Again, David paused, hoping the jury were taking this in.

"Under a threat that you could be charged with perjury if you did not?"

"Yeah."

David turned to the judge. My lord, I note that Detective Splinter is in court. I had no objection to him remaining in court when I considered his evidence to be inconsequential but now after the evidence of the last two witnesses, I suggest that he should leave the court during the remainder of this witness' evidence."

The judge turned to Richard, "Mr Thornbrite?"

Richard rose, "I've just asked the officer to leave court."

All heads turned to see a slightly red-faced Detective Inspector Splinter leave the courtroom muttering something, fortunately, incomprehensible to others.

David waited until he had left before asking, "Did Detective Inspector Splinter specifically state to you that Mr Rogers had stabbed the man before he asked you to give another statement, threatening you with perjury if you stuck with your first statement?"

"Yeah he did."

"Nevertheless, you never stated you saw Mr Rogers with a knife?"

"I never did see him with no knife."

David ignored the double negative.

"You never saw him stab anyone or make any gesture that looked like a stabbing motion?"

"No."

"All you saw was Mr Rogers put his right arm around the man's shoulders and lead him away."

"Yeah."

"It looked like Mr Rogers was trying to calm the situation down?"

As if on cue, Scott turned to the jury and replied, "That's what it looked like to me."

"You never saw how the man received his injury?"

"No."

"You turned away from the man to see how Shirley was?"

"Yeah."

"At some stage you saw Adrian Simons' girlfriend, Jamie Anderson, lead him into the house?"

"Yeah."

"I want you to think carefully about this next question."

Scott just looked at him blankly.

"Can you recall whether Jamie led Adrian away before or after the man shouted something like 'you cheeky bastard'?"

Scott looked as if he was trying to remember. After a few seconds he replied, "I can't remember now, I wasn't really thinking about it at the time."

"I am sure we all appreciate that. It was late, dark, you had all been drinking, and some of you had been taking drugs and were not expecting to recall such matters, months later."

Scott just shrugged his shoulders.

"Can you recall now, where Adrian Simons was just before the man shouted something like 'you cheeky bastard'?"

Scott hesitated and looked confused before replying, "No."

"Again, I'm going to ask you to think carefully about the next answer. You see I suggest that just before Mr Worthy shouted out and hobbled away, Adrian Simons was very close to him. Actually, within touching distance. Can you recall that now?"

Scott looked more confused than ever, "I can't remember."

"Can you recall if Mr Simons still had the knife he was carrying in his hand?"

"I think so."

"Can you recall if Mr Simons was wearing any black gloves that night."

He paused before answering, "I don't think so. I can't really remember."

"Very well, one last topic then. You and Mr Rogers are both avid pool fans?"

"What?"

"You both like to play games of pool?"

"Yeah."

"In fact, you joined a pool club in central Brighton together, called 'The Black Ball club'?"

"Yeah we did."

"And before this incident you used to meet there fortnightly to play together in a tournament?"

"Yeah."

You have known Mr Rogers for almost two years now?"

"Yeah, almost two years."

"You can confirm that he is right-handed?"

Scott paused before giving his reply in an uninterested way, "Yeah."

CHAPTER 27

THE NEIGHBOUR

Scott finished his evidence shortly before 1pm and Mr Justice Holdern QC suggested that they take an earlier lunch than normal but be back promptly at 2pm. It was noticeable that the judge looked worried as he left court and for a moment David wondered if it was something to do with the case.

The judge entered his room alone and threw his wig down on the desk with some vigour almost knocking an open bottle of ink over in the process. He did not seem to care as his mind was elsewhere. He was worried, a weighty difficult case was playing on his mind.

'Damn, did I include a reference to section 175 of the Copywrite, Designs and Patents act 1988 in my judgment' he thought. 'It may be important in this case to determine whether there was a publication or a commercial publication. Why did I press send and not keep the judgement to look over at lunch?'

At 2pm the court sat again Richard asked if he might address the judge in the absence of the jury so their entrance into court was delayed.

"Yes, Mr Thornbrite?" It was clear to everyone in court that something had upset the judge from his tetchy response.

Richard peered closely at the judge with cold eyes, determined to demonstrate once more that he was not intimidated by a mere High Court judge wearing a red 'dressing gown'.

"My lord, the next witness I wished to call in sequence was Jamie Anderson, the girlfriend of Adrian Simons. She was warned to attend court for 1pm today but has failed to arrive. We have called her home and mobile phone but no one is answering. When I discovered she had not attended court, I asked the police to send a car to her address. I am reliably informed that a police car from Brighton police station was sent and arrived there ten minutes ago but no one appeared to be present. It appears that she has disappeared."

The judge seemed unimpressed, "Well what are you asking me to do about it?"

"Nothing, my lord, I was just informing you why I would be calling witnesses out of order. I do have two other witnesses who are here and I am in a position to call them but I anticipate that we may finish a little earlier than usual and I just wanted to explain that to your lordship in the absence of the jury."

The judge looked at him and smiled, "I suspect we shall just have to tolerate an early finish! Meanwhile I am sure your officers will make all the necessary enquiries to ensure that they discover the whereabouts of Ms Anderson and bring her to court under arrest should it be necessary. Should you need a warrant to ensure her attendance I am willing to grant one."

Richard thanked him and sat down waiting for the jurors to file into court. Once they were seated he announced his next witness would be Lynn Turnbull, a resident of one of the neighbouring properties in Sangster Street.

It was a full five minutes before Lynn Turnbull, walked slowly into court. She was a large lady with grey hair aged about seventy and clearly from her gait she was suffering a variety of illnesses. In fact, she suffered from diabetes and had ulcerated legs which accounted for her slow walk. She also had poor eyesight as could be seen from the thick lenses fixed into a solid gold coloured spectacle frame.

She beamed as she entered the court and rightly was not concerned at all about the time she took, enjoying the stares of everyone in the courtroom as she made her way towards the witness box. It was a few moments before she was seated and ready to answer questions.

Richard gave her a broad grin which she returned with an even broader one.

"Mrs Turnbull, I understand that you live in Sangster Street just across from number 84?"

"No, I don't."

Richard's grin evaporated, "But ..."

"I live in Cromwell Avenue, but the rear of my property overlooks the rear of the properties in Sangster Street, including number 84."

Richard quickly looked down at her statement that said she lived just across from the rear of

Sangster Street. He regained his composure immediately looking briefly at the map in the jury bundle.

"Of course you do, my apologies. For my purposes I do not need your exact address or even the street you live in. The important matter is that your property overlooks the rear of number 84 Sangster Street."

Lynn smiled at him, happy that she had been able to assist the nice man.

David turned to his junior and spoke quietly, "Richard is from the school that believes poor preparation should not get in the way of a bad examination-in-chief."

Richard caught some of the comment and glared at him before continuing, "Mrs Turnbull, I want to take you back to the evening of 25th August last year. The Friday before the bank holiday. Can you recall where you were that evening?"

"Yes, I was at home with my husband Malcolm."

"Were you there all evening?"

"Yes, Malcolm had been ill that day, he has really bad bronchitis. The doctor has told him many times to give up smoking but he won't. Anyway, I'm not as quick as I used to be so neither of us had gone out that day. Actually, Malcolm had spent most of the day in bed."

"Did there come a time in the evening when you heard any loud noises?"

Her grin rapidly turned into a frown. "There did!"

"What did you hear?"

"When Malcolm and I first moved there, it was a quiet neighbourhood, but, over the years, a lot of young families moved in and now most of their children are teenagers! Friday night is bedlam, usually from 7pm until 2am all you hear is loud music being played from several addresses. I've complained to the local council many times but no one does anything. Number 84 is one of the worst and especially that night."

"Why that night?"

"Well because of what happened!"

"Please tell us what you recall happening?"

"Well after 7pm the music started up from about three of the properties in Sangster Street, but the noise was loudest from number 84. That's when I knew that Mr and Mrs Denley we're away again leaving their son alone in the property. Usually the noise isn't so bad when they are there, but you can always tell when they've gone away. I bet you can hear the noise as far away as Hove."

Richard tried beaming at her again but she responded with a quizzical look so he asked, "Please just tell us what you heard or saw."

"Well I would have complained but our living room is at the front of our house furthest away from Sangster Street, I went in there and switched the sound on the TV up."

"Did there come a time when you heard anyone outside the rear of your property?"

"Yes! I went to bed at about 10:00pm. Our bedroom is at the back of the house so we could still hear the music..." She quickly added proudly, "... but we've had double glazing fitted so it drowns out a lot of the noise."

"What noise did you hear?"

"I heard a man shouting and swearing outside our property. He had a very deep scary voice."

"What did you do?"

"I rushed to the curtain to look out." She smiled at the judge, "Well, I moved as fast as I could."

The judge was about to acknowledge her look with a smile but Richard did not want her side tracked at this stage in her evidence so before the judge could respond he quickly asked her, "What did you see when you looked out?"

"I saw a very large man just outside my house."

"Was he alone?"

"He was at first, but then a number of youths came out from number 84. They looked like they were carrying knives!"

Richard stared at her, "Who looked like they were carrying knives?"

"Well I saw one youth with a very large knife and I'm sure I saw another youth with a knife as well."

"Can you tell us what these youths looked like?"

"They all looked the same to me."

"Can you give any better description?"

"No, I think they were all wearing, what are they called, 'hoodies' is it?"

"Can you tell us what colour the youths were?"

"No, it was too dark."

"But you believe two of them had knives?"

"Yes."

"What happened?"

"I saw two of them approach the man and he knocked one of them out. I think he knocked a girl out because she had long hair, but you can't tell these days, they all look alike."

"After the girl was knocked out..." he paused and added, "... there is no dispute it was a girl, did you see what happened next?"

Lynn looked like she was concentrating hard trying to recall, "Yes, one of the youths went up to the large man and was threatening him with a knife."

"Can you describe that youth?"

"Not really, I think he was wearing dark clothing, but I think most of them were."

"Did you hear anything that was said?"

"The youth was threatening to stab the man and the large man kept saying, 'come on then'."

"Did you see what happened next?"

"No, they moved to my right out of sight. It seemed to calm down as I saw most of the youths return to the house. I could see the ..." She paused, "... the girl, was still flat out in the pavement with two other youths round her. As it seemed over, I went back to bed."

"Were you able to sleep?"

"No, within a few minutes, the police and a couple of ambulances arrived. I looked out again but it was all chaos. Everyone was moving around so fast, I couldn't tell what was going on."

CHAPTER 28

REPAIRING DAMAGE

It was clear to David that the witness' account of seeing two men with knives was massively damaging to his client and had to be challenged, but seeing the sympathetic smiles that the jury were giving the witness, he knew that he had to tread carefully.

"Mrs Turnbull, I would like your assistance on just a few matters."

She smiled at him, clearly happy to be of assistance. This was a big day in her life.

"You have told us that you went to bed around 10pm that night. Was that the usual time you went to bed?"

"No, usually we go just before midnight, but Malcolm was ill that day and I was tired from having to wait on him, constantly going up and down stairs with meals and drinks."

She turned to the jury, "And I'm not as fast as I used to be!"

David noted the sympathetic smiles given to the witness from one or two female jurors who had, no doubt, similar experiences with their husbands.

"Did you fall asleep and then were wakened by the man outside or were you still awake?"

"I was still awake. I couldn't get to sleep because of the loud noise."

"Presumably you were trying to sleep?"

"Yes."

"So, you had done everything that was necessary before going to bed?"

"Yes."

"You had got changed into your nightclothes?"

She looked slightly embarrassed, but answered, "Yes."

"You presumably do not sleep in your glasses, so you had taken them off?"

"Yes."

"Where do you keep your glasses?"

"On my dressing table which is on the left hand side of my bed."

She was no longer smiling finding these questions very intrusive.

"Presumably you had switched off the lights in the room?"

"Yes."

"You then heard the man outside and immediately got up to see what was happening?"

"Yes, I did."

"Did you switch any lights on?"

"No."

"Why not?"

"I didn't want to be seen in case there was any trouble."

"Perfectly understandable. Did you stop to put anything on before looking out?"

"No."

"Did you stop to put your glasses on?"

"No ...", realising where this was going she quickly added, "... but I can see well enough without them."

"Forgive me for asking, but are you wearing the same glasses now as you had then?"

"Yes."

"The lenses do appear to be quite thick. Are you short sighted?"

"Yes, but I can make out shapes."

"Are your eyes worse in the dark than in daylight?"

"Yes, but I can still see."

"This is not intended as a criticism, but that night when you looked out of the window was it difficult to make out faces?"

"A little, but I could still see what was happening."

"You told us that you believed you saw two men with knives that night. Thinking back now may it have been just one man with a knife?"

"No, I distinctly remember seeing two men with knives."

"May it be that you saw something that reflected the light and now, after all this time, you assumed it was a knife?"

"No, I saw two knives?"

"Can you describe them?"

"One was long, with a long blade."

"Was that the one held by the boy who was threatening the large man?"

"Yes."

"Can you describe the other knife?"

"I just saw the blade briefly."

"Was it held by a white man?"

"I think so."

David looked down at her witness statement and decided to deal with one last issue.

"You are being asked to deal with matters that occurred months ago now. I believe that you made a single witness statement to the police in this matter, just one day after the incident?"

"Yes, I did." She replied proudly.

"Is it likely that you had a better recollection of events the day after the incident than now, months later?"

She paused before stating, "I suppose so, but I know what I saw."

"Did you have an opportunity to read you witness statement before coming into court today."

"I was given my witness statement but I had to come into court before I had a chance to read it."

"So, you've been forced to rely on your memory in court?"

"Yes, but I know what I saw."

"I'm going to ask the usher to help you with your statement. Firstly, can you be provided with a copy of the statement and just confirm it contains your signature."

He turned to the usher who took a copy of the witness' statement to her. Lynn confirmed it contained her signature and David asked Lynn to read out a paragraph on the third page of the statement. She removed her glasses and held the statement close to her face and began reading.

"I saw a number of youths leave number 84 Sangster Street and confront the large man. Two of the youths went up to the man and started talking to him. He then punched one of them knocking him out."

David asked her to stop there, "It's fair to say that in the dark without your glasses you could not tell that the large man knocked out a female."

"No, it was very dark though."

David asked her to continue reading.

"I saw another youth approach the man. This youth had a knife and was threatening to stab him. I did not see anyone else with a knife that night."

Lynn turned red when this part of her statement was read out to her.

David gave her a sympathetic look, "We all make mistakes Mrs Turnbull, but what you told the police just a day after the incident is that you only saw one person with a knife, is that correct?"

"I'm sure I saw two youths with knives?"

"But a day after the incident, you were adamant that it was only one?"

She hesitated before answering with clearly great reluctance, "Yes, that's what I told the police but I'm sure now it was at least two."

"And that is even though; you weren't wearing glasses, it was dark outside, and you were only observing this incident for a few seconds at most."

She turned a bright red as she shouted out the answer, "Yes!"

CHAPTER 29

ANOTHER 'NEIGHBOUR'

Richard's next witness was Carl Williams, a man in his early forties who came to court wearing an expensive dark Italian suit, a blue designer shirt and an expensive multi coloured tie that looked strangely out of place in the old courtroom.

Richard looked at his witness statement before asking, "Mr Williams, I understand that you live in Cromwell Avenue, the rear of which overlooks the rear of Sangster Street?"

"No."

Richard looked startled, "Sorry, your witness statement gives your address as Cromwell Avenue?"

"No, I live in Meopham in Kent. I was visiting my mother last August bank holiday as she had been ill, so I was staying with her at her address in Cromwell Avenue. The police officer who took the statement said that I could put down Cromwell Avenue as my address."

Richard's face reddened as he looked back towards Detective Inspector Splinter, who deliberately ignored his glance.

Richard looked back to the witness, muttering soto voce to himself, 'Can't these bloody idiots do something simple like take a witness statement?'

Carl looked at him perplexed, "I'm sorry, I didn't catch that!"

Richard assumed his best smile, "Nothing Mr Williams, let me ask you this. You were visiting your mother on the August bank holiday and I presume from your witness statement, at about 10pm you were occupying one of the rear bedrooms in the property?"

"Yes, that's right."

"Were you asleep at that time or just about to go to sleep?"

"Neither."

Richard's beaming smile turned into a frown as the witness continued, "My mother had gone to bed early because of her cold so I decided to go to the spare room and watch some TV in the room."

"Why didn't you stay downstairs and watch TV?"

"Even in August the living room gets very cold, and she has no central heating and refuses to warm the place. The spare room gets quite warm though because it's directly above the kitchen."

Richard shrugged off the response as irrelevant, "How much of the rear of Sangster Street can you see from the spare bedroom?"

"My mother's house is on the end of the block so I could see quite a lot, including the car park where that poor man was stabbed."

"Well please commence by telling us what is the first thing you remember from that night?"

"Yes, certainly. I was watching the 10 o'clock news when I heard some loud shouting outside, so I went to the window to see what was happening."

"What did you see?"

"There was a large white man outside the house, shouting and swearing."

"Did you hear what he was saying?"

"It was loud but garbled, it sounded like he had drunk quite a lot. I made out some words, like 'where the fuck are they?' or something like that."

"Was he alone?"

"He was at first, then after a few minutes I saw a large group of youths coming out of the rear of a house in Sangster Street."

"Can you tell how many youths there were?"

"There were about seven or eight of them, I think."

"Could you see if any of the youths were carrying anything?"

"Not at first, but later I saw one of the youths had a large knife in his hand."

"Did you see if any of the others were armed?"

"No, but they were quite close together so I couldn't see if any of them were carrying anything else."

"Can you describe these youths?"

"There was a mix of girls and boys. I think there were two girls and the others were all boys."

"What happened?"

"Well they rushed out of the house, I'm not sure what number of Sangster Street it was?"

"Don't worry, its agreed evidence in this case that they came out of number 84 Sangster Street. What did you see them do if anything?"

"Well I saw them go up to the large man. He was approached by one youth, he looked older than the others, and a girl joined him."

"What happened?"

"It seemed to me that the older youth was trying to calm the large man down but then the girl started shouting and swearing and telling the large man to, 'fuck off'. That seemed to really annoy him and he punched her knocking her to the floor."

"How did the youths react to that?"

"They all seemed to get very angry. I saw the youth with a knife, start to move around like he was a boxer, darting in and out and thrusting the knife at the man."

"Can you describe this youth?"

"Yes, I phoned 999 after the incident and gave the police a description. He looked like he was late teens, dark hair, it could be black but the lighting wasn't good. He was wearing casual clothing, a dark top and dark blue jeans. He was also waving a very large knife around and I heard him threaten to stab the man."

"Did you hear any threats from anyone else?"

"No, but they seemed angry, probably because the girl who had been hit looked unconscious."

"How did the large man react to being threatened with a knife?"

"He didn't seem to care, he just faced the youth and told him to try and stab him. I thought he was being really stupid as the knife looked like it could cause a nasty injury."

"Did you see if the youth did stab him or stab at him?"

"No, he was waving the knife about but it looked like bravado to me. Once the man squared up to him, he backed off."

"Did you see how this incident ended?"

"Yes, another youth, he looked darker than the others. He put his arm round the man's shoulders and seemed to calm the situation down."

"What did he do?"

"He led the man away into the car park."

"Did you continue to watch?"

"I did, but I thought the whole incident was over and I looked at the girl on the pavement as I was concerned that she had been injured."

"Did you see what happened to the large man and the youth who seemed to be calming him down?"

"Not at first as I was looking at the girl on the floor. However, I heard the large man shout out something like, 'you fucking cheeky bastard' and I then looked in that direction and saw him push the dark youth away from him. He then hobbled off reaching down to his right leg."

"Was anyone else near the two of them when this happened?"

"I saw a number of youths milling around but I'm not sure if there was anyone else close to the two of them."

Richard asked him to refresh his memory from the witness statement he had made to the police.

"Oh yes, I see I stated there was no one else around at the time."

"Did you see anything in the darker youth's hands at any stage?"

"I don't think so but he was some distance away, probably fifty feet and it was dark so he may have had something but I did not see it."

"What do you recall seeing next?"

"I saw the man hobble off towards a car and then he seemed to collapse. It was clear that he was hurt. It was then that I noticed one of the youths looking up at me so I closed my curtains and I phoned the police and told them what I had seen."

"Did you see the police and ambulance arrive?"

"I did, I heard the sound of sirens and then I looked out through the curtains again. I could see a few police cars arrive and two ambulances. One set of paramedics went to the girl who was still unconscious and another set went to the man."

"Did the police visit you that night?"

"They did. I waved down to them and said I had seen what happened."

"And did they take a statement from you the next day in which you described what you had seen?"

"They did."

CHAPTER 30

ANOTHER HELPFUL WITNESS?

David could see that the jury seemed impressed with the witness' demeanour and the evidence that he had given. He had nothing to hide and had given a clear and coherent account of what he had seen. He had not actually seen the stabbing and so was not a crucial witness either for or against Joseph, but he might be helpful.

"Mr Williams, you have told us that you were visiting your mother that bank holiday weekend. Did you regularly visit her around this time?"

Carl shrugged a little at the question, "I suppose not as often as I should."

"Sorry this is not a criticism, I just wanted to know how often you are in that area?"

"I suppose I manage to visit every couple of months and stay there for a few nights every four or five months."

It was obvious to everyone he did not visit his mother that often but David ignored the response.

"Do you know the area well then?"

"Reasonably, I was brought up in the Brighton area."

"Is this generally a noisy neighbourhood?"

"I don't know personally, I know my mother complains about the youths in the area making quite a lot of noise at the weekends."

"On this occasion, the August bank holiday weekend had you noticed any excessive noise when you went to bed that night?"

"Yes, it was quite noisy. I'm afraid my mother has not done much to the house since she and my father bought it. There is no double glazing upstairs and so you can hear a lot of noise from the neighbourhood."

"However, it was a particularly loud noise that was brought to your attention that night. It was the large gentleman outside your mother's house who was shouting and swearing."

"Yes."

"Did he sound aggressive to you?"

"Certainly, that's why I looked out of the window. I wasn't sure if he was going to try and break into my mother's house. He was right outside and was very loud."

"Is it right that it was a few seconds, minutes at most, from the time you looked out of the window to the time that you saw the youths leave number 84 Sangster Street?"

"Yes, a few minutes at most."

"Did the large man remain aggressive?"

"Well he knocked out a young girl, so I should say so."

"You saw a number of youths come out of number 84. They were all talking, but not everyone was aggressive, were they?"

"They sounded rowdy to me."

"Let me ask you about one. The youth you described as darker than the others. Did you hear him say anything aggressive or act in an aggressive way at any stage?"

Carl hesitated before answering, "I don't think so."

"Was he noticeable because he was the only black youth among the group?"

"No, I wouldn't say so. Some were wearing 'hoodies' so I couldn't tell what colour they were. I didn't see everyone's face."

"You never saw a knife in the black youth's hand at any stage, did you?"

"No, but to be fair, it was dark and there were a lot of youths milling around."

David held up Carl's witness statement and looked at it before he asked, "You never saw a knife in his hands, did you?"

"No."

"The only person you saw with a knife that night was the dark haired skinny youth who was wearing dark casual clothing?"

"Yes."

"He was moving around like a boxer, or perhaps a dancer, and threatening to stab the large man?"

"Yes, he was."

"However, the large man stood up to him. Effectively he told him to try and stab him and the youth backed off."

"Yes."

"Then the black youth seemed to calm things down and put his arm around the large man's shoulders and lead him away?"

"Yes."

"As I understand it that is when you stopped looking in the direction of the large man because your attention was now drawn to the poor girl that the large man had knocked out?"

"That's right, I was concerned that she'd not moved since she fell to the ground and that she might be seriously injured."

"You presumably looked away from the young girl and looked towards the large man after he had shouted out something like, 'You fucking cheeky bastard'?"

"Yes, it was quite loud and I thought he was starting up again."

"At that stage you saw him push one youth away from him?"

"Yes, I did."

"Were there other youths around him at that stage?"

Carl paused whilst he thought, "There were a number of youths between the large man and my position and even though I was elevated, they were partially blocking my view so I suppose they must have been close to him."

"Did you see where the youth was who had threatened to stab the large man?"

"I believe he was near the large man and the black youth."

"Within touching distance?"

"He must have been close, but I can't remember how close now."

"Did you see another girl near him at any stage, leading him away from the large man?"

He paused as he tried to recall.

"No, I don't think so. I remember there was another girl around at some stage but I really didn't take much notice of her."

CHAPTER 31

AN INTERLUDE

After Carl had given his evidence and been excused for the day, the judge adjourned the case for the day. He was still agonising over his judgment in the copyright case and wondering if he had made any glaring mistakes that would be torn to shreds in the Court of Appeal. 'Perhaps I should stick to criminal trials in the future' he thought to himself as he left court.

David watched the judge's pensive visage as he left court wondering why he was agonising so much over this case. It seemed relatively straight forward to him.

The weather was still typically cold January weather in Lewes and as there was a long wait for the next train, David did not feel like going home straight away so he invited his junior, Gavin Peacock, to come with him to his favourite pub near Lewes station.

After he had purchased a couple of pints of the local Sussex beer they both sat down in a window seat and observed the passers by making their way to the station to catch trains to Brighton, Eastbourne, London and the stations in between.

It was David who spoke first, "So Gavin, what do you think of the case so far?"

Gavin sipped his beer and then looked like he was deep in concentration before answering, "Well, the case has only just started and you have made some headway, but our client really does have problems. Not least when Adrian Simons' girlfriend gives evidence. As the prosecution refuse to charge Simons with murder, she has no reason to lie anymore. Her evidence could be the final nail in Joseph's already sealed coffin."

David nodded and then changed the subject. He had learnt at an early stage that when he met a new solicitor or an employee at a solicitor's firm, he should find out as much as possible about them to see if they would instruct him again. Gavin was a barrister, but he worked at a solicitor's offices so there was no harm in prying.

"So, Gavin, what type of work does your firm generally do?"

Gavin took another sip of his beer before replying, smiling first at the pretty girl who served behind the bar and who was clearing empty glasses away from their table. David noticed Gavin voluntarily or, perhaps, involuntarily covering his wedding ring with his right hand as she got closer. Gavin kept on looking at her with a sickly smile as he answered David's question.

"We have all types of work from the run of the mill crime all the way up to murder and some fraud work, although generally my work load is the lower quality stuff, actual bodily harms, woundings, driving offences and minor frauds."

"So, how did you end up with this case, murder isn't generally lower quality work, even these days with the general reduction in fees."

"No, I was lucky on this one. Generally, all the decent work goes to one of our senior in-house barristers, William Cox. He's great friends with the senior partner and would have presumably been given this case if he hadn't been busy when it was first sent to the Crown Court. I was the only one available to cover it and fortunately I got on well with the client and he insisted that I continue working on the case."

"Well that was good for you."

"Yes, I need it. We are supposed to bring in double our salary these days if we are to continue in the firm. That's becoming more and more difficult on the lower quality work and the lower fees. You need a serious case with a large amount of paperwork to get anywhere near it"

"Yes, but I hear the powers that be are thinking of getting rid of the page count and replacing it with higher brief fees, so that might help with the smaller work, but we shall see."

"If they do that, I doubt the increased brief fees will make up for the fees generated by the lost page count and it won't be possible to earn anywhere near double my salary, which means, I will probably be out of a job."

He thought for a moment before asking, "I don't suppose you have any tenancies available in your chambers."

David put his beer down as he contemplated the request. He had been fishing to see whether he could get any more work from this firm, now Gavin was trying to see if there was any room for him in David's chambers. This conversation was definitely not going in the right direction.

"We are pretty full at the moment, but there is always room for a busy practitioner with his own practice."

Gavin looked downhearted.

"That's me out then, there's no way my boss, Graham, will brief me if I leave his firm and return to the independent bar and I don't have any other contacts. Graham makes it quite clear that if you leave, that's it, you are completely cut off."

David took another sip of his beer whilst he thought of something to say to this young depressed barrister. As he could not think of anything that might lighten his mood, he changed the subject completely.

"So, tell me what frauds does your firm deal with?"

"Oh, all the usual ones, VAT frauds, Inland Revenue frauds, banking frauds, boilermaker frauds, wine frauds and recently a black money fraud."

David had of course heard of all of these and been instructed in every one of these types of case, save for the last one referred to.

"Black money frauds? That's a new one on me. What does that involve?"

"As I said, we had one recently. I was only involved in a couple of preliminary hearings before Cox got involved, but I managed to see the papers.

As you know when people rob security vans or cash machines there is a chance that an explosive device inside the money carrier will go off and cover the money in dye making it worthless as they can't get rid of it."

"I'm aware of that but where does the fraud come in?"

"We had a client last year arrested in a hotel in Brighton. Security at the hotel got suspicious when they saw a Muslim client carrying into the hotel large bottles of chemicals and taking them to his room. They contacted the police and anti-terrorist police swooped. The client was terrified when helmeted, black-clad police officers kicked the door of his room open and pointed machine guns at him and told him to get on the floor. They then searched the place and found hydrogen peroxide which you know can be used in bomb making. They also found thousands of pieces of black paper and some documents.

They arrested him and took him up to Paddington police station in London on suspicion of bomb making. It was only when they read the documents they found that they all said the same thing. 'Use the chemical on both sides of the notes to clean them'.

He confessed straight away worried that he would be charged with bomb making and/or terrorist offences. He told the police he was supplying people with the black paper and bottles of hydrogen peroxide and claiming that the black pieces of paper were all £20 notes that he had stolen from cash machines but that they had all been covered in dye. He claimed that he had invented a chemical that would clean the dye off the notes but he did not have the time to clean them all himself and he was offering bundles of 1,000 pieces of paper for £1,000. People were buying them thinking they were getting £20,000 of dyed notes for £1,000. He would then disappear to another part of the country, set up in a hotel and scam someone else. His bank account showed that he'd made close to hundred thousand pounds by the time he was arrested."

"So, what happened, I can't imagine any of the victims came forward?"

"No one did. The prosecution tried him on the basis of his confession but we got it excluded because he hadn't been given any access to a solicitor for two days because of the fear he was part of a terrorist cell."

David nodded, presumably Graham, his solicitor, had on this occasion argued successfully that his client's Human Rights had been ignored. It was a pity that he had not given Joseph the proper advice when he represented him at the police station. It would have been far better for him if he had answered questions stating he had nothing to do with stabbing or at least, if he had made a prepared statement, listing his defence and then not answering any questions.

David looked at the depressed Gavin now staring into an empty glass of beer and in a vain attempt to cheer him up, said, "Come on, you're looking thirsty, let me get you another beer."

CHAPTER 32

THE UNIFORMED INSPECTOR

Wednesday morning arrived and Richard announced to the judge that Jamie Anderson had still not been found but the police were following up on certain enquiries and were sure they would have her at court the following day. David was less confident. There were a few possibilities as to why she did not want to attend court, three reasons came immediately to mind; either because she did not want to carry on with her lies about Joseph, or, if she was telling the truth, because she did not want to give evidence against a friend, or because she was fearful of repercussions. It of course left him in a quandary.

The jury had heard the prosecutor say that Joseph had confessed to Jamie Anderson that he had killed Gerry Worthy. If she did not appear to give evidence and the case continued they would be told to ignore that comment, but was it likely that they would? Alternatively, if he asked for this jury to be discharged, the new trial would probably not take place for months, by which stage the police would probably have found Jamie Anderson. In those circumstances the prosecution would in any event call her to give evidence during that trial. As a result, she might be more resentful towards Joseph as by that stage she would probably have spent some time in custody.

As he pondered over his options he almost did not notice the dapper uniformed police officer Inspector Brian McNally enter the witness box.

The Inspector was an imposing figure, about 55 years of age, 6 feet two inches in height, closely cut grey hair, with a slightly receding forehead, wearing a smartly pressed uniform that looked almost brand new. He took the oath using a cultured voice and bore all the hallmarks of a university graduate, fast-track entrant to the police force, rather than someone who had learnt policing by walking the beat in the local streets.

It was noticeable that Richard treated him differently to other witnesses. There was an air of respect in his questioning.

"Inspector, I understand that you were one of the first uniformed officers to arrive at the scene, is that correct?"

Brian nodded, "Yes, that's right. I was just coming off duty and on my way home when I received the emergency call and made my way to the rear of Sangster Street. I arrived at 10:45pm. There were already paramedics there dealing with the two victims and two other uniformed officers had arrived a couple of minutes before me and were speaking to a crowd of people who had gathered outside their properties."

"What function did you carry out?"

"I checked firstly on the two victims. The young lady was coming around and although she had some blood on her face, she did not seem seriously hurt. The man was clearly in a bad way. I realised quite quickly that he was seriously injured. He had lost consciousness and was sitting, propped up against his car, surrounded by a large pool of blood. Two paramedics were busily working on him, inserting drips and trying to stop the flow of blood from his right leg. They were giving him what looked like CPR. I decided there was nothing I could do to help them so I spoke to the two police officers who were there, who told me that a man with a knife had entered the rear of 84 Sangster Street. I had one of the officers, PC Blackwell come with me and we both went to that address."

"Did you see anything on your way to the address?"

"Yes, just outside the house, partially hidden in the bushes, I could see a large knife. I told PC Blackwell to stay with it but not to touch it until the SOCO, sorry, the Scenes of Crimes Officer, arrived and had taken photographs. I then made my way to the rear of 84 Sangster Street and knocked on the kitchen door. It took a few minutes, but it was eventually opened by a young man, who gave his name as Steven Denley. He said his parents owned the address. After some insistence, I was invited into the property. I passed through the kitchen to the living room where I saw a number of youths gathered on two couches and an armchair."

"Did you notice anything of importance in the kitchen?"

"Yes, in the sink, I saw a similar knife to the one I had seen outside the property. Again, I left it in place but I made a mental note to refer it to the SOCO when they arrived."

I believe you now produce those knives as exhibits in this case. BM1 and BM2?"

"That's right."

"BM1 is the knife found outside the house, BM2 is the knife found in the sink?"

"That's correct."

"Was there any reaction from the youths when you entered the living room?"

"Yes, they were quite noisy and I concluded from their demeanour, that a number had been drinking, or possibly, taking drugs."

"Did they assist you?"

"I wouldn't say that, I thought them all quite obstructive and in some cases, openly hostile. I explained the reason I was there. I told them I was investigating a very serious assault, but no one said anything."

"Did you notice any youth in particular?"

"Yes, I had been provided with the description of a youth who had been seen outside the property waving a knife around and threatening the male victim. I saw a youth who answered that description and I arrested him, his name was Adrian Simons."

"Did he say anything to you in the presence of the others?"

"No, I remember he said nothing and just smirked at me."

"What about the others present, did they say anything?"

"Yes, there was a girl there. I later discovered her name was Jamie Anderson. She seemed very upset and very distressed and kept saying that Mr Simons had not done anything and kept asking me why was I arresting him."

"We have heard that it is admitted that the defendant Joseph Rogers, the only black youth there, was present in the living room. Did he say anything?"

"I did note his presence but I cannot recall him saying anything."

"What happened next?"

"Two more officers arrived, PCs Talbot and Reagan. I had PC Talbot take Mr Simons away from the address and I told PC Reagan to search all the youths, their coats and the girl's handbag, to see if they had any weapons on them."

"Did anyone have a weapon or anything of interest to the police?"

"No, as we had arrested the main suspect, I had PC Reagan collect the names and addresses of the others and then asked them to leave, except of course Steven Denley who lived there."

"Why did you let them leave."

"There were a number of them and only three of us and as their attitude was hostile towards us, I thought it best to get them out of the house as soon as possible so we could search the property without any interference."

"Did you supervise the search?"

"Yes, more officers attended and then did a thorough search of the house, recording what they found in a search log."

"What happened to Jamie Anderson?"

"She left the house with the others."

"Did she say anything else in the presence of the others?"

"No, not that I recall."

CHAPTER 33

HELPFUL EVIDENCE?

It was obvious to David that the Inspector was an honest witness trying his best to assist the court. There was no point in attacking his evidence even though Joseph had told him the police officers who arrived at the scene had been rude and pushed him around. It was a non-issue as far as the relevant points of Joseph's case and so David chose to ignore it and see what he could achieve.

"Inspector, you have told us you were on your way home when you received this call?"

"That's right."

"Presumably you were off duty, why did you attend the scene?"

"I heard the call on my police radio and as it was clearly a serious incident and I was just a few hundred yards away I thought I would go and be the first on the scene."

"Obviously, you were likely to be the senior officer present?"

"Yes."

"And so, you would be in charge and have to take on all the duties of a senior officer present at the scene of a serious crime?"

"Yes."

"Can you tell us what those duties were!"

"Yes, certainly. I was informed that a girl had been attacked by a man and that someone had stabbed the man. I was also told that a youth had been seen near the man, waving a knife around and threatening to stab him. The youth was described to me ..." He turned to the judge, "... may I refer to my notes, my lord, they were taken back at the police station at the first opportunity I had?"

David answered before the judge, "I certainly have no objection."

The judge added, "Then of course you may refer to them."

"Thank you, my lord. The youth was described as follows; 'late teens, dark possibly black hair, wearing casual clothing, a dark top and dark blue jeans.'

It was my function to secure the scene, secure any evidence, such as witnesses, weapons or forensic evidence, stop any person leaving the scene who might be offender and stop any person coming to the scene who might contaminate it."

"Obviously, one of your main functions was to try and locate the male who had been described waving a knife around and threatening to use it?"

"Yes, of course."

"It's clear from what you say that you were only told of one person having a knife at the scene!"

"That's right."

"And the person you arrested, Adrian Simons, answered the description of the man who had the knife?"

"That's right."

"Further, no one else at the scene or in the house answered that description!"

"That's correct."

"And as far as you were concerned, you had arrested the person who was most likely to have carried out the stabbing?"

"I believed so."

"Can you assist on this issue? Mr Simons was searched at the scene, presumably to ensure he did not have any weapons on him?"

"That's right, sir."

"You have listed in your notes that no weapons were found on him and then you have listed items that were. Is it right that in his right trousers pocket were a pair of black gloves?"

Brian looked at his notes, "That's right, sir."

"I want to ask you now about the knives that were found? You found one knife outside the property that was later seized by the Scenes of Crime Officer. Why did you decide to seize the one in the sink?"

"I had been told that a youth had been seen waving a large knife around. I didn't know if the one outside the property was the correct one or the one in the sink."

"So, you were not looking for two knives?"

"No, sir."

"You have told us that the youths in the house did not assist you and some were openly hostile?"

"Yes, sir."

"Only one youth in the house was a black man, my client Joseph Rogers. I suggest he was not openly hostile or you would have noted it as he was the only black youth there?"

"I don't recall him saying anything, sir."

"Or doing anything that might be thought hostile?"

"No, sir."

"When you arrested Mr Simons, you told us that his girlfriend, Jamie Anderson, told you he had not done anything."

"That's right, but I didn't know she was his girlfriend at that time."

"No, of course not, Presumably, you had never met any of these people before."

"That's right, sir."

"No one else in the room claimed that Mr Simons was innocent of any wrongdoing?"

"No, sir, it was just the young lady who you have just told me is his girlfriend."

"Obviously, Adrian Simons was searched for potential weapons or other potentially incriminating evidence?"

"Yes sir."

"But part of your duties would have been to ensure that no one else was involved so you ordered that searches of the other youths should take place?"

"Yes, sir."

"In accordance with your duties, which I am sure you carried out perfectly, you would also have told the searching officer to check to see if anyone had anything incriminating upon them; such as a weapon, traces of the deceased's blood or tissue, or anything else on them that might have placed them in close proximity to the man who had been stabbed?"

Without hesitating Brian replied, That's right sir."

"I suspect it is standard in such circumstances for you to insist that such individuals are checked to see if they have any injuries that might have been caused by them wielding a knife?"

Brian looked slightly uncomfortable as he replied, "Yes, sir."

David knew there was no risk in asking these questions. The Inspector should have taken these precautions and if he had not he would have been deemed negligent, so whether he carried them out or not he was likely to say he had!

"It follows that if any traces of blood or other incriminating evidence or marks were seen on any of these individuals, they would have been detained and you would not have let them leave?"

Slightly more confidently, Brian replied, "That's right, sir."

"Joseph Rogers was searched by the officer and allowed to leave?

"Yes sir."

"It follows that he had nothing incriminating upon him; he had no traces of Mr Worthy's or his own blood or human tissue on his clothing or person, no weapons on him and no discernible injuries, otherwise you would not have let him leave?"

"That's right sir."

CHAPTER 34

THE OWNER

The next witness Richard called was Mrs Angela Denley, the owner of the house. She made quite an entrance into court and all eyes turned towards her as she entered through the main door. She was wearing a perfectly cut black suit with black tights, high-heeled shoes and sporting a brand new hairstyle that had cost her the best part of ninety pounds. She had never been to court before, although there had been a time when her eldest son, William, had been arrested by the police for shoplifting a chocolate bar. Fortunately, she had avoided the embarrassment of going to court when he had accepted a police caution at the police station.

This was wholly different, she knew this was a murder trial and she was an important witness and she had spent nearly a month's housekeeping money on getting ready for this hearing. After all she would have to relay every detail of her appearance tomorrow at her friend Daphne's house when a few friends would gather to listen to her ordeal.

"Mrs Denley, we understand that you and your husband are the owners of 84 Sangster Street in East Brighton?"

She looked around the public gallery to see if any of her friends were there to watch her. A couple had said they would come to give her moral support but she could see that neither had turned up, so she replied with a disappointed, "That's right."

"We understand also that you are the mother of Steven Denley who lives at that address with you?"

"Yes."

"You and your husband were away on the night we are dealing with. Were you on holiday?"

"Yes, Malcolm, my husband, had some leave owing to him so we decided to go away for two weeks and stay in our caravan in the Lake District. We left on the Friday morning to avoid the bank holiday traffic."

"Who did you leave in charge of your home?"

"Steven still lives with us, his brother, our eldest son, William, left to move in with girlfriend last year, so Steven was going to be on his own."

"What instructions did you leave him!"

She looked slightly annoyed, "To keep the place tidy and generally look after things until our return."

"Did you leave any instructions about parties?"

She gave an emphatic, "Yes!"

"What were they?"

"We told him he could have a couple of friends around but under no circumstances was he to have any parties. We'd had problems in the past with parties."

"What happened?"

"Well a couple of years ago he and his brother held a party when we went away on holiday. When we returned the day after the party, there were cigarette burns on the carpet and the couches, red wine stains on the carpet and floors, vomit in the kitchen sink and worse still the bathroom sink had been broken away from the wall!"

"So, unfortunately, he disobeyed you on this occasion?"

"He claimed he just had a few friends round but clearly it was a party and his father and I were very annoyed with him."

"Very well, when did you return on this occasion?"

"Steven phoned us the following day and told us what had happened. We had to cancel our holiday and come straight back. His father was not best pleased, I can tell you."

Richard ignored the last comment.

"I'm going to ask you to look at two exhibits which the police seized. The first is a knife that the police found outside your house in some bushes. It has a seven inch blade. The second is a knife that was found in your kitchen sink, it has a six inch blade."

He waited whilst the usher showed the witness the knives which had both been separately tied in place in brown boxes and covered in a see-through plastic police exhibit bag.

"I won't ask you to open the exhibits as they have both been treated with chemicals in order to forensically examine them and sadly those chemicals can cause cancer if they come into contact with the human skin. Doing your best and looking through the transparent plastic, do you recognise those knives?"

She took the exhibits and looked at them closely.

"Yes, they look like the ones that were missing from my kitchen after the party. They were a wedding anniversary gift from my parents and were part of an expensive set. I've only got four left now."

She shook her head as she added, "It's so annoying."

Richard looked at her coldly, he sat down without thanking her. To his mind she did not deserve it. A man had lost his life and all she seemed to be concerned about was her cheap looking knife set!

David had a similar opinion and had very few questions for her. There seemed no point in asking her anything about the knives so he chose a different line.

"Mrs Denley, were you present when the police took your son's first witness statement?"

"No, we hadn't got back from the Lakes when he first made a statement."

"Were you present when he made his second statement?"

"I was in the house but the police took him into another room."

"Did you hear what was said?"

She looked sheepish.

"Well the walls are very thin so I heard some of the conversation."

"Can you tell us what you heard?"

"Yes, I heard the police telling Steven they thought he hadn't told the truth in his first statement. They said they believed he had seen what happened and that a boy called Joseph had stabbed the man."

"Did they say anything else, "I heard them threaten to charge him with perjury but I didn't hear anymore because a police officer came out of the room, stared at me and I decided to leave and went into the kitchen."

CHAPTER 35

THE ARREST

The next witness to be called by the prosecution was Police Constable Robert Freese. He entered the court room and went straight to the witness box. He took the oath and immediately gave his name before being asked any question.

Richard smiled at him and asked, "Officer, is it right that on 27th August 2017 at approximately 7:52pm you went to University lodgings in Fratton Street in Brighton and arrested the defendant in this case, Joseph Rogers?"

The officer turned to the judge, "May I refer to my notebook, my lord?"

To save time, David rose and said, "I have no objection, my Lord."

The judge nodded, "Then officer you may refer to your notes, to refresh your memory."

The officer took his notebook from his inside pocket, thumbed through the pages and then stated, "That's right sir. I arrived at the property in the company of DC Christopher Mather at approximately 7:50pm. We knocked on the door and it was opened by Mr Rogers. We asked who he was and he identified himself and at 7:52pm I arrested him on suspicion of murder."

"Can you describe the defendant's accommodation to us?"

"Yes sir, it was a rectangular room measuring about four by two metres with an ensuite shower room and toilet."

"Was there anyone else present when you arrived?"

"No sir, Mr Rogers was on his own."

"Having arrested him did you search his room?"

"Yes sir, we were searching for any possible weapons or anything that might link him to the murder."

"Did you find anything?"

"Yes sir, in the corner there was a pile of clothing. It contained a pair of jeans, a T shirt, a jumper, boxer shorts and socks."

"What state was the clothing in?"

The officer looked confused, "Sorry sir?"

"Can you assist as to whether it was discarded dirty clothing or clean clothing?"

"It looked clean sir. I asked Mr Rogers to give us the clothing he had worn on the Friday night. He said that he had washed it and dried it on Saturday morning and pointed out the pile in the corner."

"Did you seize that clothing?"

"Yes sir."

"Did you seize anything else?"

"He was wearing some trainers. He confirmed that he had been wearing them on Friday night as well. I asked him to take them off and I bagged them and he put on a pair of shoes that he had in a wardrobe."

"Was anything else seized?"

"We did seize a few other items but on looking at them at the police station, nothing else looked relevant."

"Was this the first time you visited this property officer?"

"No sir, we were both tasked to go to the address and arrest Mr Rogers on the Saturday afternoon. We went there at approximately 3pm and knocked on the door but no one answered. We contacted a caretaker who was responsible for all the student accommodation. We ascertained that Mr Rogers had not been seen since about lunch time on the Saturday. We left our details and asked the caretaker to contact us if Mr Rogers was seen again."

"Do you know if he did so?"

"He did sir, I received a call from him at about 7:30pm saying that Mr Rogers had been seen to enter the building. I then contacted DC Mather and we went straight to the address to arrest Mr Rogers."

"Did you know if he had been seen at the building earlier that day on the Sunday?"

"The caretaker told us that the first time he had seen him that day was just after 7pm on the Sunday."

Richard nodded and asked the officer to remain where he was as there may be some more questions.

David took the officer's witness statement and asked if a copy could be supplied to the officer.

"Officer, you made a note about the arrest and the search in your notebook which you have now relied upon in court."

"Yes sir."

"It appears from your notes that Mr Rogers was cooperative when you arrested him?"

The officer looked confused as he looked at his notes, "I'm not sure what you mean sir."

"Your notes show that; he did not struggle when arrested, he answered your questions, he pointed out the clothes he was wearing on the night of the incident, he pointed out the shoes he was wearing on the night. This all shows that he was cooperative."

The officer nodded, "Yes sir."

"You have told us that you listed all the items of clothing that you found and seized from Mr Rogers?"

"Yes, sir."

"You never found or seized any gloves, is that right?"

The officer looked through his notes, "That's right, sir."

"Just one other matter officer. It does not appear in your notes but is it right he told you that he had washed his clothes and that he always did his weeks washing on Saturdays?"

The officer looked in his notebook, "I don't have a note of that sir, but I think he said something like that."

CHAPTER 36

THE PATHOLOGIST

Dr Mark Lumley, the prosecution's pathologist entered the court room with an air of boredom mixed with annoyance. He had paperwork mounting at his office, with various urgent reports that had to be completed. As far as he saw it, giving evidence in this case was a waste of time. The cause of death was obvious and the prosecution should be able to read out his report as an agreed document. He glanced across at David with a slight scowl. Why did defence barristers insist on him giving evidence, as if his evidence could help the defence case?

Richard rose from his seat to ask the preliminary questions. Unbeknown to Dr Lumley, it was Richard who had insisted on calling him. Like a lot of prosecutors, he always thought calling a pathologist added something to a prosecution case. The gory and sometimes bizarrely fascinating details of someone's death reminded a jury what they were dealing with.

Richard took him through his qualifications quickly. Dr Lumley was well known to the lawyers from his fifteen years practising as a pathologist and no one was going to challenge his expertise.

"Dr Lumley, I understand that you conducted a post-mortem examination on the body of Gerry

Worthy on 28th August 2017, at approximately 2:30pm?"

"That's correct."

"You subsequently wrote a report that dealt with your findings and that report has been served on all the parties in this case."

"So, I understand."

"Can you assist, was that report based upon notes you made at the time of the post-mortem?"

"Yes, I dictated my notes as I conducted the post-mortem into a fixed microphone which is situated above the body. Subsequently I used those dictated notes and photographs that my assistant took, in order to produce the report."

"I don't wish to take you through all of your report as not everything is relevant here. Please just deal with your basic findings and the cause of death?"

"Of course. It might assist if I referred to the photographs that were taken at the time and a computer generated body map that was produced based upon other photographs that were taken."

Richard took the jury and Dr Lumley to the relevant part of the jury bundle and Dr Lumley continued.

"Yes, thank you. I was informed that he had been stabbed around 10:20pm on 25th August 2017, that he staggered to his car a few metres away and that he collapsed there. Paramedics arrived at the scene a short time later but he had lost a great deal of blood by then. The paramedics tried to stem the bleeding and replace fluids and apply Cardiopulmonary resuscitation, CPR. He was then taken to the hospital where further attempts were made to resuscitate him. He was operated upon by surgeons who found the femoral artery and vein.

That is a difficult operation, particularly as the veins and arteries are stretched like elastic bands in the body, so when one is severed as the vein was here, it tends to retract towards the groin area. Having located them the surgeons repaired them and tried to replace the blood loss. Mr Worthy was still bleeding out throughout the operation and the surgeons had to constantly replace his blood. They used thirteen litres of blood during the procedure. The body only holds an average of just under six litres. Unfortunately, they were not successful and he was pronounced dead at 2:12am on 26th August 2017.

My findings were as follows:

The body was of a well-nourished, twenty-seven year old man, 1.93 metres tall, in other words, six feet four inches tall, muscular build, weighing one hundred and fifteen kilos, or approximately, eighteen stone.

I could find no evidence of disease or anything other than the stab injury, that might have caused or contributed to his death. Looking at the first photograph in this section of the jury bundle you can see an injury to the index finger of his right hand. This is a deep injury and the tip of the finger is almost completely sliced through. This is a typical defensive injury, probably caused as he tried to grab the knife as it was exiting, or possibly, re-entering the leg. This injury would have bled profusely.

The second photograph shows the injury to the back of the thigh. This was a deeply penetrating injury which sliced entirely through the femoral artery and slightly through the femoral vein.

I dissected the leg to follow the path of the wound. The photographs of this dissection do not appear in the jury bundle, as they may be thought distressing, but the path does appear on the body drawing."

Everyone in court turned to the body drawing.

"As you can see there were in fact two tracts detected in the leg."

Richard quickly interrupted, "How could that occur?"

"The blade has moved within the wound. It has partly come out then gone back in again."

"Could this demonstrate that the knife was partially but not fully withdrawn and then thrust again into the leg?"

"Yes, that is a possible scenario."

Richard paused for this piece of information to sink in with the jury. He then continued.

"Dr Lumley, how deep were the tracks in the leg?"

"The longest was approximately 200 mm, about 8 inches. It almost exited the leg the other side. The second track veered off at around 120mm and went on for a further 30mm ending in the muscle."

"What type of force would have to be used to cause these types of injury."

"The knife would have to cut through the skin first, then the subcutaneous fat, then the muscle. It is often thought, wrongly that there is no resistance after the knife penetrates the skin. That is wrong as anyone who has carved a Sunday joint can attest to..."

Dr Lumley did not notice the older female juror in the front row turning a ghastly white at this comment and he continued oblivious of her distress,

"... the skin does offer the most resistance but the muscle offers some. I would say that a moderate force would have to be used and the knife would have to have been held firmly throughout."

"Is that both on the way in and on the way out."

"Most definitely. There would have been a firm grip both on the way in and on the way out."

"Can you tell which injury was caused first, the longer or the shorter track?"

"It's impossible to say which in fact deviated from the other and therefore which was caused first."

"I want you to look at a plan of the area which is in our jury bundle at tab 5."

Richard waited as everyone turned up the plan.

"You will see that marked on the plan is a trail of blood ending at the car where the position of the body has been drawn, situated in a large pool of blood."

"Yes, I see that."

"The start of the blood trail presumably shows where the injury was caused?"

"Yes, very probably."

"We can also see marked on the plan, is the position of a knife that was found outside number 84 Sangster Street."

"Yes, I see that."

"And if we turn over the page we see a plan of 84 Sangster Street, showing the inside of the property. We can see on that diagram that the position of a second knife is shown that was found in the sink."

"Yes, I see that as well."

"I am now going to show you those two exhibits that I believe you have seen before, exhibits BM1 and BM2. The first was found outside the property in the bushes and has a seven inch blade, the second was found in the sink, in the kitchen of 84 Sangster Street and has a six inch blade. Does the size of the blade help you to determine which one of these knives, if either, caused the fatal wound to Mr Worthy?"

"No, skin and muscle tissue are very elastic and compress upon receiving a force. The longest track here is about 200 millimetres, about eight inches, but either knife could have caused it. The really strong evidence as to which knife caused it, is the fact that the seven-inch bladed knife contained Mr Worthy's DNA undoubtedly from his blood and tissue. In my opinion that was the knife that was used to kill him."

"Does it make any difference to your opinion if the smaller knife may have been washed?"

"No, it seems from the evidence that there was only one major wound caused by one knife."

Richard smiled at him and continued, "Thank you Dr Lumley, I now would like to move onto another topic. You have told us that Mr Worthy had an injury to his finger consistent with a defensive wound when he might have tried to grab the knife. Did he have any other injuries to his hands?"

"Yes, he had the start of some bruises on the knuckles of his right hand and some minor lacerations to those knuckles. This was consistent with having punched someone that night before he received the fatal injury."

"Did he have any other injuries?"

"Yes, he had some bruising to his chest and some petechial haemorrhages, little spots on the skin around the eyes."

"Is there any significance to those injuries."

"In my opinion, no. Petechial haemorrhages are frequently seen if someone has been strangled but they are often seen in many other instances as well. For example, they appear in sportsmen and women who have been injured, or they appear because of vigorous CPR being applied. Here the paramedics did apply CPR and as there are bruises on the chest consistent with a vigorous CPR, I assume the petechial haemorrhages were caused by the actions of the paramedics."

"Thank you, now, can you assist as what would have happened immediately after Mr Worthy received this injury to the leg!"

"Yes, the injury to his right index finger suggests he grabbed at the knife when he felt it enter his leg. He would have suffered pain from both injuries and then a few seconds later, he would have suffered shock from the blood loss. A short while after that he would have collapsed and then a short while later he would have passed out."

"Finally, Dr Lumley, can you tell the jury what the cause of death was in this case?"

"I have recorded it as:

1a. Haemorrhage.

1b. Stab wound to the right leg.

In other words, the stab wound to the right leg caused severe haemorrhaging and he bled to death."

CHAPTER 37

POSSIBILITIES

David had not really wanted to cross examine the pathologist. He would have preferred it if the evidence had been read to the jury for the same reason that Richard had wanted to call the evidence live. The jury were bound to be influenced by discussions of blood, tissue and death. Still, now that he had been called there were a few matters that David could deal with. He rose from his seat and smiled at the pathologist. He was surprised that he was met with a scowl.

"Dr Lumley, I wish to say at the outset that your findings are not disputed by the defence. Clearly Mr Worthy died from a stab injury that severed the femoral artery, cut into the femoral vein and sadly he bled to death. There are just a few matters that I want your assistance with."

David was surprised to see Dr Lumley's scowl broaden. He began to wish that he did have challenges to his evidence.

"The first matter I trust you can assist me with relates to the timing of the injuries. Am I right in thinking that from simply looking at the body, it is impossible to give a time as to when the injuries occurred or indeed the sequence of those injuries?"

"Not quite! It is right to say that I cannot give a precise time for when each injury occurred, but the injury to knuckles of the right hand showed some evidence of the beginning of a bruise which suggested it was the first in time. The laceration to the right index finger was a classic defensive injury which suggested it occurred after the knife injury to the right leg and as a result of feeling the pain from that injury."

"Let's put aside the injury to the knuckles. It is common ground that Mr Worthy knocked out a young girl at the start of this incident and that injury was undoubtedly caused then. Let me ask you to concentrate on the other two injuries. The injury to the right index finger and the injury to the leg. They could have been caused as you suggest but there are other possible scenarios?"

Dr Lumley looked at him smugly, "If you suggest one, I will deal with it."

David was beginning to dislike the good doctor.

"Certainly. We have heard that night that a young man called Adrian Simons, was dancing around waving a knife and threatening to stab Mr Worthy."

"Yes, I was given those instructions."

"It follows then that the injury to the finger could have been caused then, before the injury to the leg?"

"That is true, although no blood and tissue were found on the second knife!"

It was David's turn to scowl slightly.

"Dr Lumley is it fair to say that you cannot tell the size of the blade of the knife that cause this injury."

"That's right, it's a slicing injury, caused by the blade moving across the finger or the finger moving across the blade or a combination of both. I cannot say which and it follows that the blade could have been of any size. The only matter one can say for certain is that it was sharp."

"It's right isn't it that there was only one injury to the index finger?"

"Yes."

"That would presumably have bled quickly?"

"Yes."

"Although it is quite feasible that no blood would have got onto the blade of the knife if the injury was inflicted quickly?"

"That is correct."

"Also, if blood had got onto the knife it could have been washed off in the sink?"

"That is true."

"Or, another possibility is that it was Mr Simons who was wielding the knife that was later found in the bushes and which contained Mr Worthy's blood and tissue on it?"

"I suppose so, as I understand it there were no fingerprints found on either knife."

"In relation to my suggestion that the injury to the index finger might have occurred earlier, the plan of the area that you have been referred to at tab 5 of the jury bundle, shows evidence that blood spots were found in different areas that night and there was not just the trail and the pooling that you have been referred to?"

"Yes, I can see that on the plan."

"In relation to the leg injury, that clearly would have bled extensively?"

"Yes, as you can see from the extensive blood trail and pooling at the place where Mr Worthy finally collapsed."

"You have referred to the injury having two tracks. That could be caused by the knife being thrust into the leg, partially withdrawn and then thrust again into the leg."

"Yes, as I've said that is a possible scenario."

"However, there is another possible scenario. These incidents are dynamic. The leg was not presumably stationary like a joint of meat in your earlier example..."

Neither David nor Dr Lumley noticed the mature lady on the front row now turn a slightly greenish colour.

"...it is quite possible that this was one thrust of the knife and the two tracks were caused by a combination of thrusting the knife once and withdrawing it and Mr Worthy carrying on walking?"

Dr Lumley thought for a few moments, "Yes, that is quite possible."

"Indeed, in a case like this is it fair to say that a victim may not realise they have been stabbed straight away, it is quite possible that a few seconds may have passed from the time Mr Worthy was stabbed and the time he realised he had been stabbed and said, "You fucking cheeky little bastard?"

"Yes, that's quite possible. There might have been a delayed reaction. He might have thought he had received a blow at first, like a punch and it might have taken a few seconds before he realised he had been stabbed."

"The injury to the right index finger would presumably have bled immediately?"

"Yes."

"However, the injury to Mr Worthy's leg may have taken a few seconds before the blood started to leave a trail on the pavement?"

Dr Lumley paused as he considered the question before answering, "The cut would have bled almost immediately but the blood may have first soaked into the trousers so that it would not have reached the pavement immediately. I seem to recall one of the witnesses described in his statement that he saw Mr Worthy's light coloured trousers change in shade as the blood presumably was absorbed by the cloth."

"Does it follow then that the place where the blood trail starts on the plan is not necessarily the place where the injury was caused?"

"Yes, it is likely to have been a few paces back from that location.

"Finally this, putting this evidence together, is it a possibility that Mr Worthy was stabbed in the leg by an assailant whilst Mr Rogers had his arm round Mr Worthy's shoulders. That assailant immediately backed away. Mr Worthy did not realise he had been stabbed for a few seconds and then pushed Mr Rogers away saying to him, 'You fucking cheeky little bastard'?"

Dr Lumley thought for a few seconds again, involuntary stroking his chin before answering.

"Yes, that is perfectly possible."

CHAPTER 38

THE FORENSIC SCIENTIST

As the next witness, a forensic scientist called Heather Taylor, was not available until 2pm the court broke for an early lunch at 12:40pm. David took Gavin across the road to the local hotel for a slightly lengthier lunch time than normal, though it still only consisted on a beef and salad sandwich for David washed down with an orange juice, and a chicken salad and a pint of local brew for Gavin. The days of the long lunches for criminal barristers were long gone.

David had a little more preparation before Heather gave evidence and he welcomed the longer lunch hour for that purpose.

At 2:05pm Heather Taylor entered the court room and went straight to the witness box where she swore an oath to tell the truth, she gave her name, her occupation as a forensic scientist and then began to list an impressive range of professional qualifications culminating in the fact that she had spent the last twelve years preparing reports and giving evidence on blood, fibre and DNA cases.

Richard beamed at the jury as she gave this evidence but was met with the stony faces he frequently faced when he conducted cases at Lewes Crown Court. Momentarily he looked at the water jug in front of him and wondered whether the contents might be affecting the local populace.

Quickly dismissing the idea, he turned to the witness to ask, "Ms Taylor, I understand that you examined clothing in this case that was recovered from; the deceased, the defendant and from a man called Adrian Simons. I also understand that you examined the two knives that were recovered. Firstly, can you tell the jury what the purpose of your examination was?"

"Yes, certainly. There were three main points to my examination. The first was to examine the two knives that were discovered at the scene to see if one had caused the injury to Mr Worthy. The second was to examine the knives and clothing to see if there were any traces of blood, tissue or clothing upon any of them. The third was to examine Mr Worthy's clothing and shoes as well as the clothing and shoes of the others to see if any fibres had transferred between them. Having conducted those examinations, I was then instructed to prepare a summary of my findings to the police."

"Let me ask you first about the two knives, exhibits BM1 and BM2. We have heard that BM1 was found outside the property in the bushes and has a seven inch blade, BM2 was found in the sink, in the kitchen of 84 Sangster Street and has a six inch blade. What were your findings in relation to these two knives?"

"I examined both knives using low power microscopy. I examined the blades, the handles, the tangs running through the handles and the rivets connecting the blade to the handles."

"The tang?"

"Yes, that's a projecting shank, prong, fang, or tongue on the blade that connects with the handle."

"Thank you. What did you find as a result of your examination?"

"BM2, the knife found in the sink had no traces of blood, tissue or DNA on it. There were also no discernible prints on the handle or the blade. The knife had been submerged in water that may have washed off some traces of blood, tissue and DNA but unless it was thoroughly cleaned I would have expected some traces to be found if it had been used to stab Mr Worthy."

"What about BM1?"

"I understand that knife was found in the bushes outside 84 Sangster Street. Again, I could not find any discernible prints on the handle or the blade but I did find traces of blood, tissue and DNA on the blade towards the hilt. There was also some minor blood staining on the handle.

I had my assistants test the blood from one side of the blade and subject the results to DNA profiling. A DNA profile which matches that of Gerry Worthy was found. Therefore, in my opinion the blood found on the blade could have originated from Mr Worthy. The probability of obtaining this matching DNA profile, if the blood tested has not originated from Mr Worthy, but from someone other than and unrelated to him, is estimated to be in the order of one in a billion, that is one in one thousand million."

"Please now help us with the clothing that you examined. Firstly, the clothes recovered from Mr Rogers?"

"Yes, I understand that these were recovered a few days after the incident and had been washed. I found a slight trace of blood on the right-hand side trouser pocket. This was a small amount and when analysed a DNA profile matching Mr Rogers was found and therefore could have come from him. Again, the probability of obtaining this matching DNA profile, if the blood tested has not originated from Mr Rogers, but from someone other than and unrelated to him, is estimated to be in the order of one in a billion."

"Did you examine the deceased's clothing?"

"I did and I found blood matching his DNA profile on his trousers and on his shirt."

"To save time can you tell us if you found any blood or other DNA on him that might have come from anyone else?"

"No, I did not."

"Did you find any blood or other DNA on Mr Simons' clothing?"

"I found some DNA that could have originated from him but not from Mr Rogers or Mr Worthy. There was some blood spotting on the right cuff of his shirt sleeve but it proved impossible to obtain a DNA profile from it."

"Let us move on to fibres, did you find any fibres on any of the clothing examined that might have come from fibres from someone else's clothing?"

"Yes, I did. I found fibres from Mr Rogers' shirts which matched fibres found on Mr Worthy's shirt in the right shoulder area."

"I also found fibres from Mr Worthy's shirt which matched with fibres found on Mr Roger's shirt in the right sleeve area of that shirt."

"Can you help us as to any conclusions you reached from these findings?"

"Yes, in my opinion, given that Gerry Worthy was stabbed just once in his left thigh, I have a low expectation that any blood would have transferred from his injury to the clothing or footwear of his assailant. This is because the knife would have been withdrawn and his assailant would have moved away from him before he began to bleed freely. If there had been no interaction between the parties once Mr Worthy was bleeding freely, it is likely that the only opportunity for transfer would have been via the blade of the knife used, assuming that sufficient blood transferred to and remained on it.

Some blood and tissue was transferred from the wound to the knife, but very little blood and tissue was found on the knife BM1. In my opinion this is probably because the skin, muscle and clothing probably wiped some blood and possible tissue from the knife blade when it was withdrawn. Therefore, I have a similar low expectation that any blood or tissue would be transferred from the knife to the assailant."

"It may be obvious to the jury, but can you assist as to what you mean by the term 'low expectation'?"

"Yes, it's a scale of testing I use, it starts at; very low expectation, then low expectation, high expectation and then very high expectation."

"So, not at the bottom of your list which is, 'very low expectation', but nearly there?"

"Yes."

"What is your conclusion in relation to the knives BM1 and BM2?"

"There is no evidence that BM2 was used to cause any injury to Mr Worthy, but there is very strong evidence to suggest that the knife BM1 was used to cause the wound."

"In relation to the fibres?"

"There is very strong evidence to suggest that Mr Worthy's clothing came into contact with clothing worn by Mr Rogers and vice versa."

Richard gave her a big beaming smile that was met with a relatively shy smile, "Thank you very much Ms Taylor."

CHAPTER 39

UNRAVELLING THE FORENSICS

Richard had managed to steer the witness to the important evidence that effectively BM1 was the knife that had been used to kill Gerry Worthy and that sometime before that death, Joseph Rogers and Gerry Worthy had come into contact with each other. David now had to try to convince the jury that none of this made any difference to the case against his client.

"Ms Taylor, I am going to ask you about three topics; the knives, the blood and DNA analysis and the fibres that you examined in this case."

She nodded as she mentally listed the items.

"Firstly, the knives. As you told us you examined two knives. BM2, the knife found in the sink can probably be discounted as no traces of DNA, blood or tissue were found on that knife?"

"Yes, in forensic science it is almost impossible to discount anything because of the number of possibilities, but it does appear here that only one knife was used to cause the fatal injury and as blood, human tissue and DNA matching Gerry Worthy was found on that knife, I would agree with your proposition."

"Now we have heard that no fingerprints or DNA were found on that knife that matched anyone other than Gerry Worthy?"

Ms Taylor briefly looked at her notes, "That's right, yes."

"So, either the person wielding the knife handle was wiped before it was discarded, or the person wielding the knife was wearing gloves?"

"Those are the likely conclusions, though it is possible for a person to use a knife without transferring sufficient DNA or prints to be useful for analysis."

"Did you find any unusable trace of DNA on this knife?"

"No."

"Did you find any unidentifiable prints on this knife?"

"No."

"So, my two suggestions are the most likely ones?"

"Yes."

"Is it possible to distinguish between the two?"

"No."

"I want to move on to the subject of the blood and DNA analysis. Were you aware that at the time of his arrest, Adrian Simons was found to be in possession of gloves?"

"I was."

"Were those gloves ever tested for Mr Worthy's DNA, blood or tissue?"

"No."

"Why was that?"

"They were never submitted to the laboratory for testing. I did make enquiries of the police when I discovered he had gloves on his person, but I was told that they had been misplaced."

"Misplaced in a murder enquiry?"

"Yes."

"Those gloves could have proved highly important to this enquiry, couldn't they?"

"Potentially, yes."

"If Mr Simons had been wearing glove and had been the person who stabbed Mr Worthy, Mr Worthy's blood might have transferred to those gloves?"

"That is possible, yes."

"But we shall never know because the police have 'misplaced' the gloves?"

"Yes."

"Let me ask you about the handle of the knife. You have told us that there were minor traces of blood on the handle. Did you subject that blood for DNA analysis?"

"I did, but again it was a very small amount and I did not obtain a full profile. If, it came from someone other than Mr Worthy, it was undoubtedly contaminated with his blood because of its location near the hilt of the knife."

"Could blood have transferred from the knife to the sleeve cuff of the assailant?"

"It could."

"You found minor traces of blood on the sleeve cuff of Mr Simons?"

"I did, but as I said I could not obtain a DNA profile so I could not say whose blood it was nor how or indeed, when it got there."

"It does not appear that Mr Worthy or Mr Simons had ever met before, so if it was Mr Worthy's blood, it must have got there that night he was injured?"

"If it was Mr Worthy's blood, but I cannot say whose blood it was."

"No doubt in your experience, often in a stabbing case, the assailant injures himself when he carries out a frenzied attack, either when he thrusts the knife into someone's body or as he withdraws it?"

"Often, but not always."

"Do you know if Mr Simons injured his hand that night?"

"I don't have any information about that."

"If the blood on his cuff came from that night and was his own, it could have been as a result of his having a minor injury as he used the knife to stab Mr Worthy,"

"It could, but such a conclusion would be pure speculation on my part because of the number of assumptions there, not based upon the actual evidence. As I have already said, I don't know whose blood it is, nor how or when it got there."

"Very well. Are you aware that Mr Rogers was searched at the scene by police officers?"

"I am aware that a search was carried out some time later when he has returned to the house."

"Are you aware that no traces of blood or injuries were found on him."

"I believe a cursory search was carried out and nothing was found."

"Who told you it was a 'cursory' search?"

"I believe that came from the police report which came with the exhibits to the laboratory.

I ought to add the flow of blood from the major wound may not have been apparent at first and may not have started to reach the pavement until he had walked a few paces. Equally although there was clearly blood and tissue on BM1, it was in tiny amounts. Some blood and tissue may have been wiped from the blade by the skin and tissue as it was withdrawn from the wound which is why there was so little found on the blade. As it was effectively just one wound which did not immediately spurt blood I would not expect any to have been transferred to the assailant such as you would get if there had been a number of injuries caused by the assailant with a knife."

"Nevertheless, some blood was found on the handle of the knife and that blood could have transferred to the sleeve cuff of the assailant?"

"As I have already said, that is a possibility but it is speculation in this case."

"Ms Taylor, the final topic I want to ask you about is about the fibres. You have told us that fibres from the clothes that Mr Worthy was wearing, in the right shoulder area were transferred to Mr Joseph's shirt in the right cuff area and vice versa?"

"Yes."

"This demonstrates that their clothing was likely to have come into contact with each other?"

"Yes."

"You are aware that the evidence suggests that Mr Joseph put his right arm around Mr Worthy's right shoulder as he ushered him away?"

"I am."

"And I suggest that is the most likely way in which fibres were transferred between their clothing?"

"I would agree."

"In a case like this where there was only one stab wound to the leg and what looked like a defence wound to Mr Worthy's right index finger, an assailant could easily have caused these injuries without transferring any fibres from his clothing to Mr Worthy, or picking up any fibres from Mr Worthy's clothing?"

"Again, I agree."

"Thank you. Now I want to see if you agree with this proposition. Am I right in thinking that your analysis does not assist you in any way to say who wielded the knife that night which caused the fatal wound."

She thought for a few seconds before answering, "I have to agree. In my opinion the work we have carried out does not enable me to answer the question who wielded the knife at the time Mr Worthy sustained his injuries."

"So, it could have been Mr Simons?"

"It could be if he was wielding BM1 at the time Mr Worthy's blood, tissue and DNA was transferred to the blade. Equally, it could have been anyone else who was wielding the knife at that time."

CHAPTER 40

THE GIRLFRIEND

Thursday morning and Richard announced to the judge that Jamie Anderson, the girlfriend of Adrian Simons, had finally been located and was going to give evidence to the court.

Once the jury had taken their seats in court, Richard announced to them that he was calling Jamie Anderson. The older white haired lady sitting in the front row of the jury gave him a beaming smile when he said this, something that caused David a slight degree of concern.

It took a full five minutes before Jamie Anderson entered the court room. She had red eyes and was dabbing at them with a handkerchief. A witness support lady guided her towards the witness box and then stood behind her as she took the oath and gave her name.

Richard looked at her over the top of his reading glasses with what looked like barely concealed contempt, but what, was in his own eyes, his most benign look.

"Ms Anderson, I am going to ask you some questions about an incident that occurred on the night of 25th August of last year. Can you recall where you were that evening?"

It was meant to be a disarming question but was met with a series of sobs from the witness.

He tried again, "Ms Anderson, I am sure we all appreciate that giving evidence can be an ordeal for any witness, but if you could answer my questions, the ordeal will soon be over."

This was met with even greater sobs.

The learned Judge had been on a recent course dealing with distressed witnesses and decided that he should take over.

"Ms Anderson, please sit down, there is a chair in the witness box."

Jamie looked behind her and took her seat.

The judge smiled at her, "Good, now the usher will give you a plastic cup of water, please take a sip and compose yourself. This is not meant to be an ordeal and I will not let anyone distress you. These gentlemen ..."

He pointed to Richard and David.

"... have a number of questions to ask you about the evening of 25ᵗʰ August. We can break now for a little time if you wish and you can come back to give evidence, or we can continue with the questioning now. It's a matter for you."

Jamie looked at him and through a few sobs said, "I'd rather get it over with please."

The judge nodded, "Of course, I think we all understand that."

He turned to Richard, "I suggest that you start asking your questions, but please keep an eye on the witness and if she shows any distress please wait."

Richard nodded at the judge barely hiding the fact that he thought the comment patronising. He had been asking questions of witnesses for over thirty five years, he did not need a civil judge to tell him how to do it. Ignoring the implied rebuke, he turned to the witness.

"Ms Anderson, can you recall where you were on the evening of 25th August last year?"

Jamie wiped her eyes again before answering, "I went to a party with my boyfriend Adrian."

"Can you tell us where that party was held?"

"It was at Steven Denley's home."

"We have heard that he lived at 84 Sangster Street, Brighton, is that right?"

"Yeah."

"Do you recall what time you arrived at the party?"

"I think it was after 8pm, I don't remember the exact time."

"Who was there when you arrived?"

"Steven Denley was there and his friend, Scott Robson."

"Was anyone else there at the time?"

"No, I don't think so."

"Did anyone arrive just after you?"

"Yes, Joseph Rogers and his girlfriend Caroline Jennings arrived just after us."

"Did they both stay throughout the night?"

"No, Caroline left after about half an hour to an hour."

"So sometime around 9pm?"

"I wasn't looking at the time, I suppose so."

"Do you know why she left?"

Jamie smiled, "I think it was because Jo kept looking at me..." She added with a grin, "... he's always fancied me."

"By Jo, you mean Joseph Rogers?"

"Yeah."

"What was Joseph Roger's attitude like when she left?"

"He seemed annoyed, I think they had an argument about him looking at me."

"Did you hear either of them say that?"

"I heard Jo saying something about it."

"Did he calm down at all?"

"No, he really seemed annoyed about it."

"We have heard that others came to the party around 10pm called Brian Williams and Shirley West. Did you see them arrive?"

"I remember others coming to the party, yeah."

"Did you know Brian Williams or Shirley West?"

She grimaced a little, "I didn't know the man but I knew Shirley."

"How did you know Shirley?"

"She was Adrian's girlfriend before me."

"Were you friends?"

"No!"

"We have also heard that there came a time when there was a commotion outside the house. Do you recall that?"

"Yeah."

"In your own words, what happened?"

"I remember that the music was quite loud in the house but we could still hear a lot of shouting and swearing coming from outside."

"Could you hear what was said?"

"No, I could make out a few words but not many, I just know someone was outside shouting and swearing."

"What did people do?"

"People wanted to find out what was happening so we all went outside."

"Did Adrian go outside as well?"

"Yes, he did."

"Did he have anything with him?"

She looked coldly at Richard, "What do you mean?"

"Did he take anything outside with him?"

"What you mean the 'shank'?"

Richard paused, "What do you mean by 'shank'?"

"A knife."

"Yes."

"Yeah, he took a knife with him."

"Where did he get it from?"

"In the kitchen. We had to go through the kitchen to get outside."

"What did you think when he picked up a knife?"

"I thought he was being an idiot."

"What did you do?"

"I followed him and told him to get rid of it"

"Did he?"

"Not at first."

"What was happening outside?"

"There was big tall bloke outside. He looked drunk and he was swearing."

"Could you hear what he was saying?"

"Yeah, can I say?"

"Please do."

"He was saying words like, 'fucking bastards.'"

"What happened next?"

"Shirley and that man who came with her went up to the bloke. He shoved the man out of the way then he floored Shirley."

"How did he 'floor' Shirley?"

"He punched her in the face. It was right out of order."

"How did people react to this?"

"People got angry. Quite a few people like Shirley a lot and they didn't want to see her get hurt".

She grimaced, making it clear she was not one of them.

"What did Adrian do?"

"He acted like a right idiot!"

"In what way?"

"He started moving around like he was a boxer threatening to stab the man."

"How did the man react?"

"He just squared up to Adrian and Adrian backed off."

"Did Adrian ever stab at the man?"

"No."

"Did he get close to the man?"

"No, he was a long way away from him."

"How far away?"

"At least a couple of metres away all the time."

Richard nodded as he asked, "Did you see Joseph Rogers outside?"

"Yeah."

"Where was he?"

"He was near the man all the time."

"Did you see what he did?"

"I saw him put his arm round the man."

"What did you do?"

"I grabbed Adrian and took him back inside the house."

"What happened to the knife he had?"

"I saw him go into the house and throw it into sink."

"What state was the knife in?"

"What?"

"Was there any blood on it?"

"No, he never got near the man."

Richard looked at the jury, hoping the witness' evidence was being followed. Satisfied that it was, he asked, "Were you the first people to go back into the house?"

"I think so."

"Did others return to the house later?"

"Yes."

"Did you see Joseph Rogers return to the property?"

She paused before answering and started to sob.

Richard changed the tone of his voice, almost sounding sympathetic, "I am sorry, I do not wish to distress you, but can you answer, did you see Joseph Rogers return to the property?"

She appeared to recover, "Yes, I saw him."

"How did he look?"

"He was grinning."

"Did he say anything?"

She hesitated before answering, "Yes."

"What did he say?"

"He said, 'I shanked him'."

"Did you understand what he meant?"

"Yes, I thought he was saying that he had stabbed the man, but just in case I asked him what he meant."

"What did he say?"

"He said he had stabbed the man in the back of the leg because the man had knocked Shirley out."

"Did he show you where he had stabbed him?"

"Yes, he pointed to the back of my right leg and said he had stabbed the man there."

"Did he still have the knife with him?"

"No."

"Did he say what he had done with the knife?"

"I asked him and he said he had thrown it into some bushes outside the house."

"We have heard that the police came to the house a short while later. Were you still there when they arrived?"

"Yes."

"What did they do?"

"They arrested Adrian."

"Did you say anything to the police?"

"I told them that Adrian hadn't done anything, but they ignored me."

"Did they arrest anyone else?"

"No."

"Did you tell them what Joseph Rogers had told you?"

"No!"

"Why not?"

"I didn't want to get him into trouble."

"Did the police allow you to leave?"

"Yes, they did."

"Did you go home on your own?"

"No, Jo walked me home."

"How long did it take for you to walk from 84 Sangster Street to your home address?"

"About twenty minutes."

"Did you and Mr Rogers discuss what had happened?"

"Yes."

"What was said?"

"He told me that he had been worried about Shirley. He said he thought the man was right out of order knocking her out like that. He said he's decided to push the man away from everyone in case he became aggressive to anyone else. He told me he had taken a knife from the kitchen when he heard the noises outside."

She started sobbing again and the judge intervened, "Ms Anderson, would you like a short break?"

She dabbed at her eyes again with her increasingly moist handkerchief and answered immediately, "No thanks sir, I'd like to get it over with."

The judge nodded and turned to Richard, "Very well, carry on Mr Thornbrite."

Richard thanked him and turned back to the witness, "Ms Anderson, you were telling us what Mr Rogers said to you on your way home with him that night. You had reached the stage where he had told you that he had taken a knife from the kitchen when he heard the noises outside. Did he say anything more?"

"Yeah, he told me that the man quietened down as he led him away and then to get him back for what he had done to Shirley, he stabbed the man in the back of the leg."

CHAPTER 41

A CHALLENGING WITNESS

Richard thanked her and sat down rather abruptly. David gathered his papers around him and then stood to question her. He noticed that she had stopped sobbing and was looking at him warily.

Her evidence, if believed by the jury, was the end of Joseph's case. David knew he would have to challenge a great part of her evidence but he needed to do so without unduly distressing her. He could see that one or two members of the jury were looking at her sympathetically and he did not want to appear as a bully and have them take against his client.

David adopted what he hoped was his most disarming look, "Ms Anderson, you were due to give evidence a few days ago. Is there any reason why you did not?"

There was no sobbing from the witness now as she almost shouted a response, "What do you mean?"

"Were you avoiding coming to court?"

"I didn't want to come."

"So, you avoided a court order to appear at court?"

"Yeah, but it's because I didn't want to come and give evidence against Jo."

"Was that because you were worried about coming here and committing perjury?"

She looked confused, "What's perjury?"

"Lying on oath!"

She looked at the judge, "Can he say that?"

The judge looked at her closely, "Ms Anderson, Mr Brant has a duty to put his client's case to you. Please just answer the questions."

She gave the judge a frown before turning back to look at David, "I'm not lying, it's Jo who's the liar."

David looked at her coldly, "Let me ask you a few questions that hopefully you will not find difficult. I do not want to find out your address, but I presume you still live in the Brighton area, is that correct?"

"Yeah."

"Have you always lived in the Brighton area?"

"No, I moved here with my parents when I was ten."

"Where did you move from?"

"Leyton."

David paused as he recalled his geography, "Leyton is in the East of London?"

"Yeah."

"The word 'shanked', is that a word you first heard used in the London area."

"I don't know where I first heard it."

"But obviously you knew what it meant when you say Mr Rogers used the word?"

"Yeah."

"I suggest it's a London word, doesn't it originate from the East end of London?"

"I don't know where it comes from, but I've heard it before from Adrian."

"From Adrian?"

She reddened slightly, "Yeah he told me a mate of his had been shanked once."

"Are you sure he didn't say it in relation to Mr Worthy?"

"What?"

"Did Adrian ever tell you he 'shanked' Mr Worthy?"

She reddened as she said loudly, "No he never. He never touched that man!"

"Are you still in a relationship with Mr Simons?"

She involuntarily stroked her stomach and proudly said, "Yes."

David paused before asking the next question, "I'm sure we all noticed you touch your stomach area when I asked that question. May I ask if you are pregnant?"

She beamed as she announced, "Yes, Adrian and I are expecting our first child in August."

"Congratulations, your relationship with Mr Simons is clearly a close one."

"Yes."

"You are no doubt looking forward to bringing up a child together?"

"We are."

"And no doubt keen that nothing gets in the way of that?"

She looked suspiciously at him, "What do you mean?"

"Ms Anderson, this is a murder trial. Mr Rogers has been charged with murder. He denies that offence and it is his case that someone else must have killed Mr Worthy. The only person seen waving a knife around that night in the direction of the victim was Mr Simons.

Have you lied about Mr Rogers confessing to you, because you fear that otherwise the truth will be revealed and the police will charge Mr Simons with murder?"

She turned bright red as she shouted out an answer, "That's a complete lie. Adrian had nothing to do with killing that man."

"That's not right."

"I suggest it was Mr Simons who stabbed Mr Worthy in the leg?"

"That's not true."

"You saw him stab Mr Worthy, didn't you?"

"No, I did not. He never stabbed anyone."

"Just after he stabbed Mr Worthy, you grabbed him and pulled him towards the house?"

"No, I didn't, I did that before the man was stabbed."

"You saw Mr Simons discard the knife in the bushes outside 84 Sangster Street?"

"I never."

"And then you concocted this story that you have told this jury, claiming falsely that Mr Rogers claimed that he had 'shanked' Mr Worthy?"

"No, it's not true, he did say that."

David sat down without saying anything further to the witness.

CHAPTER 42

THE OFFICER IN CHARGE OF THE CASE

Believing that the cross examination of Jamie Anders had gone reasonably well, David was nonetheless conscious that she had denied all the important points he had tried to make and the jury still seemed to be treating her sympathetically. He watched as she left court and Richard announced that the final witness that he was calling to give evidence was, Detective Inspector William Splinter, the police officer in charge of the prosecution case.

DI Bill Splinter, walked into court with the superior air of someone who believed that the case was going well. Although he had not been in court since he was forced to leave he had not found it difficult to keep himself informed of what was happening.

Having gone through the usual formalities, Richard asked him, "Detective Inspector Splinter, as we have heard, you are the police officer in charge of this case. You are responsible for the investigation, the collation of evidence and the submission of that evidence to the Crown Prosecution Service whose duty it was to determine what charges, if any, should be brought in this case?"

"That's right, sir."

"We have heard that there was an initial reluctance on the part of witnesses to assist the police and that having taken some witness statements you went back to a number of witnesses to obtain further statements. Why was that?"

"As a result of our initial enquiries it became clear that some witnesses must have known more than they were telling us, and that in some cases, the witnesses initial accounts could not be correct."

Richard nodded as he continued, "When confronted with a witness who has, I suppose the best term would be, 'been economical with the truth', what steps do you take to obtain the correct version?"

"The steps we took here. We visited them again and told them we did not think they had given a full version of what they had seen, or what had happened and we asked them to give a further, honest account."

He stressed the word, 'honest'.

"Were any witnesses threatened with certain consequences if they did not comply?"

"No, we told them that they must provide an honest account. We did emphasise that it must be a truthful account and we warned them that if they lied in their statements, or in court, that would amount to the crime of perjury. It wasn't a threat though, just a warning."

"Did Jamie Anderson give an initial witness statement to police?"

"No, as she was clearly the girlfriend of our chief suspect at the time and we knew she was claiming that Mr Simons had done nothing wrong, we chose not to interview her."

"As we have heard though, she did later approach the prosecution and she made a witness statement, claiming that the defendant confessed to the crime."

"Yes, sir."

With that Richard sat down. He knew that because of what had happened earlier in the case that David would attack the officer's credibility. He chose not to rely on the officer for any other evidence just in case the jury agreed with David and did not believe this witness. There was no reason to weaken his case now.

CHAPTER 43

A CHALLENGING CROSS EXAMINATION

David quickly turned to Gavin and said something quietly, then he nodded sagely, beaming at the answer and finally he shuffled his papers and stood to his feet. (In fact, David had merely said, 'Here we go', and Gavin had replied quietly, 'good luck', David was simply trying to make the witness think he had something important to put. It seemed to work as Bill shuffled his feet, slightly nervously, in the witness box.

"Detective Inspector, the jury may not be aware of this but the prosecution also have a duty of disclosure in this case and indeed in all cases?"

"Yes, sir."

"The prosecution tend to divide their evidence into two distinct types. Used material which is evidence the prosecution relies upon, and unused material which the prosecution do not rely upon?"

"That's right, sir."

"Under the disclosure rules, the prosecution must disclose to the defence any of the evidence that they have gathered that might undermine their own case or might assist the defence case?"

"That's right, sir."

"Are you the disclosure officer in this case?"

"No sir, Detective Constable Ben Sharpe is responsible for disclosure in this case".

"As the officer in charge of the case you will of course be aware of what has been disclosed to the defence in this case?"

"Yes, sir."

"In fact, very little has been disclosed in this case, has it?"

"I don't believe there was a great deal that fell within the disclosure test."

"Usually officer, phones are seized in cases like this, but there is no reference to any phones in the disclosure schedule that was served in this case."

"I believe Mr Simons' phone was seized upon his arrest but it didn't contain any relevant messages."

"So, no other phones were seized because none appear on the disclosure schedule?"

"I believe that's right, sir."

David heard a scribbling noise coming from his right where the prosecution junior Emilia Johnson was seated, but he ignored it and moved on.

"Officer, let me move on to the investigation of this case. Is it fair to say that the investigation of this case must have been frustrating at times for you?"

Bill paused before answering, "It's had its moments, sir."

"You had two victims to begin with?"

Bill looked puzzled, "Two, sir?"

"Yes, Shirley West was seriously assaulted that night by Mr Worthy."

Bill nodded, "Yes, sir, but she recovered from her injuries."

"That did not make her any less a victim!"

"No, sir."

"You then had Mr Worthy, who sadly died?"

"Yes, sir."

"And on that first night, you only had one suspect, a man seen to carry a knife from 84 Sangster Street, seen to wave it around and then heard to threaten to stab Mr Worthy. It must have seemed a relatively straight forward case at that stage?"

"We don't like to jump to conclusions, sir."

"Nevertheless, it must have seemed that Friday night that you had the right man in custody?"

"We still had to investigate and discover what had happened."

"Of course, but after taking the initial witness statements with people saying they had not seen anything, you must still have thought you had the right man in custody?"

"We were still investigating the case, sir."

"Mr Simons was arrested on suspicion of committing attempted murder. Mr Worthy then died so Mr Simons must have been the prime suspect in the murder enquiry at that stage?"

Bill hesitated, he never liked to give the defence anything if he could help it, but here he saw no harm in answering the question and putting his own slant on the answer, "Before we had obtained all the witness statements Mr Simons was our major suspect, but then we discovered that your client was leading Mr Worthy away from the scene when the fatal blow was struck and he was the only person who was in close proximity to Mr Worthy."

David grinned at him, "That was the position after you received a statement from Mr Brian Williams?"

"Yes, sir."

"Did you take his statement?"

"Yes, sir."

"Did he seem as though he was suffering in any way when you took the statement?"

"I don't know what you mean?"

"You're a police officer with a great deal of experience. You must have seen many traumatised witnesses in your life and no doubt you recognise the signs?"

"I have seen a few, but I'm not an expert."

"No, but I suggest it would have been obvious that Mr Williams was traumatised when you took his statement from him?"

"He was obviously affected by his friend's death but I don't know if I would call him traumatised."

"You saw him in court when he gave evidence, he still seems traumatised?"

"I don't know, sir."

"Witnesses who are 'affected' or 'traumatised' by what they have seen may not be the best at recording details accurately?"

"I suppose that's obvious sir, which is why we try to obtain evidence from a number of sources."

"I suggest, that you obtained a statement from one traumatised witness and the whole of your case changed. From investigating the knife wielding Mr Simons for murder, you shifted to Mr Rogers, who no one ever saw with a knife."

Bill hesitated before answering, "I don't think that's a very fair categorisation of our investigation."

"Not only is it fair, it's what happened. After that you went back to the other witnesses in this case to try and obtain accounts that fitted in with your new theory?"

"I resent that, sir, we went back to witnesses because it was clear their accounts weren't correct."

"You were in court when Steven Denley gave evidence weren't you?"

"Yes."

"You heard him say that he gave a statement and then a week later you visited him. He stated, that you told him that the police had taken many statements from people and you didn't think he was telling the truth. Did you say that?"

"No, sir, I told him that I did not think he had given the full truth in his statement."

"You said you thought he was trying to protect Mr Rogers."

"No sir, I asked if he was trying to protect somebody, I did not suggest that he was trying to protect Mr Rogers, he might have been protecting Mr Simons for all I knew."

"Really, wasn't that the theory you had formulated by that time?"

"We were still investigating the matter, I had not formed any opinions by then."

"Did you tell Mr Stevens that if he did not support your theory, he could be prosecuted for the offence of perjury?"

"No, I did not sir."

"What about Scott Robson?"

"Sorry, I don't understand, sir?"

"You were present for most of Mr Robson's evidence. You heard him say, 'The police came around and told me they thought I'd lied in my first statement and if I didn't make another I'd be charged with perjury.' Did you say that to him?"

"I told him that we believed he had seen more than he claimed and that if he had lied in his first statement, he could be charged with perjury."

"Mr Robson gave evidence that you told him that you thought he had lied and that Joseph Rogers had stabbed the man and you wanted him to tell you what he saw, under the threat of prosecuting him for perjury. Is that true?"

"No sir, I told him that we did not believe his first account where he claimed that he had not seen anything and he should give us a true account or potentially be prosecuted for perjury."

"I suggest you were the one who first stated to him that Mr Rogers was the one who stabbed Mr Worthy?"

"No, sir, I never said that."

"What I am suggesting officer is that, instead of going for the obvious candidate for murderer in this case, namely Adrian Simons, you formed your own theory that Mr Rogers was the murderer and then put pressure on some of the witnesses to adopt and support that theory?"

"No, sir, there is no truth in that allegation whatsoever."

CHAPTER 44

THE DEFENDANT'S ACCOUNT

Detective Inspector Splinter left the witness box at 12:15 and Richard announced in a self-satisfied way, that was the end of the prosecution case. The time had now been reached in the case where David would inform the court he was calling evidence as part of the defence case or he was not calling any and the case would proceed to speeches.

The case had gone quicker than David had anticipated and he needed some extra time for last minute discussions with his client. He asked the judge if he could commence the defence case at 2pm and the judge readily agreed, announcing to the jury that they could have a longer lunch hour.

David spent from 12:15 until 1pm discussing the case with Joseph in the cells. He was then ejected from the cells so that Joseph could have his microwaved lunch whether he wanted it or not.

David managed to have a sandwich before returning to the cells at 1:35pm to carry on with his conference. He used the time to explain to Joseph that he could not be forced to give evidence but if he did not, the judge would direct the jury that they could hold it against him. David explained that in his opinion the jury would want to hear Joseph give evidence and might think he was guilty and had no answer to the charge if he remained in the dock.

Joseph readily agreed that it would be in his interests to give evidence although David could sense that he was very reluctant to do so.

David also raised the issue of calling Joseph's girlfriend as a witness. He thought it might be a mistake and it might be better not to subject her to cross-examination where she would be asked in detail why she left the party. However, Joseph was adamant that she be called as a witness at the trial. As it was Joseph's decision and David could only advise, he said no more.

At 2-05pm the judge sat again and David announced that he was going to call Joseph Rogers to give evidence in the case. After the preliminaries were dealt with, David's first question was, "Mr Rogers, is it right that you have no convictions, cautions or warnings recorded against you by the police and you are therefore a man of good character in the eyes of the law?"

"Yes, sir."

"Have you ever been charged with any offences of violence before this case?"

"No, sir."

"Indeed, have you ever been charged with any offence at any stage of your life prior to this case?"

"No, sir."

It was important to David to elicit this fact at the very beginning of Joseph's evidence. He wanted the jury to know that they were not dealing with a man with previous convictions for violence or dishonesty, which would undoubtedly affect how they viewed him.

"Mr Rogers, I understand that in August 2017 you were a student at Sussex University. What were you studying there?"

"I was studying Mechanical Engineering, I was about to start the second year of a three year course."

"Had you decided what your future plans would be with such a qualification?"

"Yes, I was hoping to obtain employment in a company dealing with renewable energy sources; solar panels, wind energy, wave energy and the like."

"Those plans are of course on hold now?"

"Yes, I was unable to start my second year of the course due to my arrest and imprisonment."

"We have heard that at the time of this incident you had a girlfriend, Caroline Jennings. When did you first meet her?"

"In my first year at university. She also studied at Sussex University."

"Was she on the same course as you?"

"No, she was studying astrophysics ... she still is."

"Are you still in a relationship?"

"Yes, although because of my arrest I have not been able to see much of her. The only time I see her is when she visits me in Lewes prison. I did tell her she should leave me because it was not fair to her to have to wait for the outcome of this trial ..." He added proudly, "... but she said she wanted to stay with me and support me."

"Let me ask you about the night of 25th August 2017 and the party that was held at 84 Sangster Street. Firstly, who invited you to attend that party?"

"I met Steven Denley in my first year at Sussex University and we became friends. He invited Caroline and I to the party."

"Did you know everyone at the party?"

"I knew most of the people who were there, though I'd never met Brian Williams before."

"What time did you arrive?"

"Caroline and I arrived just after 8pm."

"We have heard that Caroline left the party before the incident with Mr Worthy occurred. Can you tell us why she left the party?"

"Yes. Caroline and I had a few relationship problems at the time. We had been arguing a lot about general matters. Caroline was unfortunately insecure and thought that I was interested in Jamie. I wasn't, but she wouldn't believe me and that night she accused me of constantly looking at Jamie even though I wasn't. We argued about it and she decided to leave."

"Why didn't you leave with her?"

"Caroline made it quite clear that she didn't want me to. I decided to stay and enjoy the party ..." he added sadly, "... I wish I had followed her now!"

David looked at the cold expressions on the faces of the jury and hoped his client would not make any more comments like that, they clearly thought he was trying to gain sympathy and it did not help when he was accused of killing somebody.

"How did you feel when Caroline left?"

"I was upset."

"Were you angry?"

"No, I thought she was being silly. There was no reason to get angry."

"We have heard that drink was flowing that night, we have also heard that Scott Robson was smoking 'weed', as he put it, and maybe others were as well. Can you tell us what you had that night?"

"I had a few drinks of lager and some of the food that had been left out, although there wasn't much food."

"How many drinks of lager?"

"About 4 big cans."

"Did you take any drugs?"

"No, I don't use drugs."

"Were you drunk?"

"I was merry, but I wouldn't say I was drunk."

"There came a time when Mr Worthy appeared outside the property. Do you recall that happening?"

"I do remember someone turning the music down and making a comment that there was a loud noise coming from outside."

"What did you do?"

"Everyone wanted to see what was happening, so we all went outside."

"We have heard that Mr Simons armed himself with a knife from the kitchen. Did you arm yourself with anything?"

Joseph faced the jury before replying firmly, "No, sir. I did not! I did not pick anything up. I just went out to see what was happening."

"Did you see anyone other than Mr Simons with a knife or other weapon?"

"No, I didn't sir."

"So, the only person you saw armed with a knife was Mr Simons?"

"Yes, sir."

"What did you see outside?"

"I saw that Mr Williams went up to the large man and started talking to him. Then I noticed Shirley went up to the man and started shouting at him and a few seconds later the man knocked her out."

"How did that make you feel?"

"I was annoyed that he could do that, but before I could say anything, I saw Adrian Simons go up to him and threaten him with a knife. I decided that everything was getting out of hand, so I went up to the man to try and calm things down before anyone else got hurt."

"What did you do?"

"I tried to get in between the man and Adrian and then I put my arm around his shoulder and told him, it wasn't worth getting upset about what happened and it would be best if he left."

"How did he react to that?"

"I was a little surprised that he seemed to calm down straight away. I had tried to show him that I was not carrying anything and was not a threat."

"What happened then?"

"I led him away talking to him. He was upset and was saying that he had driven Shirley and the other man to the party and they had just left him and ignored him."

"We have heard that you placed your right arm around his shoulder, is that correct?"

"Yes."

"Are you right or left handed?"

"I am right-handed."

"Did you see where everyone else was as you led Mr Worthy away?"

"No, I had my back to them."

"Do you know where Adrian Simons was?"

"He had been close to the man just before I led him away."

"How close?"

"About a metre away ... within touching distance."

"What happened next?"

"The man suddenly shouted out in pain and pushed me away, saying, "You fucking cheeky bastard."

"Did you know what had happened?"

"No, I was shocked when he pushed me away. I had no idea what had happened to him."

"Did you discover what had happened to him?"

"I saw him start to limp away and I noticed his right trouser leg become stained. It was obvious he had been stabbed."

"Did you stab him?"

"No, sir, I did not."

"Did you see who stabbed him?"

"No, sir, I did not."

"Was there anybody near to you when you were pushed away?"

"I didn't see anybody when I was pushed away, but after Mr Worthy was limping away I saw Adrian Simons was still within a metre or so of the man."

"Was he holding anything?"

"He was still holding the knife."

"Did you notice anything about the knife?"

"No sir, it was dark."

"What happened to Mr Simons?"

"Jamie grabbed him and pulled him towards the house."

"Did you return to the house?"

"Yes, I did, just after Adrian and Jamie."

"Did you speak to anyone when you returned to the house?"

"I remember someone asking what had happened to the man outside. I said, 'Someone stabbed him'."

"Were you grinning?"

"No, I was in a state of shock at what had happened."

"Did you speak to Jamie Anderson?"

"I might have said something to her."

"Can you recall what?"

"No."

"We have heard her evidence, did you say you had 'shanked' the man?"

"No, I have never even heard the word, 'shanked' until I saw Jamie Anderson's written statement to the police."

"Did you say you had stabbed the man?"

"Certainly not."

"Did you say you had stabbed him because he knocked Shirley out?"

"Certainly not. I didn't stab him."

"Do you know why Jamie Anderson has given this evidence?"

"I don't know, but I think she's trying to protect Adrian."

"Did you ever tell her where the man had been stabbed or did you point to the back of her right leg and say that was where you had stabbed him?"

"Certainly not."

"Did you ever tell her what had happened to the knife that had been used to injure Mr Worthy?"

"No, I didn't, I didn't know what had happened to the knife!"

"Did you say you had thrown it into some bushes outside the house?"

"No, I did not."

"Had you had a knife in your possession, any time that night?"

"No, I never had a knife."

"We have heard that the police arrived a short time after you all returned to the house. Do you recall how long after you returned to the house that they arrived?"

"It was within a few minutes or so."

"We have heard evidence that no one in the house appeared to cooperate with the police. Did you cooperate with them?"

"I didn't tell them anything because I was still shocked by what had happened and I wasn't sure who had stabbed the man."

"Did you tell them what you had seen Adrian Simons do?"

"No."

"Did you try to prevent his arrest?"

"No, I didn't say anything when Adrian was arrested because I had seen him with a knife and I had seen him threaten to stab the man."

"We have heard that the police asked to search you, did you cooperate with them then?"

"Yes."

"You allowed them to search you?"

"Yes."

"What did the police do during the search?"

"They checked all my pockets and they looked at my clothing and my hands."

"Did they tell you why they were doing this?"

"No, they just told us to stand up and put our arms up in the air when they searched us."

"How thorough was the search?"

"It seemed very thorough to me."

"Did you have any injuries?"

"No."

"Did you have any blood on your clothes?"

"No."

David took hold of a witness statement and asked, "We have heard that when police came to arrest you two days later, the clothes you had worn that night were washed and piled up in your room. Why was that?"

"I'd been wearing my jeans all week. I always wash my clothes on Saturday morning, so I washed and dried them that Saturday morning and then put them back in my room, stacked in the corner. That's where they were when the police arrived that night."

"Did you have any gloves that night?"

"No, sir."

"We have heard that the police eventually allowed you to leave 84 Sangster Street. Did you leave the property with Jamie Anderson?"

"Yes, I did."

"Why did you leave with her?"

"She was upset. Adrian had just been arrested on suspicion of attempted murder. She was crying and I thought I should walk her home to see that she would be alright."

"Did you walk her home because you were attracted to her?"

"No. I liked Jamie, but I wasn't attracted to her."

"Do you like her now?"

"No, she's lied about me, she's trying to get me convicted of murder!"

"Did you say anything to her about stabbing the man?"

"No."

"What did you talk about?"

"We just talked about Adrian. She was just saying she was worried about what would happen to him."

"What did you say?"

"I just told her I hadn't seen Adrian stab the man."

"What did she say?"

"She didn't say anything."

David paused as he picked up a witness statement. "We have heard that you were arrested on the Sunday night, 27th August 2017 at 7:52pm. You were at your University lodgings. Is that where you returned to on the Friday night when the police let you leave 84 Sangster Street?"

"Yes."

"Did you stay there on the Saturday?"

"No, I got up about 10am and phoned Caroline to see if we were alright and if she wanted to see me. She said we were ok and she would like to see me. I did my laundry and then I went around to her address. She lives in a flat with friends in Hove. We went out to Brighton and just walked around talking and then I stayed with her Saturday night and part of Sunday and only returned to my place around 7pm."

David looked down at the client's written proof of evidence, provided by his instructing solicitors. It was the document that he was examining Joseph from. The proof said that Joseph returned to his home at 4pm for fifteen minutes and then he went out again. David had asked him earlier in conference where he had gone at about 4:15pm and Joseph said he could not recall but would try and remember. He did wonder why Joseph had changed his recollection, but it was no part of his job to cross examine his own client so he continued.

"We have heard that you were arrested on the Sunday 27th August 2017 at 7:52pm?"

"Yes, sir."

"You were taken to the police station and there you were allowed to see a solicitor?"

"Yes, sir."

"You were then interviewed?"

"Yes, sir."

"You made 'no comment' to the questions asked?"

"Yes, sir."

"Why was that?"

"I was advised by my solicitor to make 'no comment', so I took his advice."

David looked up from the proof of evidence and turned to observe the jury before asking the final question.

"Mr Rogers, you are charged with the most serious offence in our criminal calendar, namely, 'murder'. Did you have anything to do with the death of Mr Worthy?"

Joseph followed David's gaze towards the jury. He scanned their faces and said. "No, sir, I had nothing at all to do with it. I just wanted to calm the situation down. I never wanted to hurt anyone and I never did!"

CHAPTER 45

A DEMANDING TIME

As David sat down he noticed Richard look back at his junior, Emilia Johnson, and give what David viewed was a sickly grin at her. He then turned to face Joseph. He looked at him for a few seconds before asking any questions and then turned his gaze towards the jury.

David had seen this approach before from a number of old school prosecutors. Some liked to stare at the defendant as they cross-examined, hoping that the defendant would avoid eye contact and look shifty or uncomfortable. Others, like Richard, would not look at the defendant when cross-examining him, as if to indicate complete contempt for the individual and anything that came from his mouth. Richard was clearly from the latter school.

"Mr Rogers, do you love your girlfriend?"

"Sorry?"

"It's a simple question, do you love your girlfriend?"

"Yes."

"Does she love you?"

"I think so."

"Surely after this period of time you know the answer to that question?"

"Yes, she loves me."

"No doubt you would assist each other if one of you finds yourself in difficulty?"

"Of course."

"If she was attacked by a man in the street, no doubt you would go to her aid?"

"Of course."

"No doubt you feel the same way about any vulnerable person?"

"Yes."

"So, as an example, if a young girl were attacked in the street by a large man, you would go to her aid?"

Joseph paused before answering, "Yes."

"You would want to protect her?"

"Yes."

"If she was injured, you would no doubt want her attacker to be punished?"

"I think anyone would."

"Is that how you felt on the night of 25th August 2017, when Shirley West was hit and knocked unconscious by Mr Worthy?"

Joseph hesitated, "No."

"Why not, didn't you want him to suffer for knocking out one of your friends?"

"No."

"Didn't you want to get revenge on him for assaulting this small, defenceless girl?"

"I didn't want to get revenge."

"Well what do you say you wanted when you put your arm around Mr Worthy?"

"I just wanted to calm the situation down."

"Oh, come now Mr Rogers, you had just seen the very large, muscular Mr Worthy knock a small, petite girl out. You did not want to calm the situation down, you wanted to avenge her and you did!"

Joseph shouted out the answer, "That's not true."

Richard paused and still refused to look at Joseph as he asked, "Let me ask you a few questions about earlier that night. You have told us that you arrived at the party after 8pm that night and you were in the company of your girlfriend, Caroline?"

"That's right."

"Why did she leave?"

"I've already said, she thought I fancied Jamie and that I was staring at Jamie."

"Did you 'fancy' Jamie?"

"No."

"Why not?"

"She's not my type."

"We have seen Jamie give evidence. She is young, attractive. Are you sure you were not attracted to her?"

"As I said, she's not my type ..." He smirked as he added, "... even though she's obviously yours."

David looked up from his notes as a frown spread over his face. Why did clients always try to be clever in the witness box, even when he told them not to be? The jury looked at Joseph impassively as the judge intervened.

"Mr Rogers, please remember that you are in a court of law. Prosecuting counsel has a duty to put questions to you. You must answer them and flippant remarks like that will not assist your case."

To David's consternation, Joseph just stared at the judge instead of looking suitably contrite.

Richard was not concerned, he believed, rightly, that he was getting to Joseph and he welcomed more comments that might alienate the jury against him.

"Is Caroline an unreasonable person?

Joseph looked suspiciously, "What do you mean?"

"Is she the type of person who would lie?'

"No."

Richard smiled, he knew from the Defence Statement that Joseph had to serve pre-trial that he was calling Caroline as a witness. Joseph could hardly brand her a liar before relying on her evidence.

"Is she paranoid?"

"No."

"Is she prone to bouts of serious jealousy?"

"No."

"So, what made her think you were staring at Jamie ... unless of course, that is what you were doing?"

Joseph hesitated before answering, "I don't know.'

"Come now, you have told us, Caroline does not lie, she did not make this allegation up. You must have been staring at Jamie?"

Joseph paused before answering, "I may have done once or twice."

"Once or twice, or a few times?"

"Maybe a few times, but I didn't mean anything by it."

"I suggest you did. You were obviously staring at Jamie in such a way as to make Caroline jealous. Not only jealous but so upset that she left the party?"

"She just said she was leaving."

"Why didn't you go with her?"

Joseph did not answer.

"After all, it was getting dark outside. It was hardly chivalrous to let her walk home on her own?"

Joseph gripped the sides of the witness box with his outstretched hands, "She told me she didn't want me to come with her."

Richard looked at him for a few seconds, with contempt etched on his face, then looked away and asked, "Even if she did say that, you could have insisted?"

"No, she wanted to leave, I wanted to stay."

"Is that so you could possibly get closer to Jamie?"

"No, Caroline made it clear she was leaving and didn't want me to walk her home. The party had just started getting going. Everyone was getting merrier. I didn't want to leave and Caroline didn't want me to go with her."

"We have heard witnesses say that you were annoyed because of her leaving. Is that true?"

"No, at first I was upset because she had left after wrongly accusing me of staring at Jamie, but after a short time I just started to enjoy the party."

"As you have told us, you went outside when the loud noise was heard. Did you have any idea what was happening?"

"No."

"You were aware that there was someone outside making a loud noise, were you scared?"

"Not really, I just followed others out to see what was happening."

"Did you leave after Mr Simons?"

"Yes."

"Did you see him arm himself with a knife?"

"Yes."

"What did you think of that?"

"I thought he was just taking it to protect himself."

"Did you think it a good thing?"

"I didn't really think about it."

"I suggest that having seen him arm himself with a knife you decided to do the same thing?"

"That's not true!"

Richard picked up exhibit BM1, "I suggest you armed yourself with this sharp knife with a seven inch blade in order to, 'protect' yourself?"

Joseph hesitated before answering, "That's not true."

"Did Mr Worthy appear afraid of you and your friends?"

"No, not all."

"He was a large man, did it look like he could handle himself?"

"Yes."

"Indeed, we have heard that he wasn't afraid when Mr Simons was waving a knife in his face, threatening to stab him. It was Mr Simons who backed off."

"Yeah."

"Is that why you tried a different strategy?"

Joseph looked puzzled, "What do you mean?"

"Is that when you decided to lull him into a false sense of security before attacking him?"

"What?"

"You pretended that you were calming the situation down?"

"No, I was trying to calm the situation down!"

"I suggest that far from trying to calm the situation down. You had concealed the knife BM1 with a seven inch blade and you waited until Mr Worthy was no longer a threat and then you plunged the knife into the back of his right leg?"

"Well why did no one see me do that then?"

David again looked up, his advice to Joseph to just answer the questions and not to get involved in arguments with the prosecutor was being ignored.

Richard looked at Joseph briefly before looking away, "I am not here to answer your questions but I suggest you know the answer to that one. Everyone was looking at Shirley West at that stage, as we know, she was laid out on the floor. You knew no one would see you."

Joseph shouted out, "I didn't stab him, it's a lie."

Richard paused for a few seconds before asking, "If you are telling the truth, you wanted to calm the situation down, avoid anyone else getting hurt and generally you wanted to be a peacekeeper?"

"Yes."

"You didn't want Mr Worthy to be injured?"

"No, I did not."

"If that's true, why didn't you go to his assistance?"

Joseph looked nonplussed, "What do you mean?"

"You didn't want this man to be injured or hurt, but you saw that he was hurt, you saw the blood seeping into his trousers. If you did not cause that, why did you just leave him and go back into the house."

Joseph was looking extremely stressed now, "I don't know, I guess I didn't want to get involved. He'd called me a fucking cheeky bastard, I didn't think he wanted me near him."

"Or, is the reality that you had deliberately stabbed him and now you were making your escape?"

"No!"

"You entered number 84 Sangster Street and told everyone there that you had stabbed or 'shanked' the man?"

"No, I didn't."

"You even tried to impress Jamie Anderson by showing her where you had stabbed Mr Worthy?"

"That's not true."

"You told her where you had thrown the knife?"

"I never had a knife."

Richard looked at his papers and then asked, "We have heard that the police arrived and no one at the party cooperated with them. Is it right that you didn't say anything to them?"

"I didn't want to get Adrian into trouble."

"Or is it that you did not want to get yourself into trouble?"

"No."

"Why not tell them that you had tried to usher the man away?"

"I thought they might arrest me."

Richard paused and gave a quizzical look towards the jury, "Why, according to you, you had done nothing wrong?"

"Yes, but the man clearly thought that I had stabbed him. I didn't want the police to think that as well."

Richard paused.

"Mr Worthy clearly thought you had stabbed him?"

"Yes, that's why he called me a 'cheeky little bastard'."

"That was because no one else was close to him. You were the only one?"

"That's not true, Adrian Simons was close to him and he had a knife."

"I thought you couldn't recall where Mr Simons was?"

"He was nearby."

"But you were the one who stabbed Mr Worthy?"

"That's not true."

"Adrian Simons was arrested and you took an opportunity to get closer to Jamie. You, who had not escorted your own girlfriend home when she left, now escorted Jamie home. Why was that?"

Joseph paused again before answering, "It was later, it was dark and I felt sorry for her because her boyfriend had been arrested."

"Did you discuss the stabbing?"

"Not really, Jamie was too upset, she kept crying because Adrian had been arrested."

"Isn't it true that you did discuss the stabbing and you told her you had done it to get back at the man because of what he had done to Shirley?"

"No, that's not true."

"Were you worried that you might have Mr Worthy's blood on your clothing?"

"No."

"Even on your case you got close to the man, your arm was round his shoulders. Didn't you think you might have some of his blood on you?"

"I never thought about it."

"Is that why you washed your clothes on the Saturday morning, to wash out the bloodstains?"

"No, I always wash my clothes on Saturday morning."

Richard turned to the record of Joseph's interview with police. "We have heard that you made no comment in interview and this was because of your solicitor's advice?"

"Yes, sir."

"Needless to say, you did realise that this was only advice and it was still your choice whether to answer questions or not?"

"Yes, I did."

"Why didn't you give the account that you gave today?"

"My solicitor advised me not to?"

"You could have easily answered questions and said you had not stabbed the man, if that was your case?"

"Yes, but my solicitor advised me not to."

"Or is it you are hiding behind that advice?"

Joseph looked puzzled at the question. Richard paused a few seconds before adding, "I suggest the reason you did not answer any questions was because you did not know the full extent of the case against you and you wanted to wait to see the prosecution papers before inventing a defence?"

Joseph grabbed the rim of the witness box again with both hands, he had angry expression on his face as he shouted out, "That's not true."

David looked up from his notes and glanced at the faces of the jurors. They were mostly stern faced. He could see that Joseph was making a bad impression and his bursts of anger did not assist in a case alleging murder.

Richard now changed his gaze and looked at Joseph for a few seconds before looking away again and staring at the jury.

"Do you easily lose your temper Mr Rogers?"

Joseph seem to realise that he was not helping his case, "No, I don't."

"Are you angry now, just because of my questioning?"

"No."

"I suggest you are and that we have gained a real insight into your character. You easily lose your temper, don't you?"

"No, I don't."

"And you did that night because of what you had seen happen to your friend, Shirley?"

"No, that's not true."

"You then decided that you would lull Mr Worthy into a false sense of security and stab him when he wasn't looking?"

Richard sat down at the same time as Joseph was saying quietly, "That's not true."

CHAPTER 46

THE DEFENDANT'S GIRLFRIEND

Joseph returned to the dock with his head held low. David tried to distract attention from him by immediately announcing to the court that he was ready to call his next witness, the defendant's girlfriend, Caroline Jennings. He then added quickly, that as it was now just after 4:15pm and she would not finish her evidence tonight and he asked if he could call her the next day so she could give her evidence in one tranche. The judge readily agreed and the court adjourned for the day.

David chose not to see Joseph in the cells that night. He was probably upset at how his evidence had gone and no words of David would have helped. Alternatively, if Joseph thought he had done a good job, David did not want to tell him the truth and upset him!

At 10:15am on the Friday morning a lady from witness services brought Caroline into court. She was ushered towards the witness box where she was quickly sworn and gave her name.

Some members of the jury seem to react to her presence by moving forward in their seats as if to seek a better view of the defendant's girlfriend and try and read something from her demeanour.

David had met her briefly on the previous day and had noted then that she was an attractive girl, well dressed, composed and she was well spoken without betraying any nerves, despite the fact that she was being called to give evidence on behalf of her boyfriend, a man who was charged with murder. He hoped that the way she presented herself might assist the case and repair some of the damage that Joseph had done with his outbursts.

"Ms Jennings, when did you first meet Joseph Rogers?"

Caroline turned to the jury as she had earlier been directed to by David and smiled at them.

"We first met at the University of Sussex. We started our courses at the same time in October 2016. I started Astrophysics and he started an Engineering course. We met in December that year, at a party held by a mutual friend, Peter Lennon. Joseph's then girlfriend had recently broken off their relationship and he was very upset. We just started talking to each other and shortly afterwards we were meeting each other regularly."

"Are you still in a relationship?"

"Yes...", she paused before adding, "... though of course I only see him once a week now, when I visit him in prison."

She looked down for a moment before composing herself again. David waited a few seconds before asking her, "By the time of the tragic incident we are dealing with, you had known Joseph for almost a year then?"

"Yes." She smiled at the thought.

"How often did you see him in that time?"

"The first few weeks we met every couple of days. After a month it almost became daily except when one of us had an important piece of coursework that had to be completed urgently."

David smiled, students never changed, everything was left to the last minute which is why it became 'urgent'.

"Do you think you were able to judge his character in that time?"

"Oh, yes!"

"Can you tell the court something about his character?"

"Yes, certainly. He is one of the sweetest, most caring people I have ever met. He cares about everyone. He feels that his parents were distant to him and they did not provide great emotional support for him as a young child and he has reacted to that by reaching out to, and helping everyone he can."

David smiled, she seemed to be laying it on a little thick, but the jury appeared to like her.

"In the time you have been together, have you ever fallen out?"

"Yes, of course, all couples do, but that's mostly been my fault. I am slightly insecure. My parents divorced when I was twelve years old because of my father having several affairs. I then had a boyfriend at school who constantly cheated on me with some of my best friends and those experiences have made my relationships with other men difficult. I am prone to jealousy and I have sometimes accused Jo of being interested in other women when in fact he is not."

"Can you give us an example?"

"Yes, the night of this ..." She paused before adopting David's phrase, "... tragic incident. I went to the party with Jo. We were both looking forward to it but I acted stupidly. I thought he was taking too much of an interest in Jamie Anderson and I became concerned and I left."

"What do you mean by the phrase, 'too much of an interest'?"

"I thought he was looking at her a lot. I accused him of being interested in her and told him I was leaving. He told me at the time he wasn't interested, but I didn't believe him and I left."

"Did he follow you?"

"He tried to but I told him to go away, I didn't want to see him again."

"Do you think now that he had an interest in Jamie?"

"No. I realise it was my own insecurity."

"In all the time you have known him, has he ever been violent towards you?"

"No, never."

"In all the time you have known him, have you ever seen him being violent towards anyone else?"

"Certainly not, he's not like that. If he has a problem with someone, he tries to sort it out peacefully. He never resorts to violence."

"Have you ever seen him carry a knife in a public place?"

She smiled again, "Only in a restaurant!"

David frowned a little, more at himself for the looseness of the question, "I mean having a knife in the street or somewhere like that, for an offensive purpose?"

"No, certainly not. He is anti-knife. He has often read of some stabbing in London or Manchester and complained to me about people carrying knives. He would never carry one, let alone use one."

"Is he the type of person who is capable of taking a knife from a party, going out into the street and slyly stabbing someone in the leg whilst pretending to befriend them?"

She looked horrified at the suggestion and answered, "Certainly not."

David looked down at his papers and then looked at her again, "There is just one further matter I want to deal with and that's after you left the party, did Joseph contact you again?"

"Yes, he contacted me the next day, in the early morning, I think about 9 or 10am."

"Did you discuss the party?"

"He told me someone had been stabbed?"

"Can you recall what he said?"

The judge looked directly at the prosecutor. Technically this was asking for a previous consistent statement and therefore inadmissible but Richard had no objection.

"Yes, he told me a man had been stabbed but he didn't know who had stabbed him."

"Did you make any arrangements to meet with him that day?"

"Yes, he always does his week's laundry on Saturday morning so we arranged to meet after he had finished that, at about 12pm."

"Did you meet him?"

"Yes. He came around to my place and we went out and spent the day together."

"Where did he stay that night?"

"We returned to my place and we spent the night together. He left the next day in the afternoon."

David thanked her and sat down. He thought that she had come across reasonably well and had helped Joseph's case. He looked towards the jury, hoping they shared his opinion!

CHAPTER 47

REVELATIONS

Richard rose from his seat almost immediately that David sat down. He looked at the witness and beamed at her, keeping her gaze as he addressed her.

"Ms Jennings, you have just told us that Mr Rogers left your flat on the Sunday in the afternoon. Do you recall now what time Mr Rogers left you?"

She thought for a second or two before answering, "I think it was around 3pm?"

Richard turned his smile towards the jury, "Did he say where he was going?"

"He said he was going home."

His beaming smile widened into a grin, "It presumably does not take him four hours to travel from your flat to his?"

She laughed, "No, it's only about a mile away."

Richard nodded sagely, "You see Mr Rogers has told us he arrived home at 7pm that night, do you know where he went after he left you."

She hesitated before replying, her smile had been replaced with a look of concern, "No."

Richard paused before asking, "Was he carrying anything when he came to your flat?"

She looked surprised at the question, "I don't think so."

"Did he have a bag with him?"

She looked worried as she answered, "He had a small rucksack, but he always has that."

"Did you see what was inside the rucksack?"

"No...", she quickly added, "...He usually has a few books and spare clothing when he visits me."

"Was there any clothing in the bag that day?"

"There must have been because he changed his clothing when he was at my flat."

"Can you recall seeing any other clothing or items in his bag, such as gloves?"

"No, but I didn't really look."

"Did he mention that he may be going somewhere else before he went home?"

"No, he just told me he was going home."

"Has he ever told you where he went after leaving you?"

She looked puzzled, "No."

"Did he ever tell you he was going to get rid of any clothing, such as gloves, for example?"

She looked concerned, "No."

"Very well, let me deal with another topic. You have told us that Mr Rogers is not a violent man?"

"No, he's not."

"He has never hit you or anyone else in your presence?"

"No, he's never."

"Does he get angry?"

She hesitated before replying, "Sometimes."

"If a large male knocked out a small defenceless female, would that anger him?"

She hesitated, "I don't know."

"Come now Ms Jennings, you have known him now for well over a year. You tell us you are able to assess his character. If he saw a large angry male knock out a small defenceless female, that would surely concern him?"

"I suppose so."

"Even anger him?"

"I suppose so."

"Such that he would want to do something about it?"

"Maybe."

"Did he ever tell you that was what happened."

She looked confused, "What do you mean?"

"Did he tell you he had stabbed Mr Worthy as an act of revenge because Mr Worthy had assaulted Ms West?"

She looked to the dock before answering quietly, "No, he never said that."

Richard stared at her, "You seemed to hesitate before you answered that question, why?"

She reddened slightly, "No reason, it's just nerves."

"Or is it that he did tell you he stabbed the man, albeit in revenge for the man's assault on Ms West?"

She almost shouted the answer, "No, he never said that."

"You have told us that you left the party because you thought he was paying too much attention to Jamie Anderson?"

"Yes."

"You didn't imagine that, it must have seemed to you at the time that he was paying too much attention to her?"

"He has told me he has no interest in her and I believe him!"

"That may well be the case now, but let us deal with the night in question. You saw him staring at Jamie Anderson?"

"It looked like that but I could have been wrong."

"You could have been right?"

"No, I'm sure it was my insecurity."

"But you thought at the time he was paying too much attention to her?"

"Yes."

"Such that you had an argument and you left the party?"

"Yes."

"Did he really offer to go home with you?"

"Yes."

"But you refused his offer?"

"Yes."

"It must have been clear to you that annoyed him?"

"Yes."

"Even angered him?"

"I suppose so."

"And how does he act when he's angry?"

Again, she hesitated, "He gets upset."

"Does he get violent?"

She looked towards the dock and caught Joseph's eyes, "No, he does not."

"You are still in love with him. He has obviously impressed you with his qualities?"

"Yes."

"Is he the type of person who would try to impress young girls?"

She hesitated, "What do you mean."

"Is he the type of person who might try to impress Ms Anderson by stabbing a man and then boasting about it?"

She looked nervously at Richard as she answered quietly, "No he's not like that, he's kind, he's not aggressive."

"Even when he has seen a young woman seriously assaulted?"

"Yes."

"I suggest you are not telling us the truth. You are still trying to protect the man you love?"

"No that's not true!"

"I suggest you are lying and you are covering up for him. You know he killed Mr Worthy, don't you?"

Richard sat down as Caroline quietly and almost inaudibly, sobbed the answer, "No."

deliberately waited until the last possible moment on Saturday evening before serving the evidence, but soon dismissed such thoughts as he read through the statements that had been taken dealing with the phone analysis. He sipped at the remains of what had been a large glass of Rioja Reserva as he made notes on the statements, his mouth developing into a large grin. Wendy was next to him in bed, sleeping soundly with a gentle snore.

It had been an exhausting evening for her as Rose had developed a hacking cough that night and was frequently waking and needing attention. David wanted to wake Wendy to discuss the case and share the new material, but he knew that would have to wait, Wendy needed her rest. So, did he, but he couldn't resist preparing his cross examination tonight. He crept out of bed and went downstairs. He was looking forward to seeing Jamie Anderson again.

CHAPTER 49

THE RECALLING OF THE GIRLFRIEND

On Monday morning Richard announced to a bemused jury that he was recalling a witness as a result of information that had only come to light on Friday. David knew the statement was misleading and Richard was trying to protect his paymasters. The reality was that the Crown Prosecution Service had been bedevilled by disclosure problems for years and it was rapidly becoming the norm in cases for there to be disclosure failings.

As he announced that he was recalling Jamie Anderson all the jurors eagerly looked towards the door of the court wondering what the new information could be.

After a few minutes Jamie came into court followed closely by a man wearing a three piece suit wearing bifocals and carrying a briefcase.

The court staff and the barristers in court knew him to be a local solicitor named Rodney Grace who practised in criminal law.

Jamie Anderson did not look well as she entered the courtroom. Her hair was dishevelled, her, clothes looked like she had slept in them (which she probably had) and she looked exhausted.

Richard gave her some time to compose herself before he asked the judge in her presence. "Is Ms Anderson still subject to the oath she took earlier in these proceedings?"

The Judge had been served with all the information that the defence had and he quickly answered, "Normally I would say that a witness who took an oath less than a week ago would still be subject to that oath but in the light of the unusual circumstances in this case I consider it appropriate that Ms Anderson be sworn again."

He waited until Jamie took the oath once more and then he addressed her, "Ms Anderson you have been called back to this court because information has been obtained that may cast some doubt about statements that you made in this case. I must now give you a warning about your evidence. You are normally obliged to answer questions in this court, however, there is one important exception. You are not obliged to answer any questions which might incriminate you. That does not mean that you can refuse to answer all questions on that basis, so innocuous questions must be answered. It means you may only refuse to answer questions which might cause you to admit a crime by yourself. Do you understand."

Jamie looked blankly at the judge before nervously looking towards Rodney Grace. He knew everyone in court was looking at him and he did not acknowledge her gaze and looked down at his notebook where he scribbled something. Most of those in court assumed he was making a note of the judge's comments. Those closest to him could see he had drawn a picture of a rabbit standing under the glare of dazzling headlights.

She finally said she understood and Richard did not waste any time before asking her his first question.

"Ms Anderson, you gave evidence in this court last week. Was that evidence truthful?"

Jamie looked towards Rodney Grace again, who this time acknowledged her gaze. He gave a wry smile as she answered, "I refuse to answer that question on the grounds that it might incriminate me."

"Was any part of your evidence truthful?"

She looked at Rodney who stared back at her.

"I refuse to answer that question on the grounds that it might incriminate me."

Richard frowned, "Did you attend a party at 84 Sangster Street on 25th August 2018?"

She again looked at Rodney who looked away from her, "Yes."

Richard slowly took her through the evidence she had given. Each time she was asked a

"Do I take it from your answer, that no one else used your phone?"

"I refuse to answer that question on the grounds that it might incriminate me."

"The text could only have been sent by you, couldn't it?"

"I refuse to answer that question on the grounds that it might incriminate me."

"Who else could possibly have sent the message on your phone, 'What the fuck were you doing? I told the police that you didn't do anything, but I saw you right next to him when he screamed out!'?"

"I refuse to answer that question on the grounds that it might incriminate me."

"So, it appears that Mr Simons did not return to the house with you before Mr Worthy was stabbed, but was, right next to Mr Worthy when he received the mortal wound?"

"I refuse to answer that question on the grounds that it might incriminate me."

There were a few murmurings from the jurors who clearly did not appreciate Jamie Anderson's refusal to answer any of David's questions. David preferred it that way as it meant that provided he phrased his questions in such a way as to ensure she claimed privilege, she would not deny anything that he put to her.

"You clearly saw what Mr Simons was doing?"

"I refuse to answer that question on the grounds that it might incriminate me."

"You were clearly outside and not inside the house when Mr Worthy received the mortal wound?"

"I refuse to answer that question on the grounds that it might incriminate me."

"You were close enough to see who stabbed him?"

"I refuse to answer that question on the grounds that it might incriminate me."

David had one last question, "You were close enough to see and I suggest you did see, Mr Simons stab him?"

She opened her mouth to speak but looked towards Rodney who was staring at her.

"I refuse to answer that question on the grounds that it might incriminate me."

CHAPTER 50

THE PROSECUTION CLOSING SPEECH

Jamie Anderson left court at 11pm. The judge then sent the jury away until 2pm so that he could discuss the law with Counsel before speeches. As was anticipated by all counsel, there was very little law to discuss and at 11:45 the court rose. The judge went off to have a long lunch whilst Richard and David found rooms in the court building to put the finishing touches to their speeches.

At 2:05pm the court sat again and Richard rose to give his final address to the jury.

He scanned their faces before addressing them to try and assess what they were thinking. Realising, he could not, just like in every case he conducted, he began his address.

"Ladies and gentlemen, we anticipate that some time tomorrow afternoon or Wednesday morning at the latest, you will withdraw from this courtroom and sit around a table and begin your deliberations in this most serious case.

You are probably wondering why you can't go now?

The law requires you to listen to counsels' speeches and His Lordship's summing up before you deliberate, so that you have all the arguments before you and a framework of law from which you can attach the facts. The good news is that my address to you will not be a long one because you have heard all the evidence in this case.

I hope to provide you with a succinct summary of the significant parts of the evidence and the questions that reasonably arise from that evidence.

To deliberately plunge a large kitchen knife into Mr Worthy's leg with or without the intention of striking an artery or vein is an intent to kill, or at least an intent to cause really serious harm. Either way, as his Lordship will direct you, it is murder.

We have called before you all the available evidence that we submit demonstrates this defendant's guilt. I am going to highlight the evidence of a number of witnesses, many were former friends of this defendant, none of whom have any reason to lie about him.

Even Jamie Anderson had no reason to lie about the defendant, despite the efforts by the defence to suggest that she does.

No doubt my learned friend will make some points, some no doubt better than others and some will undoubtedly make you think whether there is anything in the defence case and you will want to consider them. He will no doubt refer to the fact that no one, with the possible exception of Mrs Turnbull; saw his client with a knife or saw his client stab Mr Worthy. He will point out that his client's fingerprints were not on the knife that clearly was used to kill Mr Worthy. He will point out that his client's DNA was not on the handle or any other part of the knife. He will point out that, neither Mr Worthy's blood or DNA was found on the defendant or his clothing save for the area where he put his arm around Mr Worthy.

However, we do know someone stabbed Mr Worthy that night and yet; no one was apparently seen to do so, no one's fingerprints were found on the murder weapon, no one's DNA was found on the murder weapon save for Mr Worthy's. Mr Worthy's DNA was not discovered on either the defendant or Mr Simons or their clothing save for the area on Mr Rogers that I have already referred to.

You heard from Dr Lumley in this regard. There was only one stab wound and one defensive wound caused undoubtedly at the same time or within milliseconds of each other. It is not surprising in the circumstances that blood and DNA was not found on the defendant. Of course though, the assailant would not know this.

Remember that the defendant washed his own clothing on the morning after the incident. Was that mere coincidence because he washed his clothing every Saturday as he claimed or was it because he deliberately washed his clothing to remove traces of Mr Worthy's DNA or blood which he thought may be present?

I have no doubt that my learned friend will point out that the defendant was searched by police at the party before they let him leave that Friday night. But how thorough was that search of a relatively large number of youths by very few officers? A search conducted when the police thought they had already arrested the culprit. In any event would they have seen traces of blood and DNA that could be seen on dark clothing that night?

Also, what do you make of the evidence of the defence witness, Caroline Jennings, who flatly contradicts the defendant as to when he left her flat on the Sunday. He said he arrived home about 7pm, he lives less than an hour away from her address so he would have left around 6pm. However, she gave evidence that he left much earlier, three hours earlier at 3pm.

Where did he go for three hours? Was he getting rid of something, maybe clothing or perhaps gloves?

I am going to ask you to look at the evidence carefully with me. We the prosecution say that the evidence is clear and proves so that you will be sure, that the defendant, Joseph Rogers is guilty of murder. There is no other reading of it.

As you have heard, through misguided loyalty, a number of witnesses originally withheld what they knew about the defendant. Eventually though their tongues were loosened, probably because their consciences compelled them to tell the truth. After all, a man did lose his life that night!

The defence have made some suggestions in this case that the witnesses were compelled to give a misleading account to support a police theory. There is no evidence whatsoever to support such a suggestion. What possible motive could the police have for doing so? Why would they want an innocent man convicted and a guilty one to get away with a minor offence?

Are the police to be criticised for pointing out the truth to witnesses, namely, that if you lie on oath you will be guilty of perjury?

No, we suggest that a number of witnesses did not want to give incriminating evidence against the defendant because he was a friend. Those witnesses of course include Steven Denley and Scott Robson, but they also include Jamie Alexander, who as you will recall, was reluctant to come to court to give evidence against him.

Steven Denley gave evidence to you on oath that he had first claimed he had seen nothing because he was protecting the defendant. Now he may have been protecting Adrian Simons too. Of course though, if Mr Rogers had done nothing wrong, why did Mr Denley feel the need to protect him?

Scott Robson gave similar evidence, as did Jamie Alexander. Their evidence was not given because they were supporting a police theory, they were finally being truthful after trying to protect a friend.

What is the evidence then?

The defence have made great play of the fact that Mr Worthy was aggressive that night. There is no doubt that he was. He had been disciplined at work, driven friends to a party and then been ignored and as we know, he knocked Shirley West out. However, none of that will help you with the question of whether he was murdered or not. No one is suggesting that this killing was carried out in self defence. The evidence suggests this killing was a cold calculated act of revenge because Mr Worthy had knocked out Shirley West.

At the time he was stabbed, there is no suggestion that Mr Worthy was a threat to anyone.

You will no doubt recall the evidence of Brian Williams in this regard. A friend of Mr Worthy's, who told you candidly that Mr Worthy had been aggressive that night but as he also told you, although Mr Worthy was initially aggressive and knocked out Shirley West, he was calm when the defendant was seen to usher him away. All the aggression had gone by that stage, he was not a threat to anyone.

On the other hand, what does the evidence tell us about the defendant's attitude that night. You may think the evidence is clear. Just as Scott Robson told us. The defendant was angry after the argument with his girlfriend Caroline. She left the party because he was looking at Jamie Anderson. Despite what he says to you now, he undoubtedly found her attractive, he could not take his eyes off her which is why his girlfriend left the party making him angry.

This was a clear case of murder!

CHAPTER 51

THE DEFENCE FINAL SPEECH

David was impressed, Richard's address had almost convinced him. He could see that it had been well received by some members of the jury so he knew he still had a lot of work ahead of him.

He stood up and without an initial scan of their faces, launched into his speech trying to look at each of the members of the jury as he addressed them.

"Ladies and gentlemen, it is always gratifying to listen to the closing remarks of an able and experienced prosecutor who can construct a compelling argument ... even when the evidence does not exist!"

Some members of the jury looked at him a little harshly and he wondered if he might have gone too far, after all this was a Lewes jury and in his experience, they tended to be pro-prosecution.

Undeterred, he carried on.

"Mr Thornbrite has suggested to you that there is a lack of evidence in this case because witnesses were trying to protect Mr Rogers. That is in fact mere speculation and in reality, the evidence tends to show that witnesses, like Steven Denley, were closer to Mr Simons than Mr Rogers and had more reason to protect him and therefore, more reason to continue to protect him when they gave evidence before you.

This opinion that witnesses were out to protect Mr Rogers was formed early on by the police in their investigation and we suggest it has coloured their approach to the whole case.

It seems clear from the evidence of Steven Denley and Scott Robson that the police assumed Mr Rogers was guilty because he had his arm around Mr Worthy when he was stabbed and they then sought evidence that would support that theory, so much so that they put pressure on witnesses like Scott Robson and Steven Denley, to support their case, under the threat of perjury if they did not!

You will recall what Steven Denley said about this and what his mother, Angela Denley told you she heard through the door when the police were talking to her son.

You may think that these witnesses were not protecting Mr Rogers, they were protecting Mr Simons and we saw a prime example of how they are continuing to do so when Steven Denley gave evidence before you.

You will no doubt recall that when Steven Denley first gave evidence he stated that Adrian Simons was a few feet from Mr Worthy, in other words, within stabbing distance when Mr Worthy shouted out and pushed Mr Rogers away. He later retracted this when reminded by the prosecution what was in his statement. However, you may think it appeared to be a genuine recollection when he first gave evidence before you. His retracting it when his statement was shown to him was not an example of him assisting Mr Rogers. It was an example of him assisting Mr Simons.

I am not suggesting that he deliberately lied about what Mr Rogers did, far from it, but he had more reason to protect his friend Mr Simons than Mr Rogers and he continued to do so in this court, when encouraged to do so by the prosecution.

Please put aside any suggestion that witnesses were trying to support Mr Rogers in this case and just consider the evidence you have heard.

We suggest the prosecution have effectively ignored important pieces of evidence that assist Mr Rogers. Indeed, I suppose it could be called, important pieces of missing evidence.

Of all those witnesses there that night, not one ever saw Mr Rogers plunge a knife into Mr Worthy's leg.

Not one witness ever saw a knife in Mr Roger's hand. Now with one or two witnesses at a scene you might expect them to; miss the carrying of a knife, to miss a person plunging a knife into someone's leg. What you do not expect it is that not one witness, whether it be a party goer or an independent witness, ever saw Mr Rogers fatally wounding Mr Worthy.

Indeed, apart from Mrs Turnbull, every single witness who gave evidence before you stated there was only one knife they saw that night and it was being wielded by Adrian Simons.

Now it may be that friends might cover up for a friend and say they did not see a knife, but in this case, they all said they saw their friend Mr Simons with a knife so that is not a strong prosecution point.

Putting aside the evidence of Mr Rogers' so called friends though, it is noticeable that, the wholly independent witness, Carl Williams, who probably had a better view than anyone else that night, only saw one youth with a knife and it is clear from his description, that youth was Adrian Simons.

Mrs Turnbull told you she thought two youths had knives that night. Importantly, even if she is right, she gave important evidence that it was not the black youth who had a knife.

Nevertheless, we suggest she was wrong and there was only one youth with a knife that night. Please remember the circumstances at the time. She told you she had just got up suddenly from either being asleep or just going to sleep and she looked out of the window without putting her glasses on. Clearly, her distance vision would have been impaired.

Further and undoubtedly more importantly, she made a statement to police a day after the incident when matters would have been fresh in her mind and she said she only saw one knife that night.

We for the defence, suggest that you be very careful about her evidence in those circumstances. No one is suggesting that she is lying, but experience in these courts tells us that human beings do not make good witnesses to confusing, rapidly moving events and often they mistake what they have seen. For a person who has just woken up and has not put on their glasses who has a fleeting glimpse of an incident, it is not surprising if they make mistakes.

What else would you expect to see in this case and yet is surprisingly missing?

Whoever, carried out this killing clearly got close to the victim. Surely if Mr Rogers plunged a knife into Mr Worthy, some traces of his DNA, blood or tissue would be found on Mr Rogers' clothing, but it was not. Now, it is right that Mr Rogers washed his clothing on the Saturday morning before his arrest on Sunday evening. However, before he did, we know the police searched him when he was at 84 Sangster Street, checking for signs of injuries, cuts, blood and anything else that might indicate that he had been involved in a fight.

Nothing was found.

Inspector McNally accepted that Mr Rogers had nothing incriminating upon him. He had no traces of Mr Worthy's blood or human tissue on his clothing and no injuries that could have been caused when wielding a knife. If he had, the police would have detained him at the house.

Mr Thornbrite has tried to suggest to you that the search was not thorough. There is no basis for that suggestion and it is wrong for the prosecution to malign the police inspector's integrity in this way. He came across as a perfectly respectable and able officer who was telling the truth when he said a thorough search was carried out.

The prosecution called him before you as a witness of truth, there is no basis for them now suggesting that he did not tell you honestly what occurred, just because his evidence does not fit the prosecution theory.

It has been suggested by Mr Thornbrite that the clothing was washed deliberately that Saturday morning in order to remove traces of DNA or blood, but again there is no basis for that suggestion. We have heard from Mr Rogers and his girlfriend Caroline Jennings, he always washes his laundry on Saturday morning. That is not a recent invention by him made since the service of the prosecution evidence to explain why his clothes were washed! As we heard from PC Freese, when Mr Rogers was arrested he said then, in August last year, that he washed his clothes every Saturday.

Please be careful. When there is no evidence, do not try and fill the gap by speculating as the prosecution has. For example, it was suggested by Mr Thornbrite that Mr Rogers might have been getting rid of clothing or gloves when he left Ms Jennings' flat on the Sunday. That we suggest is a laughable idea. There is no evidence that he had any gloves that night. No one ever suggested they saw him wearing gloves or saw him with gloves on his person.

There is also, no evidence he ever got rid of any clothing at any stage. If he had wanted to get rid of clothing, surely, he would have done that on the Friday night or the Saturday morning at the latest and not waited until Sunday afternoon! There is no evidence that he got rid of anything after the incident and as his lordship will direct you, you must not speculate in this case, you must base your conclusions on evidence, not guesswork.

It is obviously an important point that you do not convict a man on what the prosecution say he may have done. You can only convict him if you are sure, on the evidence you have heard, that he did carry out this murder.

When assessing the evidence in this case, please remember, it is noticeable that no one describes Mr Rogers as being aggressive outside the property that night. Neither the people he knew and perhaps more importantly, nor the independent witness Carl Williams, describe him in that way.

Nor is there any evidence he was aggressive or hostile when the police arrived. As he was the only black man there, someone would have noticed if he was angry or hostile, but no one did. That suggests he was calm and not someone who had just taken another person's life!

You may recall that Carl Williams even described the black youth, which is clearly Mr Rogers, seeming to calm things down. The prosecution claim he was just putting on an act, lulling Mr Worthy into a false sense of security, but couldn't a more credible explanation be, that he was simply trying to calm the situation down?

You may think that Mr Worthy thought Mr Rogers was his attacker when he called out words to the effect, "cheeky fucking bastard". But does that really help you at all? He could not have known who stabbed him in the back of the leg. He would not have seen his assailant. He would have felt the pain, seen Mr Rogers and made an assumption, a wrong one.

We suggest that he made the same mistake that the prosecution have here in bringing this case against Mr Rogers and ignoring the obvious suspect, the same mistake they want you to make."

David noticed a few jurors were taking notes which meant they were at least listening!

"One matter you may want to ask yourselves is, how could Mr Rogers have stabbed Mr Worthy? His right arm was around Mr Worthy's right shoulder. Mr Rogers is clearly right handed as Mr Scott Robson confirmed from their pool playing days. If he was going to wield a knife it would have been with his right hand, yet he was hardly likely to have been carrying a knife in his right hand with his arm around Mr Worthy. Mr Worthy would clearly have seen the knife and no doubt had something to say about it.

Another question you will no doubt want to ask in this case, is which knife caused the injury to Mr Worthy?

If it was the one carried by Mr Simons, then only he could be the murderer. If on your view of the evidence it was or may have been the one carried by Mr Simons, then Joseph Rogers is not guilty of murder.

Noticeably no fingerprints or DNA were found on any knife that was recovered, that linked Mr Rogers to that knife. True no fingerprints were found from anyone else on any knife found in this case. Maybe that is not surprising when we recall the evidence of the uniformed Police inspector, Brian McNally. He told us that when Adrian Simons was searched, a pair of black gloves were found in his right trouser pocket.

Obviously, if he was wearing gloves when he wielded the knife, he would not have left prints on the knife handle. This was confirmed by the forensic scientist Heather Taylor in evidence, though it is no doubt obvious to you all.

Heather Taylor, also confirmed that some of Mr Worthy's blood may have got onto those gloves if it was Mr Simons who stabbed him. Yet those gloves were never tested. As you heard, the police misplaced them. They denied you the opportunity of discovering whether Mr Worthy's blood was on them and probably denied you the opportunity to discover who the true murderer was in this case!

Noticeably, we were told by PC Freese, the officer who arrested Mr Rogers, that he seized from him a large amount of clothing and searched his accommodation, but never found any gloves. Further, as we have heard, no witness ever refers to Mr Rogers wearing gloves that night.

Nevertheless, Steven Denley did give important evidence that was of assistance to Mr Worthy's case and may assist you in determining what happened that night.

Firstly, Steven Denley stated that Mr Rogers was trying to calm Gerry Worthy down. He also gave evidence that he saw Adrian Simons within touching distance of Mr Worthy just after he shouted out. In other words, Adrian Simons was within stabbing distance at the time the fatal wound was received.

Further, when they all went back to the house although he heard Mr Rogers utter the words, "stabbed him", he accepted that he could have missed the word, "someone", before that phrase.

Steven Denley also gave evidence about the knife that contained Mr Worthy's DNA, blood and tissue. He accepted that the knife that he saw Mr Simons holding, could have been the murder weapon.

He gave evidence that the second knife could have been placed in the sink after cutting up a lemon and in other words was never taken outside by anyone.

Carl Williams, the independent witness gave similar evidence that assists Mr Rogers. He said that he saw, "another youth, he looked darker than the rest, he put his arm round the man's shoulders and seemed to calm the situation down."

Mr Williams also gave evidence that there were other youths milling around Mr Worthy and Mr Rogers when Mr Worthy pushed Mr Rogers away. In other words, all the youths were very close. Mr Williams was then reminded by my learned friend of his police statement where he said there was no one else around at that time. However, we know that statement was taken by the police who had their own theories by then and may have unintentionally or worse, intentionally misled him. When I asked him questions he said, "There were a number of youths between the large man and my position and even though I was elevated, they were partially blocking my view so I suppose they must have been close to him."

He gave evidence that he believed the youth who we know is Mr Simons was near the 'large man' Mr Worthy and the 'black youth', Mr Rogers."

David paused and looked at the jurors before continuing.

"This evidence points to Mr Roger's innocence of this offence and points towards Mr Simons being the true culprit.

So, what do the prosecution finally rely upon? The evidence of Jamie Alexander!

What did you make of her when she first came into court sobbing. She came across as a reluctant witness. Someone who did not want to give evidence against her friend Joseph Rogers but was being forced to. You may think the truth came out a little during my cross examination when she reddened at any suggestion that Adrian Simons was the killer.

We suggest the truth finally came out when the prosecution, fairly and properly, albeit very late in the day, disclosed that her phone had sent a text to Adrian Simmons phone on the night of the murder,

'What the fuck were you doing? I told the police that you didn't do anything, but I saw you right next to him when he screamed out!'

It proved she had lied to you. Had you found her a convincing liar? We suggest she continued to lie. She had been found out in her lies about whether Adrian Simons was present at the scene so she no longer gave that evidence as she was no doubt advised by her lawyer about perjuring and incriminating herself. However, she could still do her bit to protect Adrian Simons by lying about Mr Roger's involvement and that, we suggest, is what she continued to do.

Her lies are unravelled a little when you realise that everything she said could have been gleaned from the prosecution papers in this case served on her boyfriend. Those papers gave her the details needed to concoct these lies. Mr Thornbrite has suggested that she has told the truth because only the killer would know there was one stab wound and where it took place.

By the time she gave her witness statement in December 2017 she had seen that information in the prosecution papers and had had ample opportunity to discuss the case with the future father of her child, Adrian Simons.

If he was the killer, he knew from the time Mr Worthy was stabbed that there was only one stab wound and where it had been inflicted and he had months to convey that information to Jamie Alexander.

There is also one other piece of evidence which she gave which we suggest points to her concocting this story. It is her use of the word, 'shanked'. There is no evidence apart from hers that Mr Rogers ever used that word or even knew it. Yet Jamie Alexander states he used it when he came back into the house from the street. No one else in the house heard him use that expression. Yet Jamie Alexander let it slip that one person had used that phrase before.

That was her own boyfriend, the father to be, Adrian Simons.

It is not an expression that Joseph Rogers uses. It is not an expression from the Brighton area but it is an expression used in East London where Jamie Alexander originates from. I suggest she lied when she said Joseph Roger had said he had 'shanked' the man. She lied to protect her boyfriend and has continued to do so even when confronted with the undeniable fact that she lied about her own boyfriend's presence when the stabbing took place.

This was the same man, Adrian Simons, that Shirley West tells us had threatened to stab Mr

Worthy. Isn't it highly likely that is what happened?

You heard the evidence of Dr Lumley, the Pathologist. He accepted that a possible scenario in this case was that, "Mr Worthy was stabbed by an assailant whilst Mr Rogers had his arm around Mr Worthy's shoulders. That assailant immediately backed away. Mr Worthy was not aware he had been stabbed for a few short seconds and then he reacted and pushed Mr Rogers away, saying to him, 'you fucking cheeky little bastard'."

David paused again and looked around their faces which gave nothing away.

"The question in this case is can you be sure that scenario didn't take place here. If you have any reasonable doubt, you must give the benefit of that doubt to the defendant. Of course, it is a matter for you but we suggest that upon the evidence you have heard you cannot be sure of guilt in this case and the one proper verdict is 'not guilty'.

David scanned their faces once more and noted that they continued to give nothing away.

He added with a smile,

"Thank you for your patience in listening to a speech that lasted longer than I intended and probably longer than you hoped for."

At least that elicited a smile from two of the ladies on the front row of the jury.

CHAPTER 52

THE JURY DELIBERATES

The judge had summed up the case fairly as was to be expected from most High Court judges and now David watched as the jurors filed out of court towards their jury room, to consider the fate of Joseph. David had watched their faces carefully when the judge summed up the evidence but few had given any reaction and he still had no idea what they were thinking and could not predict what their verdict would be.

It was part of what made his job interesting to him and at the same time terrifying for the clients. He had his own idea of what the verdict would be, he had looked at the evidence as a juror might, but with the added advantage or disadvantage, of seeing it through the cynical eyes of a lawyer. He did not think it looked good for Joseph, but you never know.

He chose to have another coffee at the still functioning WRVS before seeing his client. He knew Joseph would be extremely nervous at the moment and a little delay in seeing him, might calm him down.

In the jury room there was the usual tussle between the most dominant jurors as to who should be the foreman of the jury. There were two mains contenders. Doris Nathan, sixty three years of age and chairperson of the local Conservative Woman's Association and Reginald Prior, Chairman of the local Rotary club. Both had chaired numerous meetings in the past; both felt suitably qualified for the role of foreman and both had taken an instant dislike to each other on day one of the trial.

For some days now, they had both been urging the others to select them as foreman. The other jurors had avoided doing so as they thought the atmosphere in the jury room would be even worse than it already was if they made an early decision.

After twenty frustrating minutes of arguing who would be the best foreman Mary Forest made a constructive suggestion. "Perhaps it might be easier if we selected someone else to be a foreman. I think Michael here..." She pointed towards the thirty eight year old Michael Lamb who had caught her eye in the first few days of the trial and who she now secretly pined for. She had married young at age twenty two and had twenty six years with her husband, an accountant called Derek who managed to find new ways to bore and annoy her every day. Throughout the trial she had been day dreaming about a possible liaison with the gorgeous Michael and, although she would not admit this to anyone, she had probably missed some of the forensic evidence when she was reinventing a trashy scene from the latest book by Deirdre Sheman, titled, 'The Dominatrix And The Callow Youth,' only this time she and Michael were in the exhausting position of the title characters.

Michael gave her one of those, 'keep me out of this' looks, thinking to himself that this woman was mad. She had pestered him constantly throughout the trial, always trying to sit next to him in the jury room and invariably asking inane questions about gardening and the like. He hated gardening and although he tried to be polite, he wished she would simply go away.

Doris also gave Mary a stare that clearly said, 'shut up you silly idiot'. Reginald's stare was even more pointed and he almost added to it verbally, but in the end, he chose not to.

After another twenty minutes, they had a secret ballot and Doris became foreman by just two votes, 7 to 5. Reginald retreated to a corner of the room, determined not to take any further part in the trial.

Doris took her seat at the head of the table and invited Reginald to join them. "We do value your opinion Reginald and I am sure it would benefit our discussions if you join us."

Reginald looked at her with clear contempt. "I am, comfortable here. I can hear everything you say and I have every intention of joining in the discussion, when it is necessary to do so."

Doris looked at him coldly and muttered, "Good."

She then turned to the others. "I suggest we start with a preliminary vote just to see how far we are apart, if at all."

Reginald grunted his disagreement from the corner but Doris ignored him. Ian Herbert, a television engineer, saw this and boldly spoke up. "I think Reginald is opposed to this idea and so am I. If we vote now, people are in danger of being entrenched. I think we should discuss the evidence first before we have any vote."

He was quite proud of himself. He had only just come across the word 'entrenched' in a tabloid newspaper and he had been dying to find a time to use it.

Doris looked at him sympathetically as if he was a child making his first big mistake in life, "I understand your position, Ian, but nevertheless, as foreperson, I see it as my duty to guide our discussions. I believe it will help those discussions if we have a preliminary vote and unless the majority are against that, that is what is going to happen!"

Mary quickly glanced at Michael and noted that he was looking at Doris as though she was power mad. In an effort to impress him she spoke up, "I agree with Ian, although I think a vote is a good idea soon, I do think we should discuss the evidence first. What do you think, Michael?"

Michael was tempted to argue for an immediate vote just because of Mary's intervention, but he thought the ideas of voting straight away was foolish and so he added, "I agree with Ian, it is far too early to vote."

It was soon obvious that the vast majority of the room disagreed with an immediate vote and Doris withdraw the idea with as good grace as she could muster to this ungrateful stupid lot.

Doris chose the first topic for discussion. Jamie Alexander's evidence. "I think we should discuss her evidence first because if she was telling the truth, the defendant confessed to being the murderer and that's an end to the case!"

"Rubbish", Reginald's voice boomed round the room."

Doris looked at him, shocked and horrified at his aggressive intervention. She was about to say something when Reginald, ignoring her glance, stated, "I'm simply saying that her evidence was rubbish. I tended to believe her when she first gave evidence, but that text changed all of that for me. She clearly lied to us and I wouldn't convict a dog, based on her evidence."

There were a few murmurs of agreement around the room, save for Lynne Talbot who ran a kennels for stray dogs.

Michael decided to lead on the discussion, "I think a proper starting point is to consider the independent evidence first, to see where it leads and then to consider the forensic evidence. Finally, we should consider the evidence of the party goers, including that of Jamie Alexander and the defendant, although we should consider those two in a different way because they both have reasons to lie."

Mary quickly agreed with him but Ian butted in. "The judge directed us to consider the defendant's evidence just like any other witness' evidence, I don't think we should treat it differently just because he is charged with a criminal offence."

Reginald could not wait any longer, without noting that he seemed to be arguing contrary positions he almost shouted, "Poppycock! Of course, a defendant has a reason to lie. The judge wasn't directing us to believe what the defendant said but to use our common sense."

Doris felt she was losing her authority and quickly intervened, "I think we should all calm down, there is quite a lot of evidence to consider in this case and I think we need to be careful in the way we approach it and consider the questions the judge has asked very carefully. It might help our discussions if we had a cup of tea, or coffee for those who prefer it, Mary, would you be a dear and put the kettle on."

As Mary got up from the table, asking Michael what he wanted, Doris opened her copy of the judge's legal directions and the document headed, 'Route to verdict' which contained a number of questions that the judge told them they were expected to answer before reaching a verdict.

Reginald saw what she was doing and just stared at her, before muttering some almost inaudible profanity.

CHAPTER 53

'GLAMPING'

"What's wrong with Rose."

David woke suddenly to the noise of a Wendy frantically pulling Rose from her cot. He could hear Rose coughing and vomiting and immediately he was concerned as he saw her waxen pale skin in the bedroom light.

They had gone 'Glamping' to a place called, "Forest Dale' in Kent. It was near Box Hill and was somewhere that Wendy had always wanted to visit since she had first heard of it during a hair appointment.

David put it down to an idiot hairdresser and to Wendy's uncle's influence. As David had learnt to his regret, her uncle was a Bohemian type who professed a love of nature and a disdain for the material world, providing someone was providing him with all his needs!

Wendy similarly loved nature and wanted to stay in a log cabin for two nights on 10th and 11th March 2018 to celebrate Mothering Sunday. David had gone along with the idea. It was after all Mother's Day and therefore Wendy's day and she should have the choice.

However, he loathed the idea. His idea of a weekend away might involve staying in the country, but preferably staying in a four or five star hotel, not staying in a log cabin. His opinion had not changed when they arrived at Forest Dale.

They had been met by the owner, Daffodil Jones. She was dressed in fishing waders that came up to high over her waist and tied over a loose fitting T-shirt. It was clear she was not wearing a bra underneath and had chosen not to wear anything on top of the T-shirt, despite the chill in the air.

She was about seventy and had closely cropped grey hair. She had refused to shake their hands because, "I'm making compost." David had immediately looked at her hands and was grateful that she had refused to take his.

They were then shown to the log cabin, two hundred metres from the grass car park and past a roped off stagnant lake. The cabin itself had looked all right but first impressions could be deceptive. The toilets, showers, sinks and running water (save that which ran down the inside of the cabin after a bad rainfall), were one hundred metres away from the cabin.

Heating was supplied by a log fire, fuelled by logs that Daffodil was selling for £9 a bag. David had soon worked out that they would need three or four bags a day to keep the place tolerably warm. Inside the log cabin was one room about two thirds the size of their bedroom at home. It had a pull-out sofa in one corner and a gas hob directly opposite.

Daffodil provided them with a ten litre plastic jerry can of water for 'teas and coffee'. Their whole room was divided in half by a large ladder type staircase which led to the 'mezzanine' level, a small area where there was a double bed but no readily discernible way of getting into it because of the low ceiling.

The views outside were pleasant but if this was 'Glamping' David felt it was for others. Wendy though was ecstatic. It was part of her wish to, 'get back to nature', so he did not express his own opinion that the lack of a sink, toilet or shower made him feel it was back to the Stone Age. Now to add to the experience, poor little Rose had been taken ill at three in the morning on Mothering Sunday.

For the next twenty minutes they wondered if they should take Rose to the Accident and Emergency Department of the local hospital, wherever that was! They still had access to the internet on their phones so they looked up her condition.

They feared meningitis but fortunately after Wendy gave her Homeopathic remedies, Rose responded and their fears subsided. Rose was ill but not seriously ill.

David was still cynical about homeopathic remedies, not seeing how they could possibly work, but as they seemed to work for Rose and because of her age it could not be a placebo effect, he was not going to voice his doubts.

They had made their bed downstairs on the pull out sofa as it simply was not practical to sleep on the Mezzanine level and keep Rose in her cot downstairs. They now placed her in the bed and Wendy cuddled up to her to provide warmth, whilst David tried to sleep on the two discarded cushions from the sofa, that he had placed near the stove. It proved impossible to sleep and he stayed awake thinking how, instead of being here, he could have been on a cruise round the Mediterranean now, with all expenses paid by Dr Sanda.

The jury in Joseph's case had taken two days to deliberate. In the end they had reached a majority decision and acquitted Joseph of murder and manslaughter. Juries were never asked to give the numbers of a majority verdict that ended in an acquittal, so he did not know how many voted against Joseph for a guilty verdict, but he noticed two stony faced men on the jury looking daggers at Joseph when the verdict was announced. He assumed therefore that the verdict was 10-2 as at least ten jurors had to agree on their verdict.

Joseph had said a peremptory thanks to him when David visited him in the cells in Lewes Crown Court, waiting for his release. Gavin, in probably the only question he had asked in the entire case suddenly said, "Go on, you can tell us now ..."

David was horrified that he was going to ask if Joseph was guilty of murder. There were some things that you never ask an acquitted defendant. Fortunately, Gavin merely asked, "...where did you go on the Sunday afternoon before you were arrested?"

Joseph had looked at him quizzically until a smile had crossed his lips and he volunteered. "I went to see my other girlfriend."

Gavin was unable to draw him any further as to who the other girlfriend was and they had left the cells wondering.

Two weeks after the verdict, David received an invite for Wendy and him to join Dr Sanda and his wife for dinner at the Ritz in London. A week later they were having a sumptuous meal with fine wine paid for by the Sandas.

Dr Sanda profusely thanked him for securing Joseph's acquittal.

"I shall always think it was fate that drew us together on that cruise. I know you Queen's Counsel like to be known as 'Silks'. Forever more

I shall think of that holiday as 'the Silk's Cruise'."

David grinned at the reference and as he did Dr Sanda offered, "As a token of our appreciation, we would like to offer you another such cruise around the Mediterranean, at your convenience and entirely at our expense."

Mrs Sanda beamed at them both as her husband made the offer.

David looked at Wendy. Both obviously wanted to accept but it was one thing to accept a dinner, an entire cruise was something else and would in his opinion breach some Bar Council rule or other.

"I am sorry Dr Sanda, we must decline your remarkably generous offer. Although we are very grateful, the rules of our profession prevent us from accepting such a trip."

Dr Sanda nodded wisely understanding David's decline of his offer was made reluctantly and for professional reasons.

As the evening progressed, David eventually asked how Joseph was. Dr Sandra's face saddened as he recounted how Joseph had, for the first few days, been polite towards them and apparently happy to be in their company.

"Then it all changed, he left us and went to see his new girlfriend and did not contact us again. I managed to get through to him once, when he told me he was in a happy relationship and did not want to contact us anymore."

David wondered for a moment, "Did he mention his new girlfriend's name?"

Dr Sanda thought for a moment, "I believe she is called Jamie?"

"Jamie?", David was clearly surprised.

"Yes, why do you know her?"

"Do you know her last name by any chance?"

"I believe he said Jamie Anderson."

David put his glass of wine down, "Did he say how long he had been in a relationship with her."

"No, I gathered it had started shortly before the tragic incident that resulted in that man's unfortunate death and then stopped because of Joseph's arrest and then was renewed on his release."

David's mind fought to take in this information. Had Jamie and Joseph planned the false confession so that it could be unravelled by her text, sent sometime after Joseph had taken her home that night from the party?

Surely not, that was too far fetched! What if they had never learned of the text? In any event, she had continued to claim that the confession was true even after the text was discovered.

He put such thoughts out of his mind. One undeniable fact of his profession was that you never really knew what actually happened in one of your cases. You could merely speculate, put two and two together and although you might come up with a four now and again, more often than not, you probably came up with a five.

The meal had ended shortly afterwards and David never expected to see or hear from Dr Sanda again.

David turned over on his two cushions wondering how on earth he had allowed Wendy to persuade him to come here. He glanced at his watch. It was now 8:07am. He looked at his phone, fortunately he had a spare charger that he had charged up in the car yesterday, so he still had some power despite the frantic internet searches he had made for hospitals.

Suddenly there was a 'ping' and David noticed a text appear from Dr Sanda as Wendy rose slightly from her bed and then fell back into a deep sleep.

He read the text wondering what Dr Sanda could possibly want at this time of day.

"Dear David, I am sorry to bother you this early on Mothering Sunday but I wonder if I can ask another favour from you. Do you mind if I call you in five minutes?"

David wondered what it was but so far the 'favours' had worked out well for him so he replied, "There's no harm in asking. I'll expect your call."

David got up and put some warm clothes on and went outside so as not to wake Wendy or Rose.

It was a lovely morning and he could see the sun rising through the forest, but it was incredibly cold and David was beginning to regret his decision.

A few minutes later Dr Sanda phoned, "Thank you David for taking my call so early, but I was speaking to a friend until early this morning who has a serious problem. He is an immigration advisor, a qualified but none practising barrister, and he has been charged with what he called, 'a tier one immigration fraud' that is to be tried in September this year in Southwark Crown Court. Do you have any experience of such cases?"

Fortunately, David had and was able to answer informatively, "Yes, 'tier one' applicants are foreign nationals who are in this country on a limited basis. They then apply to remain in this country based on the fact they either have a substantial income or substantial assets. They are allowed to remain on a points system based on their income/capital. Unfortunately, there are people out there who will fabricate documentation to suggest they earn a great deal or have substantial amounts of capital and that is a 'tier one' fraud."

His fingers were beginning to feel the cold and he wished he was wearing gloves, but he thought he could smell a good fraud brief in the offering.

Dr Sanda spoke in a serious tone, "Yes, my friend told me the prosecution are alleging that he was behind the creation of several companies which then claim to have employed these applicants. The prosecution are saying that the applicants paid £10,000 a month into these companies who then paid it back as a supposed salary. The money was then paid back into the company and each month the same thing happened suggesting the applicant had an income of £10,000 per month. Obviously, they claimed that tax was deducted but none was paid over to the Inland Revenue and the companies went into liquidation once the applicant was given leave to remain in the country indefinitely. My friend is involved in the companies but he states he is innocent of any fraud and I believe him.

I have told him about the great service you have done for our family and he has expressed an interest in being represented by you, if you are willing to offer your services. I understand that the case is a Very High Cost Case, whatever that means."

David grinned at the phone, but tried to remain nonchalant, "That's alright, I know what it is and I would be delighted to represent your friend."

The conversation finished a few minutes later and a cheerful, but cold, David returned to the cabin. As he thought about the conversation now, trying to sleep on the sofa cushions, he started to feel a lot happier. Even the cabin was beginning to look better and the sofa cushions even felt comfortable.

Life was beginning to look very good indeed.

Rose was improving in health, Wendy was looking radiant and it was likely that the September case of Dr Sandra's friend would generate a significant amount of money. Enough that the three of them might be able to put this glamping adventure behind them and in the very near future, they would be able to afford yet another 'Silk's Cruise'.

Books by John M. Burton

THE SILK BRIEF

The Silk Tales volume 1

The first book in the series, "The Silk Trials." David Brant QC is a Criminal Barrister, a "Silk", struggling against a lack of work and problems in his own chambers. He is briefed to act on behalf of a cocaine addict charged with murder. The case appears overwhelming and David has to use all his ability to deal with the wealth of forensic evidence presented against his client.

US LINK

http://amzn.to/1bz221C

UK LINK

http://amzn.to/16QwwZo

THE SILK HEAD

The Silk Tales volume 2

The second book in the series "The Silk Tales". David Brant QC receives a phone call from his wife asking him to represent a fireman charged with the murder of his lover. As the trial progresses, developments in David's Chambers bring unexpected romance and a significant shift in politics and power when the Head of Chambers falls seriously ill. Members of his chambers feel that only David is capable of leading them out of rough waters ahead, but with a full professional and personal life, David is not so sure whether he wants to take on the role of *The Silk Head.*

US LINK

http://amzn.to/1iTPQZn

UK LINK

http://amzn.to/1ilOOYn

THE SILK RETURNS

The Silk Tales volume 3

David Brant QC is now Head of Chambers at Temple Lane Chambers, Temple, London. Life is great for David, his practice is busy with good quality work and his love life exciting. He has a beautiful partner in Wendy Pritchard, a member of his chambers and that relationship, like his association with members of his chambers, appears to be strengthening day by day.

However, overnight, things change dramatically for him and his world is turned upside down. At least he can bury himself in his work when a new brief is returned to him from another silk. The case is from his least favourite solicitor but at least it appears to be relatively straight-forward, with little evidence against his client, and an acquittal almost inevitable.

As the months pass, further evidence is served in the case and begins to mount up against his client. As the trial commences David has to deal with a prosecutor from his own chambers who is determined to score points against him personally and a co-defending counsel who likewise seems hell-bent on causing as many problems as he can for David's client. Will David's skill and wit be enough this time?

UK LINK

http://amzn.to/1Qj911Q

US LINK

http://amzn.to/1OteiV7

THE SILK RIBBON

The Silk Tales volume 4

David Brant QC is a barrister who practices as a Queen's Counsel at Temple Lane Chambers, Temple, London. He is in love with a bright and talented barrister from his chambers, Wendy, whose true feelings about him have been difficult to pin down. Just when he thinks he has the answer, a seductive Russian woman seeks to attract his attention, for reasons he can only guess at.

His case load has been declining since the return of his Head of Chambers, who is now taking all the quality silk work that David had formerly enjoyed. As a result, David is delighted when he is instructed in an interesting murder case. A middle class man has shot and killed his wife's lover. The prosecution say it was murder, frustration caused by his own impotency, but the defence claim it was all a tragic accident. The case appears to David to be straightforward, but, as the trial date approaches, the prosecution evidence mounts up and David finds himself against a highly competent prosecution silk, with a trick or two up his sleeve.

Will David be able to save his well-to-do client from the almost inevitable conviction for murder and a life sentence in prison? And what path will his personal life take when the beautiful Russian asks him out for a drink?

UK LINK

http://amzn.to/22ExByC

USA LINK

http://amzn.to/1TTWQMY

POISON

VOLUME 2 OF THE MURDER TRIALS OF CICERO

It is six years since Cicero's forensic success in the Sextus Roscius case and his life has been good. He has married and progressed through the Roman ranks and is well on the way to taking on the most coveted role of senator of Rome. Meanwhile his career in the law courts has been booming with success after success. However, one day he is approached by men from a town close to his hometown who beg him to represent a former slave on a charge of attempted poisoning. The case seems straight forward but little can he know that this case will lead him on to represent a Roman knight in a notorious case where he is charged with poisoning and with bribing judges to convict an innocent man. Cicero's skills will be tried to the utmost and he will face the most difficult and challenging case of his career where it appears that the verdict has already been rendered against his client in the court of public opinion.

UK LINK

https://goo.gl/VgpU9S

US LINK

https://goo.gl/TjhYA6

THE MYTH OF SPARTA

VOLUME 1 OF THE CHRONICLES OF SPARTA

A novel telling the story of the Spartans from the battle of the 300 at Thermopylae against the might of the Persian Empire, to the battle of Sphacteria against the Athenians and their allies. As one reviewer stated, the book is, "a highly enjoyable way to revisit one of the most significant periods of western history"

UK LINK

http://amzn.to/1gO3MSI

US LINK

http://amzn.to/1bz2pcw

THE RETURN OF THE SPARTANS

VOLUME 2 OF THE CHRONICLES OF SPARTA

"The Return of the Spartans" is a sequel to "The Myth of Sparta" and continues from where that book ends with the capture of the Spartan Hoplites at the battle of Sphacteria.

We follow their captivity through the eyes of their leader Styphon and watch individual's machinations as the Spartans and Athenians continue their war against each other. We observe numerous battles between the two in detail, seen through the eyes of their most famous and in some instances, infamous citizens.

We follow the political machinations of Cleon, Nicias and Alcibiades in Athens and see how they are dealt with by the political satirist at the time, Aristophanes, who referred to all of them in his plays.

Many of the characters from "the Myth of Sparta" appear again including the philosopher Socrates, the Athenian General Demosthenes and the Spartan General Brasidas whose campaign in Northern Greece we observe through the eyes of his men.

The book recreates the period in significant detail and as was described by one reviewer of "The Myth of Sparta", is, "a highly enjoyable way to revisit one of the most significant periods of western history".

UK LINK

http://amzn.to/1aVDYmS

US LINK

http://amzn.to/18iQCfr

THE TRIAL OF ADMIRAL BYNG

Pour Encourager Les Autres

BOOK ONE OF THE HISTORICAL TRIALS SERIES

"The Trial of Admiral Byng" is a fictionalised retelling of the true story of the famous British Admiral Byng, who fought at the battle of Minorca in 1756 and was later court-martialled for his role in that battle. The book takes us through the siege of Minorca as well as the battle and then to the trial where Byng has to defend himself against serious allegations of cowardice, knowing that if he is found guilty there is only one penalty available to the court, his death.

UK LINK

http://goo.gl/cMMXFY

US LINK

http://goo.gl/AaVNOZ

TREACHERY – THE PRINCES IN THE TOWER

'Treachery - the Princes in the Tower' tells the story of a knight, Sir Thomas Clark who is instructed by King Henry VII to discover what happened to the Princes in the Tower. His quest takes him upon many journeys meeting many of the important personages of the day who give him conflicting accounts of what happened. However, through his perseverance he gets ever closer to discovering what really happened to the Princes, with startling consequences.

UK LINK

http://amzn.to/1VPW0kC

US LINK

http://amzn.to/1VUyUJf

Printed in Great Britain
by Amazon